Praise for
IN MURDER WE TRUST

"A very stylish debut."
—ANNETTE MEYERS
Author of *These Bones Were Made for Dancin'*

"IN MURDER WE TRUST is great fun. Eleanor Hyde
has given us the most intriguing and despicable
cast of characters I've met since my last high school
reunion. Her humorous take on the decadent,
affluent New Yorker and his parasitic periphery
makes for delightful enjoyment."
—MARISSA PIESMAN

"Lydia and Colombo are a fun and welcome
addition to the New York sleuth scene."
—CAMILLA CRESPI
Author of "The Trouble With" series

"Oh joy! A likable heroine and a logical plot. Lydia's
appeal lies in the fact that she's a normal New
Yorker (if that's not an oxymoron). Smart, but not
smug, and no braver than she has to be, she's the
kind of character Hitchcock would have liked—the
believable mortal who's summoned to adventure."
—LINDA STEWART
Author of *Sam, the Cat Detective*

IN MURDER
WE TRUST

Eleanor Hyde

FAWCETT GOLD MEDAL • NEW YORK

Sale of this book without a front cover may be unauthorized. If this book is coverless, it may have been reported to the publisher as "unsold or destroyed" and neither the author nor the publisher may have received payment for it.

A Fawcett Gold Medal Book
Published by Ballantine Books
Copyright © 1995 by Eleanor Hyde

All rights reserved under International and Pan-American Copyright Conventions. Published in the United States by Ballantine Books, a division of Random House, Inc., New York, and simultaneously in Canada by Random House of Canada Limited, Toronto.

ISBN 0-449-14942-0

Manufactured in the United States of America

First Edition: August 1995

10 9 8 7 6 5 4 3 2 1

In Memory of Victor

AUTHOR'S NOTE

I wish to thank Elaine Steinbeck for her hospitality and helpful information on her late husband, the writer John Steinbeck. I am also grateful to Adele Glimm for her ideas and contributions to this book, Harriet La Barre for being there when I need her, and The Group for their patience in listening to rewritten chapters. Thanks also to my editor Susan Randol and her assistant Dana Silber. And most of all, I wish to thank my perspicacious and stand-up agent, Agnes Birnbaum, for her support and unflagging enthusiasm.

All characters and incidents in this novel are dreamed up. Any resemblance to anyone living, or whom you might like to see dead, is purely coincidental.

AUTHOR'S NOTE

CHAPTER 1

"It's kind of like the year 2000, clothes have evolved, but—"

The phone rang.

She hit Pause on her tape recorder and Seventh Avenue's new young darling, Chester Tarbox, stopped his spiel.

"I need you, Vanessa," a man said, when she picked up the phone.

"Sorry, wrong woman," she told him, and hung up. She could tell he was drunk. He didn't slur his words, but she knew all the same.

It was the fifth day of the heat wave. Manhattan a microwave oven on ten. Sidewalks sweated. Assaults climbed with the temperature. Outside the window of her fourth-floor walk-up, the sky was a poisonous white. Surgeon General's Warning: Breathing could be dangerous to your health.

Under a lethargic ceiling fan, Lydia Miller, thirty-four, dark blond hair pinned up, plucked her T-shirt from sweat-sticky skin. The T-shirt was an acid green with a tasseled hem and the words "Bahama Mama" stitched across the front above a pink palm tree. In the worst kind of taste. Which was why she wore it. She was sick of chic.

Her winged eyebrows gave her a snotty look that had put her on the runways (after she'd learned to tousle her hair to cover up stick-out ears) until wholesome became the rage. She'd gotten a job on the fashion magazine *gazelle*, where she'd been ever since, writing a column called "chic to chic." Style was all she knew and she was stuck with it.

The phone rang again. This time she didn't pick up. He serenaded her on the answering machine with "Lydia the

1

Tattooed Lady" and segued into an apology. "Lydia, shit," Adam said. "I'm sorry. Now you're mad at me. You know I meant you, not Vanessa." Vanessa was his ex-wife. He had a sexy-husky voice that had once made her want to sleep with him—if she hadn't become a celibate. She'd taken the vow after Mark. No more men.

Lydia pictured Adam lying in bed, drinking and crying into his beard. Unhappier in Southampton than he was in New York. Why he even bothered going out there, she didn't know. Let Vanessa deal with him. Vanessa was AA and knew more about it.

She picked up. "I'm not mad, I'm up to here in work."

"You shouldn't be working on Labor Day weekend. You should be out here basking in the sun. Please come out, I'm depressed. Here I am forty-seven and what do I have to show for it? No wife, no children. Nothing. A fuckup and a failure. Once I expected to be somebody—a guru, talking head, on the cover of *Time*, that shit. I can't even hold down a job. All I do is lie in bed and make money," he said tearfully.

"Adam, some people wouldn't consider that a problem."

"What good does money do me when my health is shot? I'm a heart attack waiting to happen. I've got asthma, arthritis, allergies . . ."

She tuned out before he got to the *b*'s and listened instead to the gurgling toilet behind the bathroom door. In order to pay off hospital bills, she'd had to trade the enormous white-brick-walled loft she'd shared with Mark in Tribeca for a leprous-walled shotgun apartment with faulty wiring and holes in the floor. Surprisingly, she'd found the place on the so-called fashionable Upper East Side. It was cheap and the fireplace and shutters lent a certain charm. Rent for an apartment on the West Side from below New York University to above Columbia University had been out of the question—far too expensive.

Silence at the other end. Even drunk, on the phone, with Bach playing in the background, Adam had a way of not being heard, like a powerful engine on idle.

"You're not listening," he said.

"I have to get back to work. I've got bills to pay."

"You let people take advantage of you."

Any minute now, he'd turn mean.

"You should have divorced Mark and let Medicaid pay his bills. You enjoy playing the martyr," he said.

"You're spoiling for a fight. Mark gave me the most wonderful times of my life." Also the worst, she thought, hanging up.

She took an iced tea break. Cooling the back of her neck with an ice cube, she glanced at the Metro section of yesterday's *Times*, which she'd been too busy to read. A dancer charging rape at a New Jersey bachelor party, four women missing out on Long Island (serial murderer suspected), and the bodies of women and children discovered in an East New York apartment (drug-related murders). Depressing. She pressed REW/REV and returned to Chester Tarbox.

The interview was an extracurricular assignment that her boss, Milke Forte, had thrown her way. They were all very nice to her at *gazelle*. Too nice.

A lot of whispering went on behind her back as soon as Mark had gone to the hospital. For supposedly sophisticated people, they acted like a bunch of hicks.

When the phone rang again, she made no move to pick up.

"I deserved that. Forgive me," he begged. "Just speak to me so I know you don't hate me. Please."

Which was worse, his humility or hostility? Still, she owed him. Despite the fact that Adam scarcely knew Mark, he'd been one of the few people to stick around during Mark's last days at St. Vincent's. He'd even offered to send Mark on an all-expenses-paid trip to a hospital in Paris. "You'll get better care there," Adam told him. "It's where Nureyev went."

"And where he died," Mark pointed out. "He doesn't give a damn about me," Mark told Lydia later. "He just wants to get rid of me so he can make the move on you. If he's so worried about hospital bills, why doesn't he pay the ones I'm running up here? Not that I'd let him."

No, he'd left that to her.

Lydia picked up. "Adam, I do not hate you, okay?"

"Thank you," he said humbly.

She looked up at the ceiling fan for help from above, and for a heart-stopping moment thought it had lost speed, but it hummed reassuringly on.

"Lydia, listen. Come out here and work. I won't intrude, I promise. You can take a dip in the pool whenever you feel like it."

She didn't remind him that she was afraid of water ever since she'd almost drowned in Girl Scout camp. She pictured herself lounging beside the tree-shadowed pool under blue sky and lazy clouds. Then she thought of Adam lying on a pool mat, his Buddha stomach jutting up toward the sun, watching her every move. No.

"I'll send a car. I'll come in and drive you out," Adam said.

"I have a car," she reminded him.

"That junk pile? Get yourself a new one. My treat. I mean it."

"It gets me where I want to go."

"You and Colombo are the only two who don't care for my money." Colombo was his dog.

"Don't be so sure about Colombo."

Adam laughed for a brief moment, then said, "I'm seeing Jared Evans at National Trust and leaving everything to you."

Sure.

"I mean it," he said, and went into one of his impromptu rages. Not at her, but at his first ex-wife, Carolyn, his second ex-wife, Vanessa, her lover, Todd, and his neighbor, a certain Dr. Carlos Fernando Alejandro Urzaga, who, after blasting away all summer, was now giving him headaches with a concrete mixer, contributing further to his depression.

"That pool he's enlarging will be Lake Erie by the time he's finished. I'm reporting him to the zoning board Tuesday, the day after Labor Day. That shit's not getting another cent from me for his Institute for Bipolar Disorders."

"What's that? Something to do with Arctic exploration?" she asked.

"Research on depressives. Like me. I told you about it.

You read his book. Or so you said. And met him. He makes a good impression, doesn't he?"

"He's a very charming man."

"You think so? Well, I think he's a goddamned quack and phony, and so do you. I've been making some discreet inquiries and come up with enough ammo to shoot him down. I'm also seeing someone on the hospital board Tuesday. He'll end up behind prison bars after they hear."

"Hear what?" she asked.

"Come out and I'll tell you."

"By tomorrow you two will be friends again," she said, sidestepping the invitation.

"Never. I've had enough of that slick-Spic, slimy sleazy, scumbag. He's just been stringing me along for his own personal gain. And here I am in bed with a depression weighing down on me like a stone, and what the hell does that quack care? No one cares. That's why I drink. Not the main reason but a contributing factor. I wish you were out here. I need you. You listen to me."

"Adam, call Vanessa and ask her out. She can help you more than I can."

"She's narcissistic. Her universe is Vanessa Auerbach. Anyway, she won't come. Claims you have AIDS, and she'll get it from the pool. Jealous. And you won't come out because you don't trust me. I know you're still sorting things out since Mark died. I respect that. You can have the green room you two had before. Or my room. I'll take a guest room."

Lydia said her computer was too big to haul out and hung up before he offered to buy her a laptop. Once again, she returned to Chester Tarbox.

"What I've done is create a basic piece for the future. The twenty-first century's answer to a bodysuit without those inconvenient snaps at the crotch. It's revo—"

The eager young voice cut off. Her screen went blank. The refrigerator went silent. The blades on the ceiling fan turned slower and slower. Stopped.

Shit! Now what?

Lydia checked the hall light. Off. No point in knocking on the door across the hall. The apartment was vacant. In fact, the whole damn building was vacant, except for her and old Mrs. Nagy in 1W, and today not even Mrs. Nagy was here. Off on a picnic with her daughter and grandchildren. No sooner had Lydia moved in six months ago than everyone had started moving out. She didn't take it personally. The super never showed up when he said he would, and if he did, he left things worse than they were to begin with. On purpose, Mrs. Nagy said. She claimed the landlord was warehousing the building and wanted them out.

Lydia looked out the front window of her apartment. The neon light was on at the Super Locksmith's across the street. Not an area blackout then, just a fuse blown in her building. The fuse box was in the basement. Sal, the super, kept the basement door locked. He was the only one with the key, and she knew she'd never find him on a holiday weekend. Terrific!

She telephoned Sal just in case and got his machine.

Lydia considered her options. She could either suffocate here or go out to Adam's, where she could take refreshing dips in the pool—at the baby end. She pictured a sun fractured between green leafy branches. Cool breezes. To hell with it, she'd go.

She punched 1-516 on the phone, and checked her address book for the rest of his number. And got the electronic Adam. Probably cooling off in the pool or passed out dead drunk in bed. Maybe he'd still be out of it when she arrived—if she was lucky.

"I'm on my way," she announced.

The clock had stopped at 4:33.

She stepped out of her apartment building into the tropics. Rounding the corner to Second Avenue, she spotted Sal the super—black T-shirt, blue tattooed arms, and needing a shave—resembling an aging biker up to no good. He sat drinking with his cronies at a table outside Harry's Hula Hut and looked too bombed to fix a blown fuse.

"Hey, come join us for a drink," Sal called.

She pretended she didn't hear and walked on. Out of the corner of her eye she saw Sal stumble up from the table, nearly knocking over an empty chair as he started after her.

"What's the hurry?" he yelled, sounding thick-tongued.

"I'm late," Lydia called over her shoulder, and hurried on.

Hearing footsteps behind her, she turned.

"Hey, honey, I invited you for a drink; didn't you hear me?" Sal demanded.

"Get lost," she said sweetly. His buddies looked up from their beer. Lydia wheeled around and headed toward her car. As she pulled away from the curb, she glanced in the rearview mirror. Sal stood on the sidewalk looking as if he were plotting her murder.

"You're not going to get a fuse put in your box that way, kid," she told herself, and drove off, happy to get away from Sal the super, the heat, and the city.

CHAPTER 2

Traffic was bumper to bumper on Route 27. Lydia drummed her fingers on the steering wheel of her thirdhand Datsun. She was stuck in a line of rental cars of day trippers and weekenders and the BMWs, Infinitis, and Mercedeses of the summer people. A Hamptons Jitney zipped by, going back toward the city. It was the only bus she knew of whose second-language instructions were written in French instead of Spanish.

The setting sun left a red swath on the horizon streaked with feathery purples, one of those spectacular sights that played so often near the ocean. Then slowly, almost imperceptibly, the purple took over and the sky turned ominous. Lightning zigzagged, thunder rumbled. A fat raindrop splashed on the windshield.

When she reached North Sea Road, it was raining seriously. One windshield wiper limped across the glass, leaving a smeary arc. The other wasn't working. By the time she came to the tavern turnoff, the limping wiper had conked out, too. It was close to nine. She considered calling Adam from the tavern to tell him she was running late, but she wasn't dressed for the occasion. She'd been in too big a hurry to leave to bother changing. The summer people would think nothing of it if she walked into a pub wearing a midthigh tasseled T-shirt, but if she wore it into a tavern where the locals hung out, there'd be a lot of hooting and hollering. She'd forgo the pleasure.

Lydia drove with her head out the window, peering through the liquid dark, hair in her eyes and water streaming down her face.

At Bridie's Lane she turned left, driving up and downhill looking for the white mailbox with the number 5. Adam's house, a long, gray-shingled affair designed by a student of Frank Lloyd Wright's, blended in with its woodsy surroundings. Difficult to find even when you were on top of it. He lived in the unfashionable part of Southampton, north of the highway, preferring hills and trees to the shore on the southern, more expensive side.

"When you have his kind of money you don't have to prove anything," his best friend Neil had said, admiringly. His ex–best friend. Back before his and Adam's big blowup.

She'd met Adam through Neil, who had taken her under his wing when she'd come to work for him at *gazelle*. Neil was gay and proud of it. Later, he'd told Lydia he knew Mark was gay the minute they'd shaken hands. "How?" she'd asked. "Some secret handshake like the Masons?"

Of course, Neil was inclined to think most men were gay, particularly those with talent.

Stupid, stupid, stupid. How could she ever again trust her judgment when she'd been so wrong about Mark? They'd lived together for a year before the three years they were married, and she'd never guessed. If anything, she'd suspected him of sleeping with the gorgeous female models he accompanied on shoots. At least if he had engaged in risky sex, he hadn't wanted to put her life in danger. He had insisted on using condoms on the grounds that men bore equal responsibility.

When the truth came out, she'd felt anger at her naïveté, then terror. For him. For herself. Terror and betrayal. How could he have loved her and slept around—regardless of what sex he had sex with? It still hurt when she thought of it. Don't, then. Think of something else. Think of Adam.

He cut an imposing figure, broad-shouldered and hefty. With his girth and blond-gray beard, he looked like a cross between Hemingway and Orson Welles, with a dash of Henry VIII. It was the Henry VIII part that bothered her. Once she'd seen the way he wolfed down food, she knew he'd make a lousy lover.

Not that she was out shopping. From now on men would play no part in her life, other than friends. So far her tests had proved HIV-negative—thank God and knock wood—so it wasn't completely fear of destroying someone's life. She just didn't want to get hurt again. At the age of thirty-four, she'd only had three men in her life. The first, Jamie, whom she had latched on to in her freshman year in high school, had dumped her in their freshman year at Ohio State. She'd dropped out and gone to New York to forget him, and at age nineteen become involved with a guitarist named Lyle in a rock group called the Nervous Wrecks. Their romance hadn't lasted a third as long as her misery after Lyle left her for a groupie admirer. Then she'd met Mark. And he'd abandoned her, too.

Damn! She'd overshot Adam's house and reached the highway. Lydia turned the Datsun around and headed back. It was tricky finding Adam's place, especially at night. And in the rain.

Finally she spied the tipsy mailbox half-hidden by shrubbery. Had the mailbox always been tipsy and she'd just not noticed? Someone might have run into it turning around when they discovered the lane was a dead end. It went only as far as Alec Urzaga's, who lived on the far side of the woods.

Of course, it could have been Adam who'd bumped into the mailbox, and he didn't necessarily have to be drunk to do it. Adam lacked coordination. Seeing his massive shoulders, people assumed he was an ex-football player until he tripped over his own feet.

Lydia turned in to the driveway, car lights cutting across the slanting rain and momentarily lighting the trees and shrubbery in front of the house.

Adam's blue BMW was in the parking area under the trees at the bottom of the hill. As usual, he'd run the front wheels up over the curb.

She drove up the hill and came to a stop before she hit the two metal garbage cans outside the garage. The house was dark. He could have turned on the lights at least. Irritated, she jerked on the hand brake. Generally, when Adam was expecting company, he turned on the yard lights, creating a Gatsby effect, spotlighting the pool, the trees, and the shrubbery.

Maybe he didn't know she was coming. Too drunk to notice the flashing light on the answering machine. She foot-fumbled her way up the flagstone steps with only lightning to guide her, the wind whipping the tassels on her soaked Bahama Mama T-shirt.

The front door was unlocked. She stepped into total darkness and shivered, partly because Adam had the air conditioner on to slightly above pipe-freezing temperature, and partly because the place spooked her. So isolated. It made her think of the movie *In Cold Blood*.

She switched on the lights. "Anybody home?"

Silence. No welcoming barks from Colombo. Maybe he was cowering under the bed, terrified of the storm.

She stepped into a puddle in the hall as she passed the pantry. The freezer was leaking again. The guest room doors were closed, but Adam's bedroom door stood wide open.

"Adam, are you here?" she yelled.

Silence reigned.

She went into his room and turned on the light. Branches scraped against the high, narrow windows on either side of the flagstone fireplace. Rain pounded on the wooden deck beyond the glass wall. The bed was a tangled mess of blue sheets. A bottle of Stolichnaya and a nearly empty glass of vodka sat on the night table.

Lydia stooped and looked under the bed. No Colombo. Where was he? More important, where was Adam?

His wallet, surrounded by loose change, lay on the dresser alongside the unzipped blue canvas bag he used to transport the books he intended to read but seldom got around to.

It struck her that Adam might have patched things up with Urzaga and gone over there. Before the storm. Or maybe they'd gone out to dinner in Urzaga's car. But in that case, Adam would have taken his wallet. Adam always ended up paying with Urzaga. With almost everyone, for that matter.

His tan slacks, blue guayabera, and huaraches lay in a heap on the floor. This wasn't like him. Although he was generally messy, his mother must have laid down the law when it came to making his bed and picking up his clothes.

Lydia tapped on the bathroom door and called Adam's name, hesitant to go in.

Silence. The only sounds the scraping branches and the rain.

She peeked into the bathroom. A damp blue towel lay scrunched up on the tile floor. An assortment of pills crowded the long glass shelf under the medicine closet—Elavil, Prozac, Halcion, lithium, and Valium. Another nearly empty glass of vodka sat on top of the clothes hamper next to a British newspaper on international economics.

Lydia gingerly pulled aside the shower curtain, but no one lurked behind.

The red light on the answering machine wasn't blinking. Which meant Adam had gotten her message and knew she was coming. Maybe he'd decided to take a nap before she arrived, and because his bed was such a mess, opted for a guest room.

She checked the guest rooms out. They were all identical except for different-colored flowers on the vine-patterned wallpaper with bedspread and curtains to match: yellow, blue, pink, and green.

Her straw cartwheel hat still rested on the seat of a white wicker rocker in the green room. Mark's sunglasses, which he'd thought he'd lost, were on top of the dresser. She looked at them and felt an ache. That had been in June, his last time anywhere other than St. Vincent's.

The kitchen was a slum. Adam snacked throughout the day, leaving everything out. A banana peel sprawled on the beautiful Spanish tile floor near the garbage can. Adam was a lousy shot.

The dining room table held the remains of a second breakfast and the financial section of the Sunday *Times*. Adam always had his first breakfast in the village where he drove to pick up the *Times*. When she and Mark were here he'd buy three, one for each of them.

"Why didn't you just get some other newspapers?" Mark had asked.

"What newspaper do you want? I'll go back in and get it," Adam had offered. He'd been very solicitous of Mark.

Oversolicitous, Mark said. "He's like a vulture. Waiting for me to die so he can swoop down and fly away with you."

"He's being nice."

"Oh, yeah? I'm not fooled," Mark said, and added: "You could do worse. You certainly didn't luck out with me, did you?"

If she'd denied it, he'd have said she was lying.

The rest of the *Times* lay strewn on the plump chairs and sofas in the living room, which was stagily dramatic, double-height with rectangular windows just under the ceiling. In the far corner stood a vase large enough to accommodate a fat child, holding a gigantic spray of pampas grass, artfully fanned out. Curtains were pulled back at the glass wall, the room open to the night.

A cigar butt lay crushed in a ceramic ashtray offered up on the curved trunk of a ceramic elephant side table. Two elephants, both with gold-tasseled ornate blankets. Trashy. Kitsch. She loved them. Maybe she just had a weakness for tassels.

The rain had quieted down to a gentle tapping on the front deck, the thunder had become less threatening, the lightning infrequent. Lydia became aware of a whine other than the wind. Colombo scrabbling at the door. Stuck outside during the storm. His worst nightmare come true.

"Poor thing, come in," she said, opening the door and stepping back to avoid a shower. But Colombo remained outside, dancing up and down, barking and whining. A big shaggy dog, his orange and white fur matted by the rain.

She stepped out into the rain-chilled night and stood on the wooden deck under a giant tree whose branches dripped water. Colombo, still barking, nudged her knee, nipped her ankle, ran limping down the steps and up again. Limping?

Lydia felt a chill. He wanted to lead her somewhere. To Adam? But what would Adam be doing out in a storm? She turned on the yard lights and peered out into the suddenly illuminated night, at spotlighted trees, bushes, and geraniums in urns at each corner of the tree-shadowed pool across the long stretch of lawn. The Gatsby glare made the surrounding darkness darker.

She hurried across the wet grass after Colombo, who stopped by the pool and danced about on three legs, barking. He was at the deep end by the diving boards.

Lydia crouched beside him and looked down. Blood pounded in her ears at the sight of a pale round Buddha stomach in khaki swim trunks. Adam! Her head began to spin. The backs of her knees started to give way and her whole body trembled. He couldn't be drowned. Not dead. Not Adam. Not after Mark. No one was going to die on her again. She wouldn't allow it.

The water was over her head at this end. Anything higher than her waist terrified her. Besides, there was lightning to worry about. She'd either be drowned or electrocuted. What about Adam—had lightning struck him? What was he thinking of, swimming in a storm, anyway? Now was not the time to ask questions. She closed her eyes and jumped in. And went down and down in water warmed by the rain. She fought her way up again. Panicky, she swallowed a bucketful of chlorine-tasting water as she groped for Adam. And touched his arm. Warm like the water. That meant he was alive, didn't it?

"So, okay, now just hang in there," she told him, ESP'd actually, not saying it out loud. She needed to save her breath.

She had only a vague notion of how to go about a rescue. Hooking an elbow under his chin in order to hold his head above water, she felt the scratchy wet beard. Her knees bumped his back as she kicked awkwardly in an attempt to maneuver him toward the shallow end.

He slipped from her grasp and started to sink. She caught the elastic band of his swimming trunks and tugged, dragging him along. Just get him on dry ground. Administer CPR. Then Adam would sit up and shake his head and say, "Jesus, I need a drink after all that. . . ."

"What the hell's going on here?"

She looked up to see a man leaning over the edge of the pool. Tall, dark, frowning. Alec Urzaga! A doctor. Thank God!

"Help me, goddamn it. He's drowning!"

In a minute Urzaga was beside her in the water, holding Adam up, pushing her away. Then, "Jesus Christ. He's dead!"

CHAPTER 3

Lydia drove back to the city in a daze. Numb. Several times she caught herself heading toward the headlights of an oncoming car and had to veer right sharply, nearly jolting Colombo, huddled beside her, to the floor.

She'd insisted on going to Southampton Hospital in the ambulance with Adam, still unable to believe he was dead. Heart attack, the ambulance driver had said, confirming what Alec Urzaga had said earlier.

Urzaga, who had also stuck around, had driven her back from the hospital. She resented his being able to poke his nose into the room where they'd taken Adam. A room she wasn't allowed to enter. Because he was a doctor and she wasn't family.

Staying at Adam's place without him had seemed un-
bearable. Lydia had locked up and left. She grimly remembered that less than a few hours ago, she'd hoped Adam
would be dead drunk, passed out by the time she got to his
place. Dead drunk but not dead. Mark had died in August,
now Adam in September. It was as if anyone she cared for
died. Maybe she should love only her enemies.

It was nearly daylight by the time she crossed the
Queensboro Bridge into Manhattan. Cooler. The storm
must have hit here, too. She found a parking spot not too
far from her place between Third and Lex, and headed
home along the quiet predawn street, with Colombo
limping along beside her. She hadn't been able to find his
leash.

The lights were still off in her apartment. The clock still
said 4:33. She'd forgotten about the blown fuse. In the gray
light from the kitchen window she found the magnetic
flashlight on the side of the refrigerator. She put water and
leftover chicken breast out for Colombo, hoping the
chicken hadn't spoiled in the warm refrigerator. She hadn't
eaten since yesterday at noon, but she had no appetite. Neither did Colombo. He ignored the chicken and lay by the
door, a big orange and white dog rug, as if he expected
Adam to come up the stairs any minute and take him home.

She'd have to get him some Alpo or whatever and have
the vet look at his leg to see why he was limping. After
that she'd decide what to do. Maybe Vanessa would want
him. Good God, Vanessa! She'd have to call and tell her
Adam had died from a heart attack. Or had he drowned after he'd had the heart attack? No one had said.

Maybe she shouldn't call until later when she had the
specifics. After all, early morning was no time to call and
announce someone's death. But that was a cop-out. The
truth was, she just didn't feel up to encountering Vanessa's
wrath. Behead the messenger bearing the bad news and all
that. No, get it over with. Maybe she'd get Vanessa's answering machine.

Lydia shined the flashlight on the phone book and found
a V. Auerbach on the East Side. Adam had said that after

the divorce, she'd gotten a place near his on East End Avenue.

She punched the number and listened to the phone ring, noticing the red light blinking. Good, Vanessa wasn't answering. She'd leave a message to call. Just as she was thinking this, Vanessa answered.

"Vanessa, this is Lydia Miller, I—"

"Murderer!" Vanessa screamed, and slammed down the phone.

Lydia felt as if she'd been punched in the stomach. Adam had said Vanessa was emotional. But this? And how had Vanessa found out? The police? Alec Urzaga?

Lydia pushed playback on the blinking machine and heard a voice from the dead. Adam. It hurt almost too much to listen. His voice alternately faded and grew stronger as if on short wave. He was probably walking around while he spoke on the phone. "Lydia, you there? On your way? In the bathroom? (Pause) You wouldn't believe the calls I've been getting from New York's neediest," he said gleefully.

"I've finally convinced them they've got something to worry about. I'm not answering, but enjoying hearing them beg, snivel, and grovel. This is a tape I'll keep for posterity." Colombo began barking. "We're having company. Someone you'll like." Or was it "you like"? She couldn't quite hear. In addition to the racket Colombo was making, Adam's voice had faded out again. "Gotta go. Someone's at the door," Adam yelled. Colombo's barking was distant now, probably greeting the new arrival. "See you soon, babe," Adam said, his last words loud and clear.

She wondered who Adam had been expecting. Obviously whoever it was hadn't stuck around very long. If he or she had, Adam might still be alive.

Carefully Lydia picked up the cassette and replaced it with a new one. She didn't want to accidentally erase the tape. She wanted to keep Adam's last words. She smelled chlorine and saw his body—smooth round stomach, water-dark swimming trunks and beard—half-submerged in the pool. Poor Adam, a tormented man. There were times she'd hated him, but she'd also kind of loved him.

CHAPTER 4

The day was appropriately grim—gray, rainy, and unseasonably chilly. Lydia walked home from the *gazelle* office on Madison and Forty-fourth. Too tense to sit in a cab, bus, or subway, she had to be in perpetual motion. Her brain had undergone shock paralysis and seemed stuck, blank.

She stopped off at her place on Seventy-seventh to walk Colombo. He left the apartment reluctantly, as if Adam might arrive while he was out. Since she hadn't gotten the hang of cleaning up doggie do efficiently, she took along a lot of paraphernalia—scoop, newspapers, Baggies—in a beat-up L. L. Bean bag.

She didn't have to change clothes when she got back. She could wear to the memorial service what she'd worn to the office—black turtleneck, black St.-Laurent suit of ancient vintage, black stockings, black boots, and black trench coat. Milke Forte, the editor-in-chief at *gazelle*, insisted her staff dress in style. Black was the simplest and least expensive solution. It also expressed her outlook on life.

"Move it," she told Colombo, who lay stretched out by the door waiting for Adam and blocking her way. Actually, she should take him with her to the memorial service. He probably mourned Adam more deeply than anyone.

She was running late. Lydia flew down the three flights of stairs and out, heading for the Burlington Bookstore on Madison and Eighty-second, where she was meeting Neil, who was coming in from East Hampton on the jitney. They were going to the service together for moral support. The bookstore was practically next door to the Frank E. Campbell Funeral Home.

17

Adam had ducked out of Mark's funeral. "I couldn't take it," he'd said later. "I left and got smashed."

Lydia ignored Don't Walks and dodged traffic. She struggled to keep her umbrella up in the gusty wind. Except for the trademark Hanae Mori butterfly, the umbrella was also black and folded into less than ten inches. She'd paid nearly a hundred for it back in her palmier days.

Neil was already in the bookstore when Lydia arrived. "Adam," he said brokenly, and clung to her, unable to go beyond Adam's name. She was aware only of the discomfort of their wet raincoats and that they were blocking the narrow aisle. She wondered if she was an unfeeling monster. Maybe she had a certain grief level, a saturation point she couldn't go beyond.

"I'll never forgive myself," Neil said. "Adam called me that Sunday. Crying. He said he deeply regretted the things he'd said, and I was his dearest friend. He asked me to please forgive him. I picked up, said 'Fuck you,' and hung up."

Neil had already told her this when she'd phoned him about Adam's death. She squeezed Neil's hand. "He didn't have a heart attack because you hung up on him," she said. Neil and Adam had been feuding for almost a year. Neither would say why.

Neil's face was smaller, drawn, older; his light brown hair wispier. He wore an elegantly cut beige cashmere jacket and somewhat rumpled trousers.

"Armani," he said, noticing her eye his jacket. "Left over from my *gazelle* days. It was either this or the Gap. If it weren't for Gabriella, I'd be on the dole. Steve does nothing but languish around the house drinking martinis." Gabriella, a fashion designer, had lent Neil her converted barn in East Hampton while she was back in Milan working for the Casa di Fernelli.

"Heart attack," Neil said, shaking his head. "I still can't believe it."

"Vanessa didn't. She called me a murderer."

Lydia tried to laugh it off, but her laugh came out flat. "Well, after all, love, you stole her husband."

A nearby browser gave Lydia an interested look, then

turned away disappointed. Lydia guessed someone with ears sticking out of wet stringy hair didn't meet the requirements of a femme fatale.

"Ex-husband. And I didn't steal him. Adam was wild about Vanessa. Or addicted to her or whatever."

"He told me he loved you. You look good," he added accusingly.

"I can't. I walked here. I must look like a drowned rat," she said, and thinking of Adam, wished she could retract the word "drowned."

The bookstore was small with an upstairs balcony. The narrow aisles forced passing strangers into either an embarrassing intimacy or a *High Noon* standoff. Luckily, most of the customers politely yielded right of way. This was the civilized 10028 zone.

"We should have met at a bar and had a drink," Neil said.

"The Madison Pub isn't far from here."

He checked his watch. "Ten minutes to go. No time. Let's go outside, though; it's too bloody hot in here."

Outside, the rain was scarcely more than a drizzle.

A silver stretch limo with smoked windows glided up in front of the funeral home. A uniformed driver got out, raised an umbrella, and opened the back door. A woman in a sable cape and a black dress stepped out. A dotted veil topped by a big black bow concealed her face, but the paneled dress divided in several places to reveal shapely legs. Unfortunately, the divided panels also revealed the girdled top of her panty hose.

"Thierry Mugler," Lydia said, identifying the divided-dress designer. "Nothing like making a fashion statement at a funeral. Who is she anyway?"

"Vanessa. You mean you don't know her?"

"Only as someone who hangs up on me."

Neil placed a hand on Lydia's shoulder. "Now, don't interpret this as a traitorous act, but I have to say a few consoling words to the bereaved. After all, I have a play and she has a theater."

He took a step forward, then turned back as a man climbed out behind Vanessa. "Not while that sleazeball is dancing attendance," Neil said, nodding toward a man in tortoiseshell-rimmed sunglasses and white-blond ponytail. Compact, muscular. With his deep tan, he looked like an aging California beach boy.

"Todd Bigelow?" Lydia asked.

"Alias Clyde Haggerty. Adam called them Bonnie and Clyde."

"He doesn't look like he's about to die."

"Die?" Neil said. "Why? Forgive the rhyme."

"Adam told me he didn't have long to live because of his frail health."

"No doubt something Vanessa made up to sucker more money out of Adam. Let's go in. We're both getting wet. But give those two time to get ahead," Neil said as Vanessa and Todd entered the funeral home.

Campbell's Funeral Home, Manhattan's way station to the last resting place for the rich and famous, was thick-carpeted and dimly lit, but not as opulent as Lydia had imagined. Famous people and places often failed to meet her expectations. Of course, few things could live up to the half-fairy-tale, half-trashy imaginings she'd had as a kid back in Elvira. Although she'd grown up and changed, Elvira hadn't. A town that had never caught up with the times. Call it Brigadoon, Ohio.

"Mr. Auerbach's services are being held on the third floor," a quietly pretty woman said in a deferential, nondenominational voice. She held the elevator for them.

"Shit," Neil said under his breath.

Waiting inside were Vanessa Auerbach and Todd Bigelow, presenting a striking contrast together—Vanessa pale-skinned with blue-black hair, and Todd tan and white blond. Also waiting was a smartly dressed woman. She nodded sadly at Lydia, delicately touching a lacy handkerchief in the vicinity of her tinted glasses. Lydia nodded back in a way she hoped was correspondingly sad. Her nod was intercepted by a malignant glare from beautiful Elizabeth Taylor eyes behind the dotted veil.

The ride up was in hostile silence rather than sorrow.

As soon as the door opened, Neil made a dash for it, pulling Lydia along.

"Who was the woman in the tinted glasses?" Lydia whispered.

"You don't know Francoise, Adam's cleaning woman?"

"I didn't recognize her out of uniform. She's attractive."

A clone of the pretty downstairs woman smilingly informed them that Mr. Auerbach's services were being held in the rooms to the right.

"Looks like the somber, old-fashioned funeral director has been replaced by International Pancake hostesses," Neil said.

"*Rooms?* Is Vanessa expecting a mob?"

"If everyone who Adam gave handouts to comes, it'll take up the whole funeral home."

There were two rooms, divided by a bar, with sofas and chairs scattered informally about. Standing around as if they were waiting for the show to begin were people dressed in their glitzy best. Bouquets of red and silver balloons hanging from the ceiling gave the rooms a festive touch. Lydia supposed Vanessa meant to celebrate Adam's life, but considering what his life had been like, it only made things sadder.

"Big turnout," Neil said. "Vanessa's theater friends. Not many of Adam's. You'd think with her stage experience she'd come up with something better than balloons. And why a bar and no drinks?"

"She's AA," Lydia said.

"That doesn't mean the rest of us are. It looks like she's putting on a show. That spotlight can't be Frank Campbell's doings. Oh, my, there's Adam's cousins. On his Wasp mother's side. Not his dad's. Mama cut them off before Adam got a chance to know them—too Jewish. This is the New England contingent. I'm surprised they showed up. But I guess it's their Wasp sense of duty. They don't approve of me any more than they did of Adam. Still, I suppose I should do the polite thing and say hello."

Taking Lydia by the elbow, he steered her across the room toward some tweedy, slightly dowdy, Cheeverish people who stood in closed ranks and warily eyed the other mourners—although no one but Francoise appeared to mourn Adam's demise. Lydia thought regretfully of the fifties French film based on a Simenon novel that Adam had taken her to at Alliance Française. In it, the mourners, mostly relatives, had gathered around the grave all wearing black, a bouquet of black umbrellas raised against the rain. But now that she thought of it, one of the mourning relatives had murdered the deceased.

Neil introduced her to Adam's cousins: Jane and Chap Stoddard, Charles and Helen Ruff, and Tom and Phoebe Brewster. "Lydia was a good friend of Adam's," he added.

They smiled thinly. Thin people, thin smiles.

"Pity his mother couldn't make it to the funeral," Neil added.

"Aunt Grace has been very ill. She asked Vanessa to see to the funeral arrangements. She just wasn't up to it, poor thing. She gets confused, you know. Forgets that Adam and Vanessa were divorced."

"What're you doing these days, Neil?" Chap Stoddard asked.

"Hard at work on my succès d'estime, a roman à clef about growing up in Grosse Pointe."

Which more or less finished the conversation. Neil pressured Lydia's arm, and they moved on as the cousins closed ranks again.

"They understand French," he said. "It's me they don't understand. I'm always at my worst around them."

A pale, pretty raven-haired woman who rather resembled Vanessa, if Vanessa had been taller and less curvy, floated by, and waved a delicate hand at Lydia as if she knew her. Lydia watched as the woman flitted from circle to circle, but didn't remember ever seeing her before.

Out in the hall, Todd and Vanessa stood smoking and chatting with Alec Urzaga and a tough-looking woman in a green sweater and plaid slacks, who used the floor as an ashtray for her cigarillo. "Who's that?" Lydia asked.

"Oh, she's a whatchamacallit—there's a word for it in AA—sponsor. The one who keeps Vanessa on Diet Coke and off the booze. Look at that shit Urzaga. He's already sucking up to Vanessa. What money he didn't con from Adam, he'll con from her when she inherits."

Vanessa had drawn back her veil in order to smoke, revealing a rice white face with two clown dots of rouge.

"She should keep that veil down," Neil said. "She looks like a George Grosz painting. Circa 1933."

Todd wore a Brooks Brothers suit. Adam had once told Lydia that Todd kept a dark suit handy in case he had to go to a funeral. Little did Adam know that the funeral would be his.

The heat and the mingling scent of perfumes were getting to Lydia. "When does the service begin?" she asked Neil.

"Any minute, I hope. Deadly, isn't it? Pun unintended. If Adam were here, he'd have left long ago. Excuse me, but there's Vanessa without her shadow."

Alone, Lydia wondered if Adam's first wife was somewhere around. She was searching out possibilities when a trim man with luxuriant gray hair and matching gray suit came up.

"Lydia Miller?" he asked.

She nodded.

"Glad to meet you," the man said, thrusting out a hand for her to shake. Callused. Would Adam's friends have callused hands? Well, maybe a cousin from sailing at Chappaquoit. No, not cousin material. Too color-coordinated. The tie and pocket handkerchief were of the same material, gray with blue flecks.

"You look like you're holding up okay," he said, smiling. Not a nice smile. She had the feeling he didn't intend it to be.

Lydia didn't return the smile. "Do I know you?"

"You don't remember such a memorable occasion?"

"Adam's party out in Southampton?"

She and Mark hadn't known most of the people there, but then neither had Adam. Mostly friends of Urzaga's.

"Emergency. Southampton Hospital."

"The night of Adam's heart attack?"

"Heart attack? Is that what you call it?"

"That's what Dr. Urzaga and the EMS guy said. Are you a doctor, too?"

He smiled. "Wrong diagnosis. Guess again."

"I don't like playing games," she said, and started to move off.

He put a detaining hand on her arm. "Detective Barolini, Suffolk Homicide." He pressed a card into her hand. This time the smile was definitely wintry, the gray eyes as hostile as a space alien's. "Don't stray too far. I'll want to talk to you later," he said, and walked off.

Homicide? She sidestepped Todd Bigelow, hovering nearby, and blocked Barolini's path. "Excuse me, are you saying that Adam was murdered?"

She said it too loud. Several people turned and stared.

"Did I say that?"

She lowered her voice. "You said you were from Suffolk Homicide."

"We'll be in touch later. Stick around."

"What do you mean, later? When? Do you mean stick around as in don't leave town?"

He walked off without answering. She would have gone after him if Todd Bigelow hadn't suddenly stepped in her path. They stood eye to eye, or rather eye to tortoiseshell sunglasses.

"What did he want?" Todd demanded, nodding toward Barolini.

"I don't know." She wouldn't have told him if she did.

Across the room someone applauded. Vanessa. Clapping her hands for attention. Maybe she was going to announce that Adam's murderer was about to be apprehended. Her.

Vanessa stood under a spotlight, her sable cape flung on the floor in a heap in the careless way of some late-night movie queen. The dotted veil was drawn up from her face, her lips shiny red against the rice-powder face. She was probably no more than five-two, but she stood tall, her back to the bar. An appropriate metaphor for someone in AA.

Neil suddenly appeared at Lydia's side where Todd had been a minute ago. "The curtain rises," he said sotto voce.

"Yeah, but is this a comedy, tragedy, or whodunit?"

Neil gave her a quizzical look, but now was not the time to explain.

"Since Adam didn't stand on ceremony, I've planned only a brief one," Vanessa said in a deep, throaty voice.

"First, we'll hear from Adam's oldest and dearest childhood friend—"

"She should have warned me," Neil said, stepping forward.

"—Charles Orwin," Vanessa finished.

"That half-witted jock bully! He made Adam's life miserable when he was a kid," Neil hissed.

A husky man with a lined boyish face and red-blond hair stepped up beside Vanessa. Smiling graciously, Vanessa bowed out, the spotlight following her movie-queen walk across the room, a pinkie hooked around the chain of her trailing sable.

Charles Orwin cleared his throat. "I'm not too good with words, so I'll make this short. Adam was always a clumsy kid," said the man, who stood awkwardly. "He didn't know how to handle his body. And when it came to dancing, forget it! All the girls ended up with bruised toes if not permanent limps."

Some thin smiles from the cousins.

"I thought a memorial service was supposed to be a tribute, not a put-down," Lydia whispered to Neil.

"Once I invited Adam to clip me on the chin. 'I don't want to hurt you,' he said. Kidding. 'Go ahead, clip me,' I told him. 'Give it all you've got.' And damned if he didn't deliver a stunning blow. Nearly knocked me off my feet. And that was Adam, a stunning man."

"One of the great orators of our time," Neil said through clenched teeth. Lydia, who thought it was a rather nice tribute after a dubious beginning, remained diplomatically quiet.

"And next we'll hear from Dr. Carlos Fernando Alejandro Urzaga," Vanessa announced after the spotlight flitted back to where she sat in a wing chair. "Did I leave out any names, Alec?"

"I can think of some," Neil said behind a cupped hand.

"Just Junior," Alec Urzaga said.

Laughter. Even a titter or two from the cousins.

Standing a little to their right was Detective Barolini, his eyes not on Alec Urzaga but on Lydia. He looked more Mafia than cop in all that matching gray. No, that wasn't fair, just because his name was Barolini. To hell with that. He wasn't being fair accusing her of murder. Why should she be?

As soon as this was over, she'd ask what made him think Adam was murdered and why suspect her. Had he zeroed in on her just because she'd found the body? Or had her clumsy attempts to save a dead person from drowning looked like murder? Was that what Urzaga had told him?

Urzaga looked as if he'd consulted *GQ* on what to wear to a memorial service—dark suit, startlingly white shirt, and sober tie. He stood under the spotlight as if to the theater born, an old-timey movie idol—tall, trim, and handsome with an intriguingly sinister scar between his black eyebrows. Magnetic. She almost saw why people didn't see through him. Except good-looking men didn't appeal to her. As Adam had once pointed out, she was more interested in IQ. She'd married Mark in spite of his good looks, not because of them.

A small, rueful smile appeared on Urzaga's lips. "I envy those of you who had the luck to meet Adam years ago," he said. "Your memories. I feel cheated. But I also feel blessed having known him, if only for a short time."

Francoise dabbed her lace handkerchief under her tinted glasses.

"Adam and I met two years ago on Memorial Day weekend, and a memorable day it was. I'd just moved in next door to him in Southampton. My phone wasn't working, so I went over and asked Adam if I could use his. He not only offered me the phone, but a drink, dinner, and the use of his pool—mine had yet to be put in. Also the run of his house. 'Help yourself, this is liberty hall,' he said."

Lydia gulped. It was an expression Adam had used the first time she and Mark had gone out to visit him.

"Adam wasn't just a good neighbor. He was a wonderful friend. Kind. Witty. Generous."

"Especially to that parasite," Neil whispered.

"Some of you here might be familiar with my book *Rage from Within*. I know Adam sent out copies to friends. A plea for them to better understand him. His torments, his moods, his depression. Which is what my book is about—

bipolar disorder. In a way, I wish I'd written that book after I met Adam. We'd stay up late at night discussing it. Adam gave me new and valuable insights. He was a brilliant polemicist, political analyst, philosopher, art connoisseur, and scholar. The last of the Renaissance men.

"I cherished Adam. He was larger than life and a hell of a lot of fun to be with. I didn't know Adam for very long, but I felt as if I'd known him all my life. I bid adieu to you, Adam, my brother, *mon semblable,* my twin."

"My meal ticket," Neil added.

Tears glittered in Vanessa's beautiful violet eyes as the spotlight switched back to her. Francoise had removed her tinted glasses and was crying copious tears. Even some of the female cousins turned their heads to hide something as shameful as crying. The male cousins, of course, remained stoic. But look at you, you're not crying either, she told herself. Except she wasn't trying to hide her emotions. She just didn't feel anything. And Detective Barolini, looking her way, noticed.

"Does anyone else have anything to say?" Vanessa asked, looking around. But when Neil stepped forward, she pretended not to see him. "Well, I do," she said.

Vanessa might not be beautiful, but her sexy-husky voice said she was. Lydia remembered how thrilled she'd been by Adam's voice on the telephone even though she knew the man at the other end of the line was overweight and beaky. Vanessa's voice must have the same seductive effect on men. Unfortunately, Vanessa made her speech sitting down, and the effect was spoiled as once again the skirt panels divided to reveal her girdled panty hose.

"Adam and I were meant to be together," Vanessa said. "Like Romeo and Juliet, Antony and Cleopatra, Bogey and Baby, Liz and Dick ...

"I was his princess, his queen. He was my white knight, my prince, my king. I ... I'm sorry. ..." Her voice broke. "I can't go on. This is the end of an era."

"That was beautiful, Vanessa," someone called from behind Lydia. Lydia turned to see who. Todd Bigelow.

The moment the service was over, the ethereal-looking raven-haired woman approached Neil. Lydia headed for Detective Barolini, but a kid in a pin-striped suit stepped in her way.

"Lydia Miller?" he asked, and smiled charmingly.

Up close she saw he wasn't a kid. Maybe mid to late twenties.

"Alicia Minton was kind enough to point you out to me," he said, nodding toward a woman Lydia didn't know. He held out his hand. She shook it.

"Jared Evans. National Trust. We're handling Adam's estate. I intended notifying you earlier, but I've been away. You're one of Adam's chief beneficiaries."

He pressed a card into her hand before she left. Her second that night. Two cards. Two bombshells. Not only was she a chief beneficiary in Adam's will, but also a suspect in his murder.

CHAPTER 5

"Murdered? Jesus, I need a drink," Neil said.

"Maybe I need a lawyer," Lydia said. "I doubt I'll inherit enough to hire Dershowitz. Besides, his track record hasn't been so hot lately."

"Just because that cop said he wanted to talk to you doesn't mean you're a prime suspect. You're overreacting."

"He didn't tell *you* not to leave town."

"He didn't tell me anything. He told you that?"

"That was the implication. He said stick around."

She'd told Neil about the double whammy—Detective Barolini from Suffolk Homicide and Jared Evans from National Trust—the minute they got out the door of Frank Campbell's. They'd talked in undertones, sheltered from the rain by the canopy, watching as the cousins and Vanessa's show-biz friends hailed cabs. Vanessa and Todd rolled off

in their stretch limo. Barolini had slipped out before everyone else.

"To hell with the jitney," Neil said. "I'll catch the next
one back. Let's go to the Madison Pub."

They set out in the downpour, Neil, always the gentleman, holding her umbrella aloft. A mile away the top of the
Trump Palace, lit up for the night, was wrapped in a
swirling mist. So was Lydia's mind.

"Why does that cop think it was murder?" Neil asked.

"That's what I'd like to know. Maybe Urzaga said I was
trying to drown Adam."

"That shit. *He* could have done it. He lives nearby."

For that matter, Neil didn't live so far away either. She
dismissed the disloyal thought from her mind.

"They must have an idea of the time it was done," she
said. "Adam had to be dead before I got there. Around
eight-thirty. Or maybe nine. Only I don't have any proof."

Neil caught her arm. "Here we are." She'd almost
walked by.

They entered a shadowy hall, turned left, and went down
steepish steps into a long dark room that smelled of beer,
cigarette smoke, and frying hamburger.

The Madison Pub was pretentiously unpretentious—
plank floors, wooden tables and booths. Part of the bar was
below street level, the wide plate glass window cutting off
the view of passersby from the knees down. The pub was
a little-known hangout for those nostalgic for a past they'd
missed out on. Its jukebox featured hit songs from the thirties to the nineties. At lunch, it was popular with Met Museum regulars, clerks from nearby expensive antiques
stores, and art gallery people who used to eat at the Madison Avenue Leo's before it closed.

Neil and Lydia sat in a booth bathed in the orangish
glow of a cathedral-shaped lampshade. The other booths
were unoccupied except for two of the help eating in back.
Three men and a woman straddled chair-backed stools at
the bar. Serious drinkers all. The singles crowd who lived
in the area would flock in later.

Neil ordered a double scotch, and Lydia a Bombay martini.

"Straight. Three olives. Ice on the side," she told the waiter.

"You don't drink gin," Neil reminded her.

"One of Adam's favorite drinks. You should know."

"He also asked for Perfect Rob Roys. It always reminded me of Scott Fitzgerald. Of course, Adam drank anything and everything. Why gin?"

"It's supposed to make you cry."

"Why cry?"

"I haven't shed one tear over Adam."

"You cried yourself out over Mark."

"Not really. I don't cry."

"Like the princess until a suitor showed up with an onion. You looked after Mark when his boyfriend ran off. That's the important thing. You're a tough kid. A stand-up chick, as Adam used to say."

" 'Chick' is politically incorrect." She shifted positions and kicked Neil in a shin. "Sorry."

"It's these goddamned narrow booths. Constructed for a smaller race. Like our subways. Built by the Japanese for the Japanese. Americans take up two seats. Not only does our population grow larger, so do the people. Space becomes cramped. One day this world is going to be one big Tokyo."

A man with a shaved head, looking like a skinhead would-be Nazi or a heavy-metal freak, plunged quarters into the jukebox up front near the door. The waiter brought their drinks. Billie Holiday sang "These Foolish Things Remind Me of You."

"Funny thing for someone like him to pick," Lydia said.

"How I love that woman." Neil raised his glass. "To Billie and Adam." His hand shook, sloshing his drink.

She raised her martini. "To Mark, Adam, and Billie. There were times I could have killed Adam, but I never wanted him dead."

"We all felt that way."

"Except not everyone inherits."

"Alas, not me. National Trust is like the old Morgan Guaranty. They wouldn't stoop to handling anyone less than a multi-multi. Let me be the first to congratulate you."

"Yeah, I have all the luck. I'm not only in Adam's will but a prime suspect in his murder."

"Probably the two aren't unrelated."

"Neil, I saw Adam when he was lifted out of that pool. There was no evidence of foul play. If someone held him down, there'd be bruises. Or if he'd been killed before drowning—stab or bullet wounds. And if he'd been strangled, his tongue would have protruded or his eyes—"

"Must you be so graphic?"

"Sorry." Adam wouldn't have minded. They both had strong stomachs. Which had pleased him. He gave her books about serial killers that he said his other friends couldn't handle. They'd gone to movies steeped in blood, gore, and gruesome details. Their very last movie had been a video of *Silence of the Lambs*—she's missed it when it came out. Even though Adam had seen it numerous times, he'd clung to her. The difference was, Adam enjoyed gory movies and she didn't. But like a kid on a dare, she watched to prove she could take it.

"Excuse me." She went to the bar and got change from the sad-faced bartender who'd have been more appropriate at Frank Campbell's than the pretty clones. Standing before the cigarette machine by the window, she tried to decide on a brand. Gauloises, her ex-cigarettes, couldn't be found in vending machines. Maybe that was just as well since that was how she'd gotten started smoking. She chose Benson & Hedges. Returning to the booth, she ordered another martini and lit up.

"Adam was already killing himself," she said.

"Is that what you're trying to do?"

"A little patience and the murderer wouldn't have had to do anything." She paused. "Who do you think did it?"

"Any one of his friends—except me and thee. Bonnie and Clyde? He's a sociopath and she's a paranoid schizophrenic. Adam bought her the theater so she wouldn't freak out."

"He said he was cutting off everyone's lying-around money and taking them out of his will. Except he couldn't do anything until after Labor Day. Which was why someone got to him a day before."

"There might be others we don't know about. Adam was impulsive. How long did you two know each other? Not much over a year. Did he ever say he was leaving you anything?"

"What's that supposed to mean? That he threatened to take me out of his will, too?"

"You're being paranoid, love."

"He once said if anything happened to him, I'd be a millionaire. Actually, 'millionheiress' was the word. I didn't take it seriously. In the first place, I didn't expect him to die. In the second, I knew how quickly people fell from his favor. Also, he'd said Vanessa, Todd, and Urzaga were the executors."

Neil gave a loud hoot. Shaved head and his bar buddies looked over. "I wouldn't trust any of them as far as I could throw a baby grand. Vanessa's crazy, Urzaga's a fraud, and Todd Bigelow's a petty thief, if not a criminal."

"Adam didn't mind that Todd and Vanessa were lovers?"

"He was glad. That's why he paid off Todd's gambling debts so willingly. Didn't want some enforcer to incapacitate him so he couldn't perform his function, so to speak. He worried about Vanessa flipping out. Of course, his first wife is almost as nutty as she is."

"I wonder if she inherits anything. That's only fair. Neither she or Vanessa got alimony. Was she there tonight?"

"You didn't see me beckoning you over? I thought you were pretending not to because you were jealous," he said teasingly.

"A kind of tall, thin Vanessa? Raven locks?"

"Black for mourning. She changes her hair to go with her costume."

"Adam said she was a sex therapist."

"Also a snob and a social climber."

"How can a sex therapist be a snob?"

"She has only socialite clients."

"Aren't sex therapists going out of business, what with AIDS?"

"I was once in his will," Neil said reflectively. "Before our fight."

"What was that all about anyway?"

"Oh, you know, Adam had a cruel and wicked tongue. He said unforgivable things. Nothing I hadn't heard before, but it hurt coming from him. He had a knack of zeroing in on people's vulnerabilities and zapping them when he went into one of his famous rages. Naturally, he had to bring up my sexual proclivities."

She didn't buy it. "Come on, Neil. Adam had his faults, but he wasn't a gay basher. He didn't blame Mark for what he did, but for what it did to me."

"Because he knew better. He fell for you," Neil said. "I saw it the moment I introduced you two at my reading."

"Contrary to popular opinion, I never slept with him. We were friends. Nothing more."

Neil raised a blond eyebrow, which made Lydia mad.

"He joked about Vanessa's saying I had AIDS, but I think it scared him off," she said. "It scares me. If I come out of this intact, I doubt I'll ever sleep with anyone again. I'm beginning to think there's no such thing as safe sex."

"I know what you mean. My roving days are over. That's why I put up with Steve."

"Adam once said if he were gay, he'd have chosen you."

"Oh, Jesus, did he?" New tears brightened Neil's eyes. He reached for Lydia's Benson & Hedges and lit a cigarette with shaky fingers, and ordered a Perfect Rob Roy. "Edith Piaf. *La vie en rose*." He nodded toward the jukebox. "God, how I love that woman." He sang along with her. In French. Then broke off. "Everything's too goddamned dangerous."

Even in the dim light she was aware of how he'd aged. His wispy hair. Lined face.

He reached over and touched her hand. "Did Adam really say that?"

She nodded.

"If only you'd told me sooner."

What did that "if only" mean? That he'd have patched things up with Adam?

"At Dartmouth I swiped his raincoat and slept in it," Neil said. "Adam kept asking everyone where it was. He never knew I had it."

That's what Neil thought. Adam had told her the story.

"That sleaze Urzaga," Neil said. "He's evil. I'd put my money on him. He stood to lose the most if Adam cut off the Institute's funds. Doesn't it make you suspicious that he just 'dropped by' after Adam had drowned?"

"He said he saw the yard lights on."

"Sly son of a bitch. He thought I had too much influence over Adam. If you must know, it was Urzaga who caused our fight. He was feeding Adam lines—and I don't mean from my play. Adam was sniffing heroin."

"You mean cocaine. You snort heroin, not sniff. Anyway, I don't believe it!"

The neighborhood singles had arrived, raising the decibel level. Lydia caught the waiter's attention and pointed to her raised glass. She'd lost track of how many martinis she'd had, but this was all too much. She felt like she was at a Pinter play. Nothing made sense, and yet it did. "I don't believe it," she said again, weakly.

"Believe it," Neil said. "And you're wrong, dear heart. It's 'sniff,' not 'snort.' 'Snort' is only used by the middle class trying to sound 'in.' Also, I do mean heroin. Not cocaine. A pure Asiatic heroin, referred to as Special K. A fad among the rich. Not the sort of drug kids can buy at school playgrounds. Urzaga dispensed it freely—I use the word loosely. With Urzaga, nothing comes free. He also supplied Adam with drugs from the hospital dispensary. Adam was a pill head. He'd try anything. And Urzaga had everything. A truly evil man. I told Adam that, and he exploded. Said I was bad-mouthing Urzaga because he'd spurned my sexual advances. Urzaga had told him that. He said—quote unquote—'Alec found it extremely embarrassing. He didn't know what to do.' Can you believe I'd ever do such a thing?"

"No, and if you did, I'm sure that Urzaga would be perfectly capable of handling the situation."

"True. I should have told Adam that, but I was so hurt that he'd believe such an absurd charge, I wasn't thinking clearly. Actually, I'm not so sure Adam did. He was furious that I dared criticize this talented genius. A talented liar, that's what he is. Look out for him, kid. He could have killed Adam. Planned for you to discover the body. Then just happened along."

The waiter delivered her martini along with Neil's Perfect Rob Roy; she waited until he moved on.

"Except Adam didn't know I was coming out," Lydia said. "I called him and got his machine. When I saw the light wasn't blinking on the answering machine, I thought Adam had gotten my message, but maybe it was Urzaga. He could have gone over to Adam's while I was on my way out to the house. Maybe Adam went into one of his rages and told Urzaga he was reporting him to the zoning board and Hamptons Hospital."

"Reporting him? What for?"

"For something he'd learned recently. He said he'd tell me when I came out. I mean *if* I came out, not when. A bribe to get me out there."

"You should tell Detective whatshisface Adam was going to report him."

"Barolini. I will." She struck her palm to her forehead. "My God, I completely forgot. Adam did get my message, after all. Why didn't I think of it sooner?"

"Think of what?"

"The call he left on my machine. I found it when I got back to town. What did he say?" she asked herself. "Something about having great fun listening to New York's neediest beg and grovel—I guess he meant the people he supported."

"He didn't mention names?"

She shook her head. "I gathered there were quite a few. He wasn't answering their calls, but keeping everything they said on the cassette. Maybe that's why Urzaga went over—to try to talk him out of cutting off the funds to his Institute."

"Sounds like Adam. Did he say anything else?"

"Yes, now that you mention it. I didn't think anything of it when I played it back, but then I didn't know he'd been murdered. He said—" she squinted through smoke and frowned "—he was expecting another person. I couldn't tell whether he'd said someone I like or someone I will like.

Colombo was madly barking in the background. Oh, yeah, that's another thing. There was someone at the door."

"The person he was expecting or someone else?"

She looked over at Neil. "Good question. If it was someone he was expecting, he would have mentioned the name. Of course, his expected visitor may have been early, or he may not have heard a car drive up. On the other hand, it might have been your friend Urzaga."

"Don't call him that even in jest," Neil said.

"Sorry. I don't know many friends of his, and don't like the few I do. Except you."

She didn't realize the implication until after she said it. Neil missed it. Or was he just pretending to?

"The remark could have been ironic. Someone he knew you didn't like—or wouldn't like when you met them."

"Yes, and he knew I didn't like Urzaga. Come on back to my place, and we'll listen together. Maybe you can figure out what he's saying. I saved the cassette. Put it in my desk drawer. I'll give it to Barolini. That should clear me."

Neil held his watch to the light. "Dear heart, it'll have to keep. I have twenty minutes to make the next jitney." He signaled the waiter and, after making a scribbling motion into the palm of his hand, a gesture Adam used to make, excused himself and went to the rest room.

When the waiter brought the bill, Lydia tried to figure up how much she owed, but the numbers got fuzzy. She handed the bill to Neil when he got back. "I had too many martinis. You figure it out and tell me what my half is."

"Sweetheart, since you're the heiress and I'm the pauper, I'll let you take care of it."

She thought he was joking, but he reached for his raincoat instead of his wallet.

Lydia doubted she'd be much of an heiress since there were quite a few cousins and others. Still, poor Neil, Adam's oldest friend, got nothing. The least she could do was pay.

The room lurched when she stood up. She took baby steps to the stairs, hanging on to the iron railing. "I shouldn't have had that second martini," she said. "In fact, I shouldn't have had the first."

Outside in the drizzle, she slumped against the wall and watched as Neil waved down a cab, blew her a kiss, and took off. In too much of a hurry to get to his jitney to notice how drunk she was. The decent thing would have been to drop her off, but then she'd probably have ended up paying cab fare, too. Anyway, the walk home would revive her.

Remembering the cassette with Adam's message on it, she walked as fast as she could without falling on her face. If she couldn't cry for Adam, she could at least find out who'd murdered him.

At Seventy-ninth and Park the sky opened up and the rain came down hard. Shit. She'd left her umbrella behind. It wasn't getting wet that bothered her as much as losing something as expensive as her Hanae Mori. She wheeled around and went back. Luckily, the umbrella was still there. The sad-faced bartender fished it out from behind the bar.

Outside, the rain had once again dwindled to a drizzle. Not worth the bother of raising an umbrella. How lovely it would be not to have to worry about things like losing umbrellas or being stuck with a tab. Not to worry about money. The way it had been when she and Mark teamed up, he making good money as a fashion photographer, and she contributing her bit as assistant fashion editor.

Neil had been her boss back then. Covering for her ghastly mistakes. Encouraging her to be creative. He was her soul mate, pal, and best friend. It was mean and disloyal to suspect him. Also absurd. If he'd been angry enough to murder Adam, he wouldn't have waited a year to do it.

Nearing her apartment building, Lydia spied the whirling lights of a police car double-parked in front. She hurried inside and found old Mrs. Nagy, gray hair standing on end, wearing an ancient tatty robe and wringing her chubby hands. She stood at the bottom of the stairs, looking up.

"What happened?" Lydia asked, alarmed.

"Some burglar, he broke into your apartment," Mrs. Nagy wailed in her childish voice. "I heard someone going up those stairs, and it didn't sound like you. And your dog, he started barking. So I called 911. The police, they're up there now."

CHAPTER 6

Lydia ran up the three flights. Two cops stood outside her door. She hoped that's what they were. Both wore jeans and jackets, not uniforms. She tried to get ahold of herself and appear sober. "What's up?" she asked.

"Got here in the nick of time," the cop in black jeans said. He had dark eyes and dark, curly hair. Cute. Too cute—he looked stuck on himself.

"Just getting ready to break down your door," sandy mustache put in. He was of slight build and didn't look like a cop.

"If it's still locked, doesn't that mean no one broke in?"

"Better make sure," the cute, curly-haired cop said. "The old lady downstairs says she heard someone up here. Gimme your keys. We'll have a look around inside."

She let them go first, and when she didn't hear an exchange of gunfire, went in. Her motto was, better a live coward than a dead hero. No V. I. Warshawski, she.

"Jeez," sandy mustache said. "Looks like your place got tossed."

"That's how I left it."

"Hey, at least you're honest. Gotta admire you for admitting it."

"There are worse things than being a bad housekeeper."

"Yeah, guess you're right."

Nothing appeared to be missing. Her computer, tape recorder, TV, clock radio, toaster, and costume jewelry were still there.

The curly-haired cop went into the bathroom and pulled

back the shower curtain. "Well, hi there!" he called. "How you doing, fella? Come on out."

Lydia knew that cops had to be careful of accusations of police brutality, but wasn't this leaning too far in the other direction? She gingerly stepped forward and peeked in the doorway.

"You got a great watchdog here," the cute cop said.

Colombo cowered in the bathtub.

"He's been through a lot lately," she said defensively.

"Find anything missing?"

She shook her head.

"Looks like your dog scared him off," sandy mustache said with a dirty laugh.

Lydia thanked them for their trouble and, still a little drunk and a lot weary, was glad to see them go. But as soon as the door closed, she wished they'd hung around longer. She'd forgotten she had to walk Colombo. She snapped on his leash and grabbed the L. L. Bean bag containing all the necessary paraphernalia. Better to get this over and done with.

It was raining still. Worse yet, the streetlight a few doors down was out. The little light available came from dimly lit doorways and the watery headlights of an occasional passing car.

She jaywalked Colombo across the street where it wasn't quite so dark, although the still leafy trees kept the streetlight from filtering through. Ordinarily she'd have enjoyed the sound of rain pattering on tree leaves, but now her concern was hearing footsteps behind her. Time for some happy drunks to come stumbling out of the Coconut Grill, singing some hokey out-of-tune song. But they weren't so obliging tonight.

And Colombo, who usually didn't like getting wet, seemed not to mind in the least. He stopped to sniff everything in sight. Although occasionally lifting his leg to establish territorial rights, he wasn't the least bit interested in serious peeing. Lydia grew impatient. She guessed she just wasn't a dog person. If anything, she was partial to cats. But getting a cat meant having to find someone to take care of it when she went to Paris or Italy on some fashion jaunt.

She didn't trust animal boardinghouses. The animals coming back from such places looked wretched. She'd have to find Colombo a new home. No use asking anyone at *gazelle*. They'd want only the snob dog of the year. Maybe she should take him to the ASPCA; someone somewhere would no doubt want a big orange and white mutt.

She gave Colombo's leash a jerk, then apologized for being so rough and headed home.

Mrs. Nagy popped into the hall when she reached the foot of the stairs. "I wait down here until you go up," she said. "You call down when you get inside. Those cops, they say they didn't find nobody. But I'm not some old lady who imagines things."

Lydia assured Mrs. Nagy that she knew she wasn't, almost wishing she were.

After calling down to Mrs. N, Lydia went into the living room, kicked out the pink futon, and threw sheets over the mattress. She was about to fall into bed when she remembered the cassette. She padded barefoot to her desk and opened the lap drawer. Not there. Funny, she was sure that's where she'd put it. Maybe she'd left it in the machine, after all. She tried both sides. No luck. All she heard other than recent calls was whirring.

She tried every cassette she could find. Nothing! Stolen? But Neil was the only person she'd told about Adam's message.

Except he wouldn't have had time to slip in and grab a cassette before the cops got here. Or would he? After all, she'd been delayed by going back to get her umbrella. Also, she hadn't been navigating very well. And Neil had taken a cab. It wouldn't have taken long to get here.

But Neil was no Houdini. He didn't have her keys. The only person who did was Adam, who kept them in his East End apartment. She'd given him a duplicate set in case she lost hers, identified them on a tag so that Adam—easily confused when drunk, and drunk most of the time—wouldn't confuse his keys with hers. Conveniently identifying them for the cassette snatcher, who, she was relieved to know, couldn't have been Neil since she'd given Adam her keys long after their feud.

Adam had put the keys in a pigeonhole in his rolltop desk.

So who would have access to Adam's desk? Anyone who visited Adam—which meant Vanessa, Todd, and Urzaga. Also, Francoise might have run across them the infrequent times she gave anything more than a swipe when she dusted. But Francoise would hardly have been the person he was expecting that fatal night. And he wouldn't have told Lydia it was someone she liked (if that was what he'd said), even if—as Neil suggested—Adam was being ironic, since Adam was aware that she didn't particularly like or dislike Francoise. Had Adam told the person who visited him that she'd called and he'd called back with a message? Maybe.

Certainly the police should hear about this.

Lydia called the Nineteenth Precinct and spoke to a gravelly voiced man who identified himself as Officer Swit. Officer Swit did not think a stolen cassette was of any great consequence.

"Listen, lady, if that's all you're missing, you got off easy."

"But the cassette is connected to a murder. It's important."

"Yeah, well, in that case you should call Homicide."

"The murder took place in Southampton. A Detective Barolini out there is handling it."

"Yeah, well, call him, miss. Not us. Only I'd advise you to wait until morning."

Great.

Lydia made coffee, starting from scratch, grinding the beans. Blue Mountain coffee she'd bought from Zabar's. Coffee would keep her awake all night, but she couldn't sleep anyway, aware that Adam's murderer had the keys to her apartment. Maybe there was more than one person involved. Neil knew about the tape. Francoise knew about the keys. And possibly Vanessa, Todd Bigelow, or Urzaga. The murderer might have made a wild guess that Adam had called and left some kind of incriminating message on her machine. Someone cautious and thorough, or sly and practiced. It all seemed far-fetched, but then so did Adam's murder.

She drank her coffee pacing the kitchen, too wired to stay in one place. The ceiling lightbulb, which she'd covered with a white Japanese paper lantern, left the kitchen shadowy, creepy. She made a tour of the apartment, turning on all the lights.

It struck her that someone might have left through the fire escape window. It was fire-department-approved and could only be opened from the inside. But he—or she—wouldn't have gotten far. The fire escape was like a balcony. No steps leading down and none leading up. The fire escape–balcony connected only with a neighbor's apartment. Who also had a gate. Leaving the intruder stranded. Lydia's heart began to thump. She couldn't see out with all the lights on, but anyone outside could see in.

She doused the lights, found the magnetic-sided flashlight on the refrigerator, and cautiously approached the fire escape window. She felt a nearby presence and nearly had heart failure until fur brushed her hand. Colombo! Comforting to have him beside her. Maybe he wasn't so cowardly after all. Or did he expect her to protect him? Great. But if someone was out there, he'd at least bark. Wouldn't he?

Peering through the diamond-shaped openings of the iron gate, she spied no bulky shadows. After making sure the gate was latched, she switched on the flashlight and played it over the fire escape. Nothing but her stacked clay flowerpots and a window box with dead flowers.

Once again she returned to the futon. She tried to sleep, but couldn't. Staring up at the blank, black ceiling, she realized that her proof that Adam had expected someone else to visit him on the night of his murder was gone. She had the sneaking suspicion that Barolini wouldn't believe the cassette had ever existed in the first place.

CHAPTER 7

Barolini lifted a finger from the steering wheel of the gray Toyota and pointed. "See over there? That's where Miller lives."

"Looks pretty run-down," Kramer said.

"Don't expect to find a broken-down pile of shit like that in the Nineteenth Precinct, do you? Supposed to cover the richest district in Manhattan. No wonder she's itching to get her hands on fat boy's money."

Kramer, who was some twenty pounds over regulation weight, wished Barolini wouldn't keep calling Adam Auerbach "fat boy." Even on a Saturday morning, Barolini was his usual trim, sartorially elegant self, sporting gray slacks, navy blazer, and polished loafers. Kramer wore a maroon jogging suit and sneakers. For comfort, not exercise. He knew he looked like a slob, but what the hell. This was his day off. Or supposed to be.

"I got enough incriminating evidence right now to haul the lady in," Barolini said. "Except she's already got a good criminal lawyer waiting in the wings. If we take her now, she'll call him in as soon as I read her rights. What we do first is wring out a confession."

All this was making Kramer uneasy. "How do you know she's got a lawyer?"

"Because that's her MO. What I gotta do first is find a place to park this fucking crate."

They passed luxury high-rises and squat tenements, Buon Gusto café, McLaughlin's men's store, a thrift shop called Housing Works, and McCabe's Liquor Store. Kramer was glad that Barolini was driving. After the accident—no, call it murder—driving made him nervous. Not that having Barolini behind the wheel was exactly soothing.

"What time you got?" Barolini asked.

"Nine twenty-seven. We're early."

"Nothing in the book says we can't be, huh, Einstein?" Barolini asked, grinning over. "Catch her with her guard down."

Kramer had been saddled with the name Einstein in Homicide after he'd appeared on "Jeopardy." He'd made it to the final round but blew it on a daily double, betting three thousand on American literature, a category he thought he knew. The answer was the family in *The Grapes of Wrath*. The question was "Who were the Joads?" He blanked. After that, whenever anyone mentioned Steinbeck, he winced. Since then, he'd boned up on everything Steinbeck ever wrote, including his collected letters. He knew that Steinbeck had considered it not only a duty but an honor to pay his taxes, and that Elizabeth Otis, now deceased, of MacIntosh & Otis, had been his agent.

He also knew that Steinbeck had once lived in this part of town. He wasn't sure where, but he thought on Seventy-eighth. They were on Park Avenue now. Buildings with canopied entrances overlooked a traffic island of yellow chrysanthemums.

"Damn. I thought we might find something this far over," Barolini said.

Kramer offered to take care of the garage fee.

Which raised Barolini's hackles. "Money's not the problem. It's the fucking principle of the thing. I'm not shelling out money to those pickpockets."

"Right," Kramer said, sorry he'd made the offer.

"Whaddaya mean right?" Barolini asked. "I get paid more than you. And I don't pay any fucking alimony either. Wendy doesn't need it now she's snagged Daddy Warbucks and lives in her Great Neck palace. Won't even accept child support. I want to pay. Courtney's my kid, goddammit. My daughter belongs to *me*, not that fat, bald son of a bitch her mother married."

"How old is she?"

"Forty, but I'll say this for her. She doesn't look it."

"I meant Courtney."

"Just turned thirteen. August twenty-sixth. I got her a VCR for her birthday. Know what she said? 'Thanks, Dad, but I already have one.' Anything I get her, that son of a bitch has beat me to it. Sixty-something. Older than Auerbach. Maybe richer."

Barolini belched and excused himself. "Fucking Egg McMuffins. Used to have a cast-iron stomach. Now anything I eat, I get gas."

They'd stopped off at McDonald's on their way in from headquarters out in Yaphank. It wasn't just Miller who Barolini had given short notice to today, but also Kramer. He'd counted on spending the day with his kid, but had to leave Andy with a sitter.

Barolini was heading east on Seventy-sixth in his quest for a parking space. If he'd taken Seventy-eighth, Kramer could have looked for Steinbeck's house. It was redbrick and still standing. How many brick houses were left in New York City? Probably a landmark building. With a plaque saying "John Steinbeck lived here."

Barolini was still carrying on about Wendy. ". . . She spent all her time looking for things I did wrong, told Courtney not to chew with her mouth open like her father. She's cunning and conniving—like Miller. Mom was right. I should have married a nice girl named Maria."

"What makes you so sure Miller did it?" Kramer asked, changing the subject. Also, he'd just gotten back from Toronto two days before and was completely in the dark on the details of the murder.

"Call it a cop's nose," Barolini said. "Fourteen years at this job, you smell something wrong. This is gonna be a case that isn't passed on to EIT to solve." He meant the Extended Investigation Team. "Look at that, fucking U-Haul parked right in front of a fire hydrant. They got no respect for the law in this town, you know that?"

Kramer didn't answer. Barolini didn't expect him to.

"So what's your evidence she did it?" Kramer asked again.

"Well, first, we got this Dr. Urzaga, who found her in the pool drowning him. What more evidence you need than that? He says she told him she was trying to save Auerbach. She said her husband just died and she flipped out . . . couldn't face another death. Now, that's the kinda thing could get sympathy from a jury, so what we're going for here's a confession."

"Are we?"

"You with me or against me?" Barolini asked.

Barolini was going the same route, Seventy-seventh west, Seventy-sixth east. A suggestion that he try some other streets would be construed as criticism. "I just don't know what the hell this is all about, that's all. I was away, remember?"

"So I'm telling you. Just listen. Next, Miller's got a motive—money. She's in his will. Don't know how much yet. I'm seeing that kid Monday."

"What kid is this?"

"Yeah, well, that's what he looks like, a kid. The one's handling the will. You want more? I got someone puts Miller on the scene with fat boy just before the murder. I ran across this waitress at a pub in Water Mill waited on Miller and him. They were there around five, five-thirty, she says. After she'd just come on duty. Bobbie, her name is. Auerbach ordered cheeseburgers, fries, and beer. Which was what was found in the stomach contents. That and enough drugs and alcohol to kill an ordinary man. But he didn't OD. And it wasn't a heart attack. The poor son of a bitch was drowned, bruises on his shoulder. Someone held him down."

"How'd you think of looking in a pub in Water Mill?"

"I didn't until the ME told me the stomach contents. Checked out Auerbach's kitchen. No leftover hamburger, and nothing in the garbage showed he'd had the fries or burgers home. So I figured he'd had them out. You don't eat burgers and fries at a fancy restaurant, even if you're a multimillionaire, right?"

"Yeah, I'd say so."

"So I scouted hamburger-type places. Flashed around Auerbach's picture I got from his wife. Ex-wife. The second one. She said it wasn't a real likeness. Nothing recent, but the most recent she had. Fatter he got, the more he hated having his picture taken. She didn't say fatter, something like 'as Adam put on additional weight.' The lady loved him, you can tell that. And by her account, he loved her."

"Looks like you're doing a thorough job."

"Yeah, well, I had to. I was on this case solo. Lieutenant pulled Orrie Wade off to help Nassau Homicide, and you up there chasing tail in Toronto."

Kramer didn't say he'd taken Andy up to visit her aunt, Laura's sister. Barolini would make something out of that, too. He hated working with Barolini, who up to now had treated him like he was a suspect in Auerbach's murder, telling him nothing.

Suffolk Homicide was made up of three teams, eight to a team, but they were on a skeleton staff now. Everyone except Kramer and Barolini had been siphoned off to join in an intensive manhunt, searching woods and deserted areas for the bodies of missing women. Four in less than a year. None of the women was the type to do a disappearing act. One single, three seemingly happily married, kids, steady jobs—a schoolteacher, a CPA, a paralegal, and a real estate agent, between the ages of twenty-five and forty.

Each woman had gone out alone in the evening to some community or social function and hadn't returned. The CPA had been missing the longest. Since December. The latest, a real estate agent from Quogue, had been missing a week now. All but the one from Quogue lived in Nassau County. Nassau Homicide had concluded that a serial killer was at large.

Kramer wished he'd been put on the case. He'd done a lot of reading on serial murderers—Bundy, Berkowitz, John Wayne Gacy, Juan Corona—his interest dating back to reading about Jack the Ripper when he was a kid.

"One thing about serial murderers," Kramer said. "They're all con artists."

"I don't wonder about anything but the case I'm working on. You got an attitude, Einstein."

"How's that?"

"You're not interested in this case. Forget serial murderers. This one's got it all—adultery, murder, money. Gonna have the media boys and girls swarming around when it's cracked. Provided that happens before those Boy Scouts in Nassau come up with some missing bodies and another Ted Bundy. Give Miller a few jolts, she'll break. Neurotic. Those types break easy. Auerbach's exes, they're neurotic, too. Fat boy liked 'em like that. Anorexic neurotics."

"All three women?" Kramer asked. They were back on Seventy-seventh passing Miller's building again.

"Nah, the second wife, she's got flesh on her bones. Nice boobs, too."

"What did she have to say?" Kramer had to yell to be heard above a siren behind them.

"She was rehearsing all day," Barolini said, pulling over to let an ambulance pass. It turned into Emergency at Lenox Hill Hospital. When was Barolini going to give up and go to a garage?

"Rehearsing? She's an actress?"

"Director. Has a theater on Forty-fourth Street. An actor the name of Todd Bigelow backed up her alibi. Said she was working on some scenes with him and another guy. Thing is, Bigelow's her boyfriend. But the other guy verified their alibi. Says they were at her theater from four to seven."

"Her theater?"

"*Hers.* She owns it. Fat boy bought it for her. She calls Miller the Black Widow."

Barolini was waiting for him to ask why, so he obliged.

"Her husband died a month ago. August. Only forty-one. Our age."

Kramer didn't point out he was six years younger, and Barolini three years older. "What'd he die of?"

"AIDS."

"Christ!"

"Vanessa Auerbach claims he got it from Miller. Says she killed him as well as Auerbach," Barolini said. "That van up ahead is gonna pull out. Think you can manage walking five blocks, Einstein? Better start running it off. Five feet ten and two hundred twenty-five pounds. Now, ain't that embarrassing?"

"I'm five eleven and two fifteen. That's not so bad."

Barolini's laugh was replaced by a scowl. "Shit, he's not moving. We'll circle Miller's block one more time. Then if we don't find anything, we'll put the car in the garage."

This time they went east on Seventy-eighth. On the north side of the street between Lexington and Third were some ivy-covered redbrick town houses. Which one had Steinbeck lived in?

Before he could get a good look, they'd passed. Between Third and Second were more redbrick houses. Barolini nodded toward one. "See that? That's where fat boy's first wife lives," he said. "She and Miller are neighbors."

"What's she like?"

"Ditsy redhead. A phony. Kinda snotty but not as bad as Miller. Miller looks at a cop like she's holding her nose. The way Wendy looks at me. You can tell she thinks we're all scum. Anyone not making big money is beneath her. Thinks her ass is worth a ton. She won't after I nail her."

"Who? Miller or Wendy?"

"What do you mean?"

"Sounds like you're getting them confused."

"I resent that, Kramer. Like I said, you got an attitude problem. What you don't see is, they're both alike—gold diggers. Miller's guilty. Her alibis don't jibe, and a witness says he saw her drowning the victim. Also, one month after fat boy puts her in his will, he's dead. Now, what more do you want?"

"It's too obvious. If she's going to murder him, she's not going to hang around for someone to find her."

"Yeah, well, that's what her criminal lawyer's going to say, but I say she wasn't expecting a call from the next-door neighbor."

"How about the first wife? What's her alibi?"

"Says she was home. I believe her. If she was guilty, she'd have cooked something up. Says she only 'saw' fat boy on the phone. Funny way to put it. You don't see people on the phone. Not yet. She was home alone watching a dirty movie the night he was done."

"Did she actually call it a dirty movie?"

"Nah, she called it an erotic film. Something she made as a class project. She's got a lot of fancy words for fucking. 'Equal pleasuring,' for one. 'No monster shots of genitalia. No in-and-out sex'—that's the way she talks. She invited Orrie Wade and me to have a look at it. See what you missed?"

"You enjoy it?"

"Didn't get a chance to see it. Orrie had to get home to the little woman. Pussy-whipped. But then so was I once upon a time. What happens when you get married. Don't do it, Einstein, take it from me. Grab yourself a piece and keep moving."

Barolini pointed to his head. "You heard of widows turning gray overnight, but I bet this is the first time you heard of a guy turning gray after a divorce. It wasn't losing Wendy that did it. It was losing my kid.

"She thought the sun rose and set with her dad. Now she won't have anything to do with me. Yeah, well, you know . . ." Barolini paused. "I'm out risking my life for peanuts, and Wendy, she's out finding herself a rich guy, older than God."

"So you said." Kramer might have felt more sympathetic if he hadn't heard the story so often. Also, it had happened nine years back. How long before Barolini let go?

"Should have been smart like you, Einstein, and not married."

"I was married."

"No kidding?"

"You knew I had a kid."

"Oh, yeah. Right. A boy. How old?"

"It's a girl. Andy, short for Andrea. She's eight."

"Courtney's got five years on her. How come you never mention your divorce?"

"I wasn't divorced."

"So what happened, Einstein? You murder your wife?"

"You might say that. Car crash. I was driving."

Kramer kept his eyes focused on a jogger plugged into a Walkman.

"Shit. That's tough. I'm sorry."

Real regret sounded in Barolini's voice. That surprised Kramer, and he told Barolini what he seldom talked about.

"We'd gone to Laura's co-worker's wedding in Bridgehampton. On our way back to Mom's to pick up Andrea, some teenage kids racing cars rammed into our Honda. On Laura's side. We kept spinning around until the car hit a tree. Also on Laura's side."

"Jesus. They ever catch the fuckers?"

"The car was stolen. I tracked it down and found the kids." Which was how he'd landed in Homicide five years ago. It seemed like a long time now, but the accident still felt like yesterday. So why blame Barolini for talking about his divorce after nine years when he had trouble talking about Laura's death after six?

"I give up," Barolini said. "Let's put this fucking crate in a garage."

"You two looking for someone?"

The voice sounded like a young girl's, but when Kramer looked around, he saw an elderly woman leaning on a pillow in a first-floor window.

"Lydia Miller. You know her?" Barolini asked.

"Oh, my, yes. Such a nice girl. You from the police?"

"How'd you guess?"

"I thought you'd be back again after last night. Lydia, she said she knew I wasn't imagining things, but those two, they didn't believe me. I'm glad they sent somebody else. I think maybe her boyfriend, he had something to do with it. He sent someone up there to get her."

"Hear that? A new guy already," Barolini said to Kramer in an undertone. "What's her boyfriend like?" he asked the woman.

"He's no good. I think she finally found that out. He don't come around lately. Not even polite enough to go up and get her. Sometimes he's so drunk, he can't stand up. Sits on the stoop like some bum. And Lydia, she's so sweet. Pretty, too. I don't know what she sees in that fat man."

"Yeah, well, I know," Barolini said under his breath. "I bet you see a lot from that window," he said to the woman.

"Oh, my, yes. You'd be surprised what goes on around here."

"I bet. You here on the Sunday of Labor Day weekend?"

"Oh, no, my daughter, she comes and gets me and we go on a picnic. With my grandchildren. I got a granddaughter in college, you believe that?"

"Never would've guessed," Barolini said, and winked at Kramer. "Push 4E," he ordered.

Kramer pushed 4E.

They waited.

"Nagy," Kramer said, reading the name under 1W. "Must be the lady we just talked to." One of the books he'd read on Steinbeck had pointed out that a lot of Hungarians and Czechs lived in the neighborhood. The name Nagy was Hungarian.

"The old woman and Miller are the only ones living here," Barolini told him.

"How do you know that?"

"You can tell. Those other names in the mailbox slots are so faded, you can't read them. And two don't even have names."

"Ever think of becoming a detective?" Kramer asked.

Barolini laughed. "I've thought about going into a more lucrative line of work, like digging ditches. Try 4E again. Maybe she skipped. She does that, she's in real trouble."

Kramer pressed the yellowing button and shifted his sneakered feet, noticing the broken and missing tiles in the entranceway. "She lives all alone up there under the roof. Easily broken into. That's dangerous."

"She's the one that's dangerous."

The response buzzer sounded.

They went in. A flickering fluorescent wall light threatened to go out any minute. The brown linoleum on the stairs was chewed and ancient. What was left of it.

"Good place for a sex crime," Barolini said, and laughed. He was suddenly in good spirits.

CHAPTER 8

The buzzer woke her.

After Barolini's call at the ungodly hour of seven, she'd walked Colombo, come back home, folded the futon, flopped down on it with her clothes on, and gone back to sleep, knowing the drive in from that far out on Long Island would take over two hours.

Now she sat up and yawned. Luckily, she didn't have a hangover. That was all she needed. Routine questioning, Barolini had said. Why hadn't he told her last night that he was coming in today? Trying to catch her off guard, was he? And damn it, she'd been so sleepy this morning, she'd forgotten to mention the missing cassette.

The buzzer rang again. She put last night's coffee on the burner before pushing the response button. The doorbell sounded before she got a chance to comb her hair. Lydia left the chain lock on and opened the door a few inches.

Barolini stood at the door, hatefully neat in gray slacks and blue blazer. His thick gray hair looked freshly shampooed and blow-dried.

Another man, in a jogging suit and sneakers, was heading toward the apartment across the hall where Casey used to live.

"Is he with you?" she asked Barolini.

"You're pointed the wrong way, Einstein," Barolini called.

Einstein? "No one over there," Lydia said. "It's locked."

"No it's not," Einstein said, disappearing through Casey's door.

Lydia undid the chain lock and shot past Barolini, momentarily forgetting her motto about live cowards and dead heros.

"Stand back," Barolini ordered, catching up with her at Casey's door. He stepped in front of her, barring her way.

The place smelled of stale cooking and roach spray. She peered beyond Barolini, who had stepped inside Casey's apartment, and saw nothing but an empty kitchen except for a refrigerator and stove. When Barolini's back was turned, she snuck in, and noticed the fire escape gate. "That gate was locked when Casey left."

"Didn't I tell you to wait outside?"

"You said to stand back."

Barolini rudely gave her a small shove out into the hall and shut the door behind her. She returned to her apartment and poured herself what was left of the coffee. A third of a cup wouldn't do it. She put on the teakettle and waited. She guessed if they scared anyone up over there, she'd know soon enough.

A few minutes later there was a knock on the door. She opened it to Einstein and Barolini. "Find anything?"

Barolini wasn't saying.

"A boot in the closet," Einstein said. "I locked the gate. You'd better get the super to put on a better lock. If they got in once, they can do it again." He held out a hand. "Detective Kramer." He looked the opposite of the Kramer on "Seinfeld." Not tall, skinny, and goofy, but tall, chubby, and serious. His clasp was warm and he had nice brown eyes.

"Lydia Miller," she said. "I guess you know that. But how did you know that door was unlocked?" She'd also like to ask how he got his nickname. Because he was brainy?

"He leaned against the door and fell in," Barolini said.

"I saw daylight through a crack. It could have been that the door didn't fit, but I thought I'd check."

"God, this really spooks me." She was about to tell them about the missing cassette with Adam's message when the teakettle started rocking and whistling.

"Coffee?" she asked.

Kramer said coffee would be fine.

"Got any herbal tea?" Barolini asked.

His request surprised her. She'd expect a macho cop like him to drink only hairy-chested, vile-tasting black stuff.

"Chamomile, black currant, apple cinnamon, or orange spice?"

"Chamomile."

"I'll bring it to you in the living room. It's due north overlooking the street." She pointed down the hall.

Barolini didn't take the hint. "We'll keep you company," he said, leaning against the inside window ledge that divided the kitchen from her workroom.

Great. She wasn't legally awake, her unbrushed teeth felt like they were wearing sweaters, and she had to bear his scrutiny and answer his questions while she made his damn herbal tea. She would have made coffee from scratch for herself and Kramer, but she wanted to get the ordeal over with and used instant instead.

She got cups and saucers from the bookcase. Kramer straddled a kitchen chair, his brown eyes scanning the bookcase as if he were taking inventory of the china and glassware she kept there. Although the kitchen was huge, there was just one cupboard. Its two top shelves were only within reach of basketball players.

Barolini was giving her apartment the once-over with the same look of contempt it got from repair people and delivery boys. Only her friends found the crooked doorways and listing floors charming. Which was why they were her friends.

Kramer eyed the linoleum. "I always liked Jackson Pollack," he said.

She smiled, deciding she liked him, and reminded herself that she was no longer interested in men. She'd splattered red, yellow, and white paint on the linoleum to conceal the holes and worn spots.

Barolini eyed her suspiciously as she put the tray on the counter beside the stove. Her T-shirt had shrunk. Probably he thought she was out to seduce him.

"Adam called when I was on my way out that Sunday and left a message on my tape. He said some things you should hear. I saved the cassette, but someone broke in and stole it. Actually, they didn't break in but used a duplicate key. Nothing else was disturbed. Just the cassette missing."

"You hand keys around?"

She would have thought Barolini would be more interested in Adam's message than what she did with her keys. "I gave a set to Adam since he lived nearby. In case I lost mine. He kept them in a pigeonhole in his desk. My name was on them. Anyone visiting him might have noticed. Then, of course, there's his cleaning woman, but I don't see how she'd be involved."

Lydia glimpsed a flicker in Barolini's eye. He must know who was in the will. Had Adam left Francoise a tidy sum? She knew he'd paid for Francoise's psychiatrist for what she called her *crise des nerfs*.

"Unfortunately, I'd labeled the cassette 'Adam's Last Words' for easy identification. One of the things he said was that he was expecting another visitor. Either someone I liked or would like. It wasn't clear—Colombo was barking, making too much noise. But I don't know many of his friends, and the ones I do, I'm not especially fond of. Maybe he was being ironic."

She didn't mention that Neil was the only one she'd told about the cassette since she suspected Barolini was the sort who'd be antagonistic toward gay men. He might make it tougher for Neil than for her.

"Why would he leave a message if he knew you'd left?"

"Probably he thought I was still here. In the bathroom or in a hurry to leave. I don't always pick up."

Barolini looked unconvinced. "You're saying someone walked in, stole the tape, and walked out?"

"When I came back last night the cops were here. Mrs. Nagy called them—"

"We know all that," Barolini cut in. "Tea's going to get cold."

"I haven't poured the water yet."

"Mrs. Nagy told us," Kramer explained. And got a dirty look from Barolini for imparting such highly classified information. Or were they playing good cop, bad cop? Kramer the nice, helpful one and Barolini the rotten, mean one.

"Did you play Adam's phone messages in Southampton?" Lydia asked, getting out the box of mixed tea bags and a jar of Taster's Choice.

"What messages?" Kramer said, looking questioningly at Barolini, who hadn't mentioned any.

Barolini shrugged. "The only message was from Ms. Miller here saying she was on her way out."

"But before that? Before mine?"

"Before yours was a message from his ex-wife. The second one. Sunday, I'd say. She apologized for calling Auerbach so early in the morning. Auerbach picked up. That was it."

"What happened to the messages in between? On my stolen cassette, Adam had said he was keeping the messages left by people he'd cut off. The ones he used to give lying-around money to. They should have been on the tape between Vanessa's call and mine."

Barolini made no comment except to ask what in hell lying-around money was.

"You've heard of walking-around money? Adam gave people money so they could loaf. Maybe that way he felt he wasn't the only person who couldn't hold down a job."

"I never heard of such a thing," Barolini said.

"Prepare yourself. Adam did a lot of unheard-of things. He said he was saving the messages to give him a good laugh when he was depressed. That it was great fun hearing them cry and grovel and beg him to reconsider. Someone had to have erased that tape. There must have been a gap between those two calls."

Again Barolini refused to say.

She loaded everything on a wicker tray and led them past the workroom, where Colombo hid out under the desk, into the living room.

Kramer inspected the fireplace.

"It doesn't work. Smokes," she said. The fireplace had been her first big project when she moved in. She'd set to work scrubbing the soot off blackened bricks, replacing missing ones, and filling in holes and zigzagging cracks with cement. After that, she'd painted the cement the color of the original brick, carefully adding white to red. The pro-

ject got her through Mark's last days. Sometimes she had
awakened in the middle of the night and gone to work.

Lydia handed tea to Barolini and coffee to Kramer, who
was now looking over the books on the shelves she'd put
up between the fireplace and the window. "You've got
Steinbeck's *Winter of Our Discontent*," he said. "I've been
looking for that book."

"You can borrow it if you like."

Maybe these weren't ordinary cops after all. One drank
chamomile tea and the other read books.

"Thanks. I'll take good care of it."

But Barolini gave Kramer a look when he took the book
from the shelf. Kramer put the book back. "That's okay, I'll
get it from the library."

Apparently Barolini considered book borrowing equivalent to bribery.

"You take those?" Barolini asked, nodding toward
Mark's photographs of sand dunes.

"My husband's. His last work. He took them out near
Amagansett when we were visiting Adam."

Kramer sat down on the pink futon, but Barolini still
roamed the room.

"You two visit your fat friend often?" Barolini asked.

"His name is Adam. And it was damn nice of him to offer us his place when Mark was sick."

"What was wrong with him?"

She hesitated and hated herself for hesitating. She
thought she'd taught herself better than that. "AIDS."

"Hemophiliac, homosexual, or user?" Barolini asked, sitting down beside Kramer.

Did she have to be put through this? "Bisexual."

Barolini's face showed he thought no such person existed. She wished Kramer were asking the questions. He'd
handle them with more finesse. But Barolini was clearly in
charge here. Anyway, cops couldn't care less about finesse.
But why wasn't Kramer taking notes? Wasn't that how it
went?

Colombo padded into the room and rested his head on
her thigh. She stroked the soft white fur between the orange
floppy ears. "Adam's dog," she explained. "Colombo.

Named after that sloppy TV detective. So was Adam—sloppy, that is. Which was why he liked the detective. Colombo led me to the pool that night."

"What time did you say you got there?" Barolini asked.

"Around eight-thirty. Maybe nine."

"Took you over eight hours to get from New York to Southampton?"

"Eight! How did you come up with that? It took me less than four. Not bad considering I was driving a thirdhand Datsun with windshield wipers that didn't work in a nasty storm."

"Your super saw you leave before noon."

"Sal? He's lying. He was drinking with his cronies outside Harry's Hula Hut on Second Avenue. In the late afternoon."

"Why would he lie?"

"For one thing, I told him to get lost in front of his friends. For another, Mrs. Nagy downstairs claims the landlord wants him to get rid of us so they can warehouse the building until rents go up. But trying to put me in prison seems a bit extreme."

"You said it, I didn't," Barolini said.

"I left here about a quarter to five. I remember the time because the clock stopped at four thirty-three. Not long after the fuse blew."

"Why didn't you just put a fuse in instead of going all the way out to Southampton?"

"The fuse box isn't in my apartment. It's in the basement. And the basement door is kept locked. Check it out when you leave. Adam had been after me to come out all weekend, but I was doing some freelance work and couldn't. Besides, I didn't want to."

"Why not?" Kramer asked.

"Well, for one thing, he was drunk."

"What were the other reasons?"

She shrugged. "Personal. Anyway, it was fiendishly hot, and when the fuse blew I gave up and went out. When I called Adam to tell him I was coming I got his machine. So I left a message that I was on my way. There had to be a gap between Vanessa's early morning message and mine in the late afternoon."

Again Barolini wasn't saying.

Kramer had sunk deeper into the futon than Barolini, who kept sliding slowly toward him. Lydia looked forward to seeing Barolini end up in Kramer's lap.

"What happened when you got there?" Barolini said.

"Adam's house was dark, and that seemed strange. The door was unlocked, so I just walked in. Not even Colombo was there to greet me. He usually jumps all over people. Used to. He's totally different now. In mourning for Adam, which is more than anyone else is."

"Including you?" Barolini asked.

The same question she'd been asking herself. "I don't know. Is that how it looks?"

Barolini didn't answer.

"Actually, wailing and breast-beating isn't my style. I leave the histrionics to his ex-wife Vanessa. She's the actress."

"Jealous?"

"I know I have a bad habit of falling for the wrong man, but Adam was too impossible even for me. My shrink said he was the emotional equivalent of a five-year-old. He'd go into rages accusing his friends of freeloading, then suffer fits of remorse and beg them to take his money."

"You take it?"

"I earn my keep."

"How many freeloaders did fat boy have?"

"You take a special pleasure in calling him that. So what if he was fat? When it comes to Jake and the Fat Man, I'll take the Fat Man any day."

Kramer, who was far from skinny, smiled.

"Actually," she said, "I'll take the dog."

"Looks like you got the dog."

"I assure you, Detective Barolini, I didn't murder Adam to get him. I took Colombo in because I had to. Want a pet?"

"How is he with kids?" Kramer asked.

Married then. So what? Romance was the last thing she needed. "I don't know about kids, but he likes cats."

"Why'd you wait until the cassette was missing to tell me about your boyfriend's message?" Barolini asked.

Lydia sighed. Which was worse—calling Adam her fat friend or her boyfriend? "Because I didn't think it was murder," she said, spacing each word out. "Until you dropped that bomb and walked away. Then you wake me up at seven to tell me you're coming in. You could have told me that last night. And what makes you so damn sure it was murder? Is this another of your secrets? Or maybe you don't know. Just a suspicion."

"It was murder. We got prints," Barolini said, gray space-alien eyes trained on her.

"Fingerprints would have washed off, wouldn't they?"

"*Im*prints. Bruises. No sign of a heart attack. Someone drowned him."

"But the ambulance driver and Urzaga both said it was a heart attack."

"They were wrong. The ME said differently."

"Adam was a strong swimmer. Water was his element." Her hands began trembling, clattering the cup against the saucer. Something Barolini would interpret as a sure sign of guilt.

"Someone held him under," Barolini said evenly.

"It wouldn't have been easy. Adam was a big man. He might not have been the world's greatest athlete, but he had weight on his side."

"An anorexic seven-year-old could have done it with the amount of alcohol and drugs the ME found in his blood. A normal man would have OD'd. Your boyfriend was too fucking weak to fight back. He was drowned. And Alec Urzaga said it looked like you were drowning him."

"With the yard lights on to attract attention? That's absurd," she said, her voice rising at the end. She took a deep breath to regain control. "My husband died recently. I didn't want someone else to die on me. I guess unconsciously I knew Adam was dead, but I couldn't accept it. I just freaked out. I was trying to save him, goddamn it."

She saw Barolini glance at Kramer and nod. What did that mean?

"Urzaga—not me—is the one with the motive for murder," she told them. "Adam said he had something on him that would cost him his job. And put him behind bars. He was going to report it to someone on the board at Hamptons Hospital. Tuesday. After Labor Day weekend. Also, he said he'd told Urzaga he was taking him out of his will. Or rather, taking out Urzaga's foundation."

"Was he taking you out, too?"

"Actually, it would have been to my advantage if he'd lived. He'd said that afternoon on the phone that he was changing his will and leaving everything to me." Not that she'd believed it.

"What time did you and Auerbach go to that bar on Sunday?"

"What bar? I wasn't out there until after he'd been murdered, remember?" Why was she feeling guilty when everything she said was true?

"Bar, pub, restaurant—whatever you call it. Megan's. In Water Mill. Sunday around six."

"Megan's Saloon, I think it's called. I wasn't there."

"What was the big fight about?"

"There was no fucking fight."

Barolini smiled. No doubt, in his book women who said "fuck" were killers.

"Bobbie, the waitress, tells it different. She took your order. Auerbach had a double order of fries, three cheeseburgers—one to go. You had a seafood salad and Perrier. Bobbie remembers you well."

"Bobbie was confused. It's very busy on Labor Day weekend. Adam could have been there. He liked Megan's because it's unpretentious. If you know the Hamptons, you know what he meant."

"I grew up there."

"Oh, yes? Where?"

"Noyac."

"I've been through there."

"Through. Ain't that something? I live there."

"Excuse me? I don't think I understand."

"I didn't expect you to."

And then she did. He was a local, a year-rounder. Who

hated summer people. "I don't go out often. I don't like the Hamptons scene. It's too frantic."

Barolini wasn't interested in her likes or dislikes. "Back to Megan's. You been there? Or *through* there?"

"Adam and I went there. But I definitely wasn't there that Sunday."

"You visit your, uh, friend Adam often?"

"Not after Mark got too sick to sit up in the car. But even before that, when we were visiting Adam, Mark sometimes didn't feel like lunch, so Adam and I went to Megan's. Neither of us liked to cook."

"So you never went out there after Mark died?"

"Right."

"But suddenly you decide to go out the Sunday he was murdered."

"Is that what you're accusing me of? Murder? I thought this was supposed to be just routine questioning. I'm not answering anything more without a lawyer."

She stood up. So did Colombo. And growled.

"Good dog," she said.

Kramer also got to his feet. With some effort. He'd sunk deep into the futon. "Let's get rolling," he said to Barolini.

"Sit down," Barolini ordered. It wasn't clear whether he meant her, Kramer, or both. Maybe even Colombo. "No need to get so excited. No one's accusing you of murder, Ms. Miller."

Lydia heard the unspoken "yet."

"The waitress gave a very accurate description, putting you on the scene Sunday afternoon. I just want to know how that happened."

His gray eyes were on her legs as if the waitress had described them, too.

"What did she say?"

"Tall, blond, skinny, snotty. Her words, not mine."

"I'm sure there are a lot of tall, blond, skinny women out there. I told you I wasn't at Megan's Sunday. Anyway, snotty is a value judgment." But her winged eyebrows gave her a snotty look. How could a waitress at Megan's, where she hadn't been all that often, come so close in her description? And why did the woman want to put her on the scene the night Adam was murdered? "Your Barbie is confused," she said.

"Bobbie," Barolini corrected. "Bobbie, Urzaga, the super. Sounds like everyone was confused but you."

"Gee, a mob."

"One thing Bobbie was sure of. That you two had a hell of a fight. And that your fa— that Auerbach zapped you. Said he was taking you out of his will."

"Adam zapped a lot of people. And I avoid public scenes. I would have walked out."

"Exactly what Bobbie said you did. Come on, let's go." He said it to her, not Kramer.

"You can't just take me in like this," she said. Or could he? Her mouth went dry and her knees weak.

"We're going to the Nineteenth Precinct to get you fingerprinted."

And then what? she didn't say. Afraid to ask. And she didn't even have a lawyer to call.

CHAPTER 9

Lydia had been fingerprinted and dismissed immediately. Barolini had just been trying to scare her. It worked.

She hadn't heard from him for almost a week. Maybe he was letting her sit around and worry about what would happen next. She did.

Sitting in her cubbyhole office at *gazelle*, sipping her second cup of coffee, Lydia considered calling Suffolk Homicide and asking Kramer what was going on. A nice guy. Attractive. And on her side. Or so it seemed. But maybe he and Barolini were playing good cop, bad cop.

Still, Kramer didn't seem to be as intent on nailing her as Barolini. It was almost as if Barolini held some personal grudge against her. But from his point of view she might look guilty—what with Urzaga saying it looked like she was drowning Adam, the super's lie about seeing her leave at noon, and Bobbie's misidentification. Not to mention being in Adam's will. She could be in real trouble. People had ended up in prison on far less evidence. She'd better find a good lawyer. And find out who murdered Adam. She owed him that, anyway.

She'd drive out to Water Mill this weekend and talk to Bobbie at Megan's. Maybe Barolini had asked Bobbie leading questions, guiding her to a description that fit Lydia. Was she a blonde? Tall? That sort of thing. Or Bobbie could have confused Adam with someone else. For days Lydia had been trying to remember if there were any tall, blond, skinny, snotty women at the memorial service. The only ones who came half close were Adam's cousins with their thin smiles. Or her with her eyebrows. It depressed her to think she looked like them.

Lydia had confronted Sal the super, who insisted she'd gotten into her car "near noon."

"You're lying," she'd said.

"Yeah? Ask my buddies. They'll tell you the exact same thing," he'd said with a mean little smile.

So it wasn't just her word against his but also those sleazeballs he hung out with.

Click, click, click. Milke Forte high-heeled it into Lydia's office and sailed a manuscript over her desk. It nearly landed in her coffee. The copy for her column "chic to chic."

"I want new copy by the end of the day," Milke said. She was a wiry, sharp-featured woman rumored to be in her early seventies, but didn't look it. Not that she looked younger. She just looked ageless. Milke had good bones and a slight resemblance to Coco Chanel, which she played to the hilt, wearing little black numbers with silk flowers, ropes of pearls, and gold chains.

"What's wrong with it?" Lydia asked, nodding toward her copy.

"It stinks, darling."

"No worse than the usual crap. Isn't that what you want?"

"Careful, darling," Milke said. "You don't want to get fired before you come into your money. Now, take out all that stale stuff and put this in." She handed Lydia a list.

"I don't have time. Gillian's off sick and I'm doing her job, too."

"Make time. I want new copy by the end of the day." Milke's heels clicked out of the office.

Shit. She had to be at National Trust by three-thirty for the reading of the will. She supposed if she had told Milke, she'd be let off the hook, but she still rued the day she'd been so unhinged by the news of her inheritance that she'd confided in Gillian. Word had spread around the office like wildfire.

She picked up the list of things-to-be-mentioned and went to work, snarling at anyone who stopped by for a chat. She finished by two-thirty.

She raided the office shelves stocked with accessory samples from various designers who hoped they'd be mentioned in her column. She needed something to dress up her vintage St.-Laurent suit, black with braid trim. She chose an art deco pin for the lapel, a delicate gold chain, small pearl earrings, and a cashmere scarf to drape over a shoulder. In ten minutes her outfit was complete.

Copy in hand, she strode into Milke's office.

"Here comes the heiress," Regina Fellows, the beauty editor, chortled. She sat in a chair across from Milke's desk, knees crossed, a Ferragamo dangling from a foot.

"I have to leave now," Lydia said, handing Milke the copy.

"Let's have a look at you," Milke said.

Lydia executed an old runway turn, while Milke inspected her from the top of her blond highlighted hair to the tips of her black pumps.

"Did those little items you're wearing come from the shelves?"

Lydia nodded. She should have brought the copy in first and then gotten accessorized without Milke's knowing it.

"Well, it does look fetching, but don't make it a habit. I

don't want anyone to accuse us of payoffs. For once, you look the way a fashion editor should. Where are you off to, sweetie?"

"Oh, uh, personal business."

"She means the reading of the will." Milke winked at Regina.

Lydia considered denial but knew that Milke wouldn't buy it.

"Poor thing, I hope you get millions. That dear boy," Milke said. "How I loved him." She meant Mark, not Adam, whom she hadn't met. Mark had been her favorite photographer.

"You deserve everything you get," Regina said.

An ambiguous remark if she'd ever heard one.

She walked up Fifth Avenue from Forty-fourth to Fifty-seventh Street, passing Rockefeller Center, where tourists and chrysanthemums were out in abundance. The tourists looked chunky in their layers of clothes—which they could peel off in case they got hot—and their thick-soled walking shoes. Lydia told herself not to be so smug about her appearance, considering what high heels had done to her feet back in her runway days. She saw podiatrists regularly—dancers and models were among their chief patients.

It was a perfect early-autumn-in-New York afternoon, blue skies and yellow cabs. Since she'd skipped lunch, she bought a Diet Pepsi and a hot dog from a street vendor. Munching her way to National Trust, she wondered who the other beneficiaries were and how many.

She hadn't wanted to ask Jared Evans when he'd called, in case she might sound greedy.

No doubt Barolini knew how much she was getting. Did that mean he was suspicious of her because she'd been left a bundle? Dream on, you fool, she told herself. She wiped mustard from her fingers and dropped the napkin and Pepsi can into a trash basket. Anyway, what good would money be if she rotted away in prison?

No doubt Vanessa Auerbach and Urzaga would be at the reading. Would any of Adam's cousins be present? According to Neil, they disapproved of Adam, who returned the compliment, refusing to visit them.

Adam had no children. On purpose, he said, citing a family history of defective genes and a retarded older brother. Both mother and brother were well provided for.

His mother had banned him from her home two years earlier after he'd gone into one of his famous rages at Christmas. At the family dinner table, with numerous relatives present, he'd called her old iron tits and said she'd married his father for his money. Adam always said he pitied his brother, not for being retarded, but for having to live with his mother.

National Trust was located in a massive black marble building that stood back from the sidewalk. Entering through the revolving door, Lydia crossed a lobby the size of a basketball court with highly polished black marble floors and an Egyptian sunburst design in the center. Security guards kept a wary eye out for visitors who didn't look as if they belonged. Lydia wondered how Adam had gotten past them. Maybe Jared Evans had phoned downstairs and told Security not to detain the bum in bedroom slippers.

Consulting the wall directory, she saw that National Trust was on the twenty-first floor. She shared an elevator with three suits—two men and a woman.

The huge reception area of National Trust whispered money by its total waste of space. Two tastefully dressed women, fairly attractive, eyed her from behind a horseshoe-shaped counter. Lydia gave her name. The younger of the two, a brunette wearing a minimum amount of makeup and sensible shoes, led the way down a long, carpeted hall past closed doors and into a conference room.

Lydia half expected to see Barolini lurking in the shadows but found only Vanessa Auerbach and Todd Bigelow seated at a long mahogany table surrounded by empty chairs. Vanessa looked up when Lydia walked in, then quickly looked away as if she couldn't bear the sight of her. Hard to tell where Todd Bigelow was looking in the tortoiseshell sunglasses. He would have been handsome except for a weak chin and a certain furtive look about him.

"How soon will Jared be here?" Vanessa asked the brunette, her melodious voice hinting irritation.

"Mr. Evans will be here promptly at three," the woman said, and left.

Vanessa's face was the rice-powder white of a Kabuki dancer's, her lips a shiny red. Black helmet bangs emphasized her beautiful violet eyes. Like Lydia, she wore a black suit, but hers was low-cut, revealing a bit of sexy black lace and a lot of cleavage. Not exactly daytime wear, but Vanessa obviously was of the if-you've-got-it-flaunt-it school.

Todd Bigelow's thinning white-blond hair was pulled back from his tan face into a ponytail, the way he'd worn it at the memorial service. The contrast between his blond hair and Vanessa's black hair was striking. Especially since he was so tan and she so pale. They looked good together.

Lydia decided to attempt a truce with Vanessa. After all, since Adam's death, Vanessa had to feel there was no longer any need to compete for his affection. Also, since Vanessa had handled the funeral arrangements, she could tell Lydia what had happened to Adam. Was he buried in a cemetery back in Grosse Pointe, or in some remote place in New Jersey? Or maybe he'd been cremated. What had Vanessa done with his ashes?

She leaned forward. "Hi, I'm Lydia. We spoke on the phone," she said, tactfully not mentioning that Vanessa had called her a murderer.

She got a cold stare from the violet eyes. No use trying to bury the hatchet, she decided. It just might end up in her back.

Jared Evans walked in carrying a briefcase and wearing a chalk-striped suit, looking like a kid playing businessman. He smiled in an engaging way and sat down at the head of the table. "We'll begin as soon as everyone's here."

"Who's missing, Jar?" Todd Bigelow asked.

Jared busied himself taking shiny silver, legal-size folders from his briefcase, and didn't seem to hear.

"Who else are you expecting, Jared?" Vanessa asked. The caressing note in her deep, throaty voice implied they were either friends of long standing or lovers.

"Just one more to come."

Urzaga? A cousin? Or maybe Francoise. Something had flickered in Barolini's eyes when Lydia had mentioned her name. Out of her green uniform, Francoise looked pretty dishy.

A tall, striking blond appeared. Young. Mid to late twenties. She wore spike heels and a miniskirted suit—chalk-striped like Jared's, but the stripes were wider and the suit navy. She lingered in the doorway.

Jared nodded and smiled.

Vanessa glared at her. Which made Lydia feel better. At least she wasn't being singled out.

"Are we all here?" the blonde asked.

"Not quite," Jared said.

Meaning not until she sat down and joined them? Was this Adam's secret love? The mystery woman at Megan's? She fit Bobbie's description, except she was willowy rather than skinny.

She entered the room.

"Pull up a chair," Jared said. She did. Close to his at the head of the table.

"This is my assistant, Kim Lapinna," he told them. "You can speak to her if I'm not around. She knows more about the business than I do anyway." Kim smiled. "Lydia Miller, Vanessa Auerbach, and Todd Bigelow," Jared added, introducing them.

"Call me Big," Todd said.

Lydia hoped he meant to be funny.

Heads together, Jared and Kim held a whispered consultation.

If National Trust were as exclusive as Neil claimed, then what was a thirteen-year-old and his miniskirted assistant doing running the show? High-ranking officials of moneyed organizations were supposed to be silvery-haired men with sharp eyes, smooth talk, and a falsely sincere manner. Jared was puppy-cute and informal and should be fooling around in a study hall instead of handling wills. What was Adam thinking of?

"Let's get on with this, Jared," Vanessa said. "I have rehearsal scheduled for four."

"Vanessa's doing a fabulous new play. *Dreams and Nightmares,*" Todd said. "About soldiers in a prison camp."

"Officers," Vanessa said. "An all-male cast."

"Vanessa's the star. And I'm one of the POWs."

"If it's an all-male cast, what part do you play?" Kim Lapinna asked Vanessa. A question Lydia would have liked to ask herself.

"I'm the woman every man dreams of," Vanessa said modestly.

"The show's going to be a hit. We open October ninth," Todd said. "It's at the Auerbach Theater on West Forty-second."

"Named for Adam and myself. I'll send you comps," Vanessa told Jared.

"It's a quarter to four," Todd said, consulting what looked like a genuine Rolex. "What say we get this show on the road, Jar?"

"It won't take long once we get under way. She should be here any minute."

"*She?*" Vanessa's voice made Lydia glad she wasn't the woman in question.

"I'll see if I can find why she's delayed," Kim volunteered.

Seven minutes later, Kim returned with an auburn-haired woman who looked somewhat familiar.

"Now, you just sit right here next to me," Kim said soothingly to the woman, and pulled out a chair as if she were accommodating an idiot or an invalid.

"I'm so terribly sorry to be late," the woman said. "I got lost in the corridor."

Which couldn't be easy. The corridor was long and straight.

The woman's gleaming auburn hair splayed the shoulders of a black velvet jacket, nipped in at a tiny waist. A gauzy Laura Ashley skirt skimmed the tops of pointy-toed, lace-up Peter Fox fetish boots. Lydia recognized the boots from the memorial service. Carolyn Auerbach. That night her hair had been raven, but that went with her mourning outfit, Neil had said.

Carolyn didn't fit Lydia's idea of a sex therapist, whom

she thought of as determinedly pleasant and efficient. But Lydia had a feeling Carolyn Auerbach wasn't the vague, shy little thing she pretended to be.

Kim handed out the silver folders.

"I didn't get one," Todd complained.

Jared didn't seem to hear. "Adam chose a revocable trust, meaning he had the freedom to change his will. As you can see, there are quite a few codicils and—"

"Where's my folder?" Todd asked.

"The folders are for the chief beneficiaries only," Kim said.

"—and article amendments," Jared continued. "We haven't had time for anything but a rough estimate of Adam's estate. Unfortunately, more than half the trust will go for—"

"Are you saying I'm not a chief beneficiary?" Todd asked.

"More than half the trust will go for estate taxes as well as taxes for—"

"You're saying I'm not?" Todd demanded, voice rising. He was breathing hard. "What does this mean?"

"Todd deserves an explanation," Vanessa translated.

"We're coming to that. First, the basics," Kim said in a will-you-please-shut-up voice. Surprisingly, they did.

"More than half will go for estate taxes," Jared repeated, "as well as for gift taxes—on money that Adam gave away. An uncommonly generous man. Altogether that could involve well over an additional million, maybe two.

"The approximate, before-taxes account will be around seventeen million," Jared stated. Lydia caught her breath. Whatever Adam had left her would at least cover Mark's hospital expenses. Hallelujah!

"Vanessa Auerbach receives half, and the other half is to be divided between Carolyn Auerbach and Lydia Miller, with a set amount going to charity. Paid in quarterly dividends."

"Adam didn't believe in organized charities," Vanessa protested. That, Lydia knew to be true.

"In the event of the death of one of the beneficiaries, her inheritance will be shared by the survivors. In the event of the death of all survivors, the money goes to the same charitable institution."

Made for murder, Lydia thought, and hoped no one read her mind. She didn't want to give them ideas. She hurriedly flicked through pages looking for the name of the charity but didn't find it.

"What charitable institution is that?" Vanessa asked before Lydia could get around to it.

"That's treated as a separate category," Kim said.

"What about me?" Todd asked.

"He's coming to that," Kim said.

"Besides estate and gift taxes, there are private bequests," Jared Evans said. Paused. "Now, Mr. Bigelow, if you turn to page three of Vanessa's copy, you'll see that you're listed under Section Two, C."

They all turned to page three.

The trustee shall pay the sum of Eighty-Five Thousand Dollars to TODD BIGELOW (also known as CLYDE HAGGERTY) if he survives the grantor.

Francoise Grandier, Adam's cleaning woman, was also listed under Section II, C, and received the same amount as Todd. Receiving lesser amounts of twenty-five thousand each were a José Rivera and an Aijar Ahmed. Probably, they worked in Adam's building. Maybe one or both had walked Colombo.

"Wait a minute, wait a minute. Something's wrong," Todd said. He blew into cupped hands as if he were collecting air to breathe in. His elbows were propped on the table, his ponytailed head bowed, showing a bare spot in back. "You mean I only get eighty-five K, and that's it?" He sounded as if he were ready to cry.

"I can't believe this," Vanessa said. "Todd was Adam's nearest and dearest friend. There has to be a mistake."

Jared said it was made out according to Adam's wishes. "Todd, if you'd like, you can leave. The rest doesn't concern you."

"I'm staying."

"He's staying," Vanessa confirmed.

"Of course, you're welcome to stay," Jared added.

Todd was hyperventilating, making strange sucking

noises, drawing in air. Sweat had broken out on the tan forehead above the tortoiseshell glasses. "How soon can I have it? I got expenses to meet."

Jared gave a boyish frown and thought for a minute. "We could draw up a check for you by tomorrow since it's an outright amount and presents no real problem."

"I want it today, and I want cash."

Jared told Todd he'd have to wait the twenty-four hours. Todd, who alternately looked as if he were about to cry or to kill, muttered something to Vanessa, who stroked his hand soothingly while Jared told her she inherited Adam's co-op. "And all the tangible personal property therein."

"How about his place in Southampton?" Vanessa asked.

"That's covered in the codicil to Section Three, B," Jared said, and began reading, as if he were hiding behind the print. "The grantor's right title to his property in Southampton, County of Suffolk, New York, is to be given to LYDIA MILLER (also known as MRS. MARK SEGAL) and all tangible personal property therein."

"This is a swindle!" Vanessa screamed, her rice white face splotched with red. She shot Lydia a laser look of hate. Todd let out a low whistle. Chilling waves of hostility emanated from Carolyn. In a way, Lydia couldn't blame them. She didn't know what possessed Adam to leave the place to her. She'd never expressed any particular love of it.

"His apartment is worth nothing," Vanessa said. "Nothing! And that house in Southampton, millions."

"Scarcely millions," Jared corrected.

"Adam promised it to me. Look at this!" Vanessa said, holding out the open folder, bloodred fingernail pointing to the print. "The will was changed on August seventh. A month to the day he was murdered!"

And just four days after Mark had died, Lydia remembered. Had Adam added the codicil out of concern for her? He could be as compassionate as he was cruel, suffering along with those he cared for.

She almost couldn't blame Vanessa for being suspicious. She might even suspect herself if she didn't know differently.

Lydia caught a wisp of a sexy-flowery scent that she

thought might be Delilah, a perfume that sold for five hundred dollars an ounce. "How nice for you," Carolyn whispered. Was there sarcasm behind that sweet smile? Little wonder. Lydia was getting more than poor Carolyn. In fact, in leaving her the house, Adam was leaving her almost as much as Vanessa.

Judging from the hate waves she was getting, she thought she should spend those quarterly dividends on bodyguards. That is, what she didn't spend on Dershowitz or some other good criminal lawyer.

Kim Lapinna tapped her watch.

Jared nodded, stood up, and smiled an engaging grin of dismissal. Lydia picked up the silver folder, glad to get away. Her head was spinning. She was rich, rich, rich! She could pay off Mark's hospital bills, quit her job, travel. It was like winning the lottery. And it made her nervous as hell.

She needed to be alone and think through what all this meant to her life. *Please, God, just don't let me start talking taxes and investments. And voting Republican.*

CHAPTER 10

Lydia hung back in the corridor, trying to avoid any further encounter with Todd and Vanessa. She especially didn't want to share an elevator with them. Carolyn must have had the same idea. She also lingered.

Vanessa was whispering furiously to Todd, throwing venomous glances at Lydia over her shoulder, while Todd agitatedly swung her silver folder against his thigh. When the elevator stopped they got on, and Lydia hoped she'd seen the last of them. But a well-meaning suit stood in the elevator with his finger pressed on Open. Smiling her in.

Lydia stepped back, but her avoidance tactic was foiled by Carolyn's gentle push forward. There was nothing to do but get on. Carolyn followed. Two red clown spots of anger blotched Vanessa's white face, while Todd's features were screwed up, his face small behind the glasses. He made rasping sounds as if he were having trouble breathing. Lydia prayed the elevator wouldn't break down and trap them together. Kind of like Sartre's version of hell in *No Exit*.

But the elevator made it to the lobby. Lydia got another gentle shove from Carolyn as they got off. She felt like punching her.

Vanessa suddenly wheeled around, facing Lydia. "Thief!" she said. "Murderer! You deserve to be dead!"

People walked on, pretending they hadn't heard. The only indication they had was that they moved slightly faster.

A security guard stepped forward, but Vanessa had already started for the door, clinging to Todd, hurrying as fast as her spike heels permitted across the slick marble floor.

"That awful woman! Are you all right?" Carolyn asked as if Vanessa had struck Lydia. In a way she had.

"Somehow I don't think she likes me," Lydia said, intending to be funny, but the joke fell flat.

"Those two are scary," Carolyn said. "Come on, let's get a cab. We go the same way."

"Uh, thanks, but I have to get back to work." Lydia wasn't sure she wanted to be with Carolyn either.

"It's after five," Carolyn pointed out.

She considered saying she had a deadline to meet. She was still reeling from the news of her windfall and the encounter with Vanessa. Only it seemed rude to turn Carolyn down. Besides, she was curious about Carolyn. She wished now she'd listened more carefully to Adam when he'd talked about her.

One story she remembered concerned their honeymoon at Lake Como. They'd gone out in a boat together. Adam had dived into the lake and was casually swimming when a sudden storm sprang up. Carolyn had rowed toward the shore, leaving him stranded. "Luckily, some Italian rescued me. I could have drowned or been struck by lightning," Lydia remembered Adam saying.

Lydia thought of the storm the night Adam was murdered. If Carolyn had done it, she hadn't just left him to his own devices—or to lightning.

They reached the sidewalk in time to see a limo drive up to Vanessa and Todd, who stood at the curb. The chauffeur got out and held the door open. Sensing Lydia was behind her, Vanessa turned and threw a last look of hate over her shoulder before climbing in. Lydia got a chill, and it wasn't merely because the sun had disappeared behind a cloud.

CHAPTER 11

People poured from buildings onto a sidewalk shadowed by skyscrapers. Cabs would be hard to come by.

Carolyn grabbed a taxi from two potential fares by waving a twenty in the air.

"Fuck you," a well-groomed woman called.

"New Yorkers are so impolite," Carolyn said primly. She motioned Lydia in before her, then gathered the fluttering folds of her flowered skirt, slipped gracefully into the cab, and settled back. Her pointy-toed fetish boots peeked out beneath her skirt.

"The first stop will be Seventy-seventh and Third, and the second, Seventy-eighth between Third and Second," Carolyn said, her precise directions sounding not at all like the Lost Lady of the Corridors. Lydia wasn't surprised that Carolyn knew where she lived. After all, if Adam had pointed out Carolyn's house to her, it stood to reason he'd do the same with Carolyn.

"God knows where we'll end up," Carolyn whispered. "I'm sure he doesn't understand a word of English."

The driver's Asiatic features didn't in the least resemble
the blond man on the driver's license displayed on the
dashboard, whose name consisted mostly of consonants.

"Scary, aren't they?" Carolyn said.

Chinese cab drivers? "Who?"

"Those two. Vanessa and Todd. I don't trust them. I'm
sure they're plotting right now to kill us off, too, so they
can split our share."

"Too? You think they murdered Adam?"

"I know it. Detective Barolini said they had an airtight
alibi, but I don't believe it. Isn't he a hunk? You'd take him
more for a movie star than a cop."

"I'd take him for a pit bull," Lydia said.

"Oh, I thought he was very sweet. What makes you say
that?"

Lydia shrugged. "What makes you so sure that Vanessa
and Todd murdered Adam?"

"Poor Adam," Carolyn said. "I still can't believe he's
dead. He was impossible, but I adored him. Why would
anyone want to murder him? Isn't that against the law?
They don't belong in the street."

A horse-drawn carriage was stalling traffic on Madison
Avenue. Lydia wondered if Carolyn's non sequiturs were
deliberate. She seemed to work hard at appearing fey.
Carolyn might be all sweetness and light on the outside, but
Lydia sensed steel and ice within. But steely and icy
enough to hold Adam underwater and watch him kick until
his life ran out?

"Of course," Carolyn went on, "I never thought Vanessa
was the tramp Adam claimed. He did tend to use hyperbole. And you can't blame her for looking elsewhere for
sexual satisfaction, considering."

"Considering?"

"You know."

"Gay?" Adam wasn't, was he? Had she missed spotting
it in Adam as she had with Mark?

"Impotent."

"Oh." Lydia sighed, thinking how she could have saved
herself all that worry.

"I would have told Vanessa. But she refused to be

friends. Consumed with jealousy. Very smug about what she considered winning Adam away from me. She didn't know I was absolutely delighted to have him off my hands, so to speak." Carolyn proceeded to give details in her fluttery, breathy way.

"When I married him I thought I was getting this wonderful, worldly, sophisticated man who knew every trick in the Kama Sutra. But he was a sexual disaster, poor man."

Who needed enemies if they had Carolyn for a friend? Lydia supposed, out of loyalty to Adam, she should have told Carolyn to shut up, but if she was going to find out who his murderer was, she had to keep quiet and listen. Besides, she was curious.

"You can imagine my utter bewilderment. I thought maybe all men were that way. After all, I was only seventeen. And totally inexperienced. That was what drew him to me. But isn't that always the case? They like young, inexperienced girls because they don't suffer from comparison."

The cab stopped for a red light at Seventy-second Street. A herd of five buses pulled into the right lane, one after the other—New York buses never traveled alone. The buses cut off her view of Ralph Lauren's store housed in one of her favorite buildings.

"Turn right and go up Third," Carolyn instructed the driver just as the light was changing. "After three years of marriage when sex rarely reared its lovely head, I began to flip out. Really."

Lydia had heard some of this from Adam. A different version, of course. Carolyn, he'd said, had heard the voice of Ted Bundy on the car radio telling her he was going to get her next. "She kept turning up the volume to drown him out. It didn't matter that he'd been caught and was in prison. She imagined that he'd escaped. But I didn't know what the hell was going on then. Until she told me after she left Oak Grove."

"It was horrible," Carolyn said. "Did Adam mention I was at one of those fancy funny farms? Oak Grove. Adam was very generous. He always saw to it that the people he drove mad only went to the best mental institutions.

"I still have my bad moments, but darling Alejandro has

been a wonderful adviser. Unfortunately, the AIDS scare has left me with very few clients. So now I'm considering a career in filmmaking and animal behavior."

"Aren't they rather different from what you're doing? How do you combine them?"

"That's really very simple. Everyone knows that sex therapy ties in with animal behavior. Naturally, you'll want to record all this on camera."

Naturally?

The cab stopped in front of McCabe's Liquor Store on Lydia's corner.

"Come on over to my place; I'll show you a film I made," Carolyn said.

"Love to, but I have to walk my dog." *Her* dog? Since when? Lydia wasn't sure, but she suddenly knew that parting with Colombo would be too wrenching for them both. It would be cruel for Colombo to be deserted by her after he'd lost Adam.

"Some other time," she said, taking money from her wallet to cover her half of the fare. "And then you can tell me who Alejandro is."

"Alejandro? You don't know him? That gorgeous hunk who spoke at the memorial service? Lucky you, he'll be your neighbor out there."

Urzaga, she meant. Sure. Lucky her.

"I don't really hate you for getting Adam's summer place," Carolyn said, smiling to prove it. "And I'm going to be very charming and extra nice so you'll invite me out to visit."

"You're invited," Lydia said, and could have kicked herself.

CHAPTER 12

The phone rang fifteen minutes after she'd walked in the door, while she was skimming through the will to see if the name of the charity was mentioned.

"I've been dying to hear," Neil said. "Are you a million-heiress?"

Colombo jumped up on the futon beside her, dying to hear, too. "This will is made for murder. If one of us dies, the survivors split the share."

"Maybe Adam intended you to kill each other. So how'd you fare?"

"Okay, I think," she said, playing it down. After all, Neil, Adam's oldest friend, got nothing.

"What does okay mean?"

"Jared Evans, or Jar as Todd Bigelow calls him, gave an overall explanation of the terms of the trust, but the explanation wasn't all that clear. First, the estate taxes come to half what Adam left. Then there's back taxes, including a whopping fine for all the money Adam gave away."

God, she thought, I'm already talking taxes and I haven't gotten any money yet.

"So who gets what? How about you?" Neil asked.

"I'm getting to me, okay? Vanessa gets half, and Carolyn, charity, and I split the remaining half."

"Charity? Who's she?"

"Not a person but some charitable institution. Jared ducked the question when Vanessa asked who. I was just looking for the name in the will when you called, but it isn't mentioned—only referred to as charity. What do you want to bet it's the Institute for Bipolar Disorders?"

"Agreed."

"Except why would a research institute be considered charity?"

"I don't know, but I know Urzaga. Sneaky. He convinced Adam that the Institute would benefit mankind. Some such shit. So when do you collect your money?"

"Jared didn't say. We don't get lump sums. Just quarterly dividends. To think I've become a trust-fund kid at my ripe age. It's a revocable trust."

"Naturally the trust is revocable," Neil said. "Adam revoked it every other day. So who got his place in Southampton—Vanessa or Carolyn?"

"Neither. I got it."

"That's absurd. Idiotic. Ridiculous." He sounded like Vanessa.

"I agree."

"I'm sorry, sweetie. It came as a surprise, that's all. I knew Adam was smitten with you, but not to that degree."

"Timing," she said. "Next year or next month or even next week, it could have gone to someone else. Adam was impulsive. He'd changed the will in August. Right after Mark died. I guess he felt sorry for me."

"Well, for whatever reason, I think it's terrific! Now we'll be neighbors. We can borrow cups of sugar from each other. It's fantastic! Great."

The more Neil piled it on, the less enthusiastic he sounded, until his voice faded out. His "great" was weak. Poor Neil was hurt. Damn it, Adam could have left him something, despite their feud. Well, a bit late to chide poor Adam for that.

"I suppose this just gives Barolini more proof that I drowned Adam," she said, changing the subject.

"Well, you have to admit, it does look suspicious."

She heard the bitterness in his voice. And then he hung up.

Lydia sat by the phone in shock. This was her best friend? Her buddy, soul mate, pal, her big brother? He suspected *her*? Look at the bright side, she told herself. If he thinks you killed Adam, that means he didn't do it. Or was Neil only too glad that she looked suspicious and not *he*?

Lydia was saddened by the thought that Adam's murder

had caused a rift between her and Neil instead of bringing them closer together. Didn't real friendship exclude distrust? Maybe Adam's money was at the root of it. Neil resented that he hadn't been left anything by Adam, a childhood chum, while Adam, who scarcely knew her, had left her so much. But if she offered to share the money with Neil, he'd resent it, consider it adding insult to injury. What to do?

Lydia called home. At least her mother wouldn't consider her a murder suspect. But her kid sister, Chots—short for Charlotte—whom she'd had a falling out with, was probably only too ready to believe her capable of any dark crime. Chots and her three kids had moved in with Mom after Chots's husband, Hughie, took off.

Their fight had taken place after Lydia discovered that Mark had AIDS. Stunned and at a loss of what to do, she'd flown home for comfort and advice, and gotten neither. Well, some comfort from her mother. That is, as much as her mother's Midwest morality would allow when she discovered her daughter had not only married a gay man but also one who had gotten an incurable disease. Clearly she didn't understand how such things could happen. Neither did Lydia.

It was a rotten time all around. Just after Hughie had pulled his Houdini act on Chots and the kids. Call it bleak house.

"Another deadbeat dad," Lydia had said, intending to be sympathetic. But Chots had flown into a rage. Instead of blaming Hughie, it was Mark she'd faulted. "At least Hughie's a real man and not some queer."

Which was when Lydia had slapped Chots and returned to Mark in New York. Since then, Lydia hadn't gone home, and hung up if Chots answered when she phoned her mother. Beating Chots to the draw since Chots would have hung up on her.

It wasn't Chots or her mother who answered when she called today, but four-year-old Ashley.

"Hi, this is Aunt Lydia. How you doing?"

A dumb question to ask a little kid, but Ashley didn't notice. She entertained Lydia with a repertoire of songs that she'd learned at kindergarten. Most of them Lydia remembered from her own childhood. In Brigadoon, Ohio, things never changed. Ashley was just beginning an unrequested encore when Chots grabbed the phone.

"Sorry about the serenade, I was busy in the kitchen," Chots said, sounding friendly. That would change the minute she found out who the caller was. But it didn't. That is, at least Chots didn't hang up. Neither did Lydia, who praised Ashley's singing ability.

"So . . . um, how are things going?" Lydia asked.

"Great. I've taken to the road, helping Mom with the moving. She's on a trip now. We've added another Miller. Now it's Miller & Miller Moving & Storage. Mom and I spell each other. Either she stays home with the kids or I do. I have Otis and Hank and she has Otis and Carl. You remember them, don't you?"

Lydia remembered. Otis had been in her class at school, and dropped out in the tenth grade. Carl was a husky guy in horn-rims who looked like an intellectual bouncer. Actually, he was retarded and very gentle. "Who's Hank?" Lydia asked. "Someone new?"

"Oh, yeah, he's a doll." She paused. "I hate to admit it," Chots said, "but you were right about Hughie. All the kids ever get from him is an occasional postcard from the West Coast—L.A., San Francisco, and Seattle. Of course, he doesn't send a cent for support. Thank goodness the kids are crazy about Hank. As a matter of fact, I kind of like him, too."

"You always did like men with H names," Lydia said.

They both laughed.

"Why don't you come home and join the business? We'll make it Miller & Miller & Miller."

"That's tempting. I'll be back. I hope soon. If not to stay, for a long visit."

"I wish you would. The kids miss their aunt Lydia."

"I miss them, too. Also, Mom. And I kind of miss you."

"And I miss you," Chots said. She hung up on Lydia again, but this time not before saying, "I love you, sis."

Lydia wiped an errant tear from her eye and forgave Chots for being so much prettier. Colombo wandered up and kissed her. She ruffled his ears. "As soon as this business is over, we'll go back to Brigadoon. Right now we're going out for your walk."

Maybe she could talk Chots into accepting money for her kids. Chots was proud, so she'd have to approach the subject tactfully. She attached Colombo's leash, thinking that she might funnel the money through her mother so Chots didn't know it was coming from her. Maybe get Mom to tell Chots that the money was what their father had left, that she'd intended to leave the money to Chots and Lydia, but since Chots needed the money now, she was giving it to her. But this presented Lydia with another problem: how to explain to her mother that a man had left her money. Like most people Lydia knew, her mother would leap to the conclusion that she'd been his mistress and be shocked, disapproving, and upset. She'd have to think up a good lie to tell her mother. Saying she'd gotten a raise wouldn't explain her windfall, particularly since she intended to quit her job, buy a nifty little sports car, and return home in style, the backseat loaded down with extravagant gifts for her nieces and nephew. She always enjoyed shopping in toy stores. This time she'd indulge herself at F.A.O. Schwarz.

When she and Colombo returned, Lydia ordered Chinese takeout. Running her finger down the Szechuan Hunan Cottage menu, she selected everything she'd ever wanted to eat: dumplings, soup, General Ching's chicken, crispy prawns with walnuts, and seafood deluxe. Also, a carton of Tsingtao, the Chinese beer.

"That was quick," she told the delivery guy when he arrived. "I hope no one got killed on the way over."

Lydia overtipped to make up for his climb to the fourth floor. He accepted it as his due without thanking her. Whatever happened to manners? She loaded a tray with the cartons and took it to the living room, setting it on the coffee table. Sitting at a regular table made her feel Mark's absence too keenly. She'd also bought the futon to replace the bed she and Mark had shared, and converted the bedroom into a workroom. An unconscious avoidance tactic, she thought, dipping a dumpling into soy sauce. It didn't matter that Mark was in St. Vincent's by the time she'd moved here. The association was the same. Dinner table, Mark. Bed, Mark.

Don't think about it, she told herself for the thousandth time. Think of what you won't do now that you can afford not to. No, first, what you would do. After quitting her job and visiting her family, she'd move out of this death trap. Too bad she couldn't take poor Mrs. Nagy with her. Maybe she could help her out with some money so she could move, too. She might even send Mrs. Nagy a monthly check, carrying on in the Adam tradition. Except where he'd found his friends only too eager to accept money, she knew that with her sister, and probably with Mrs. Nagy, it wasn't going to be that easy. Impossible with Neil.

After that, she'd travel, visit scenes of her favorite movies—ride the Ferris wheel in Vienna that Joseph Cotton and Orson Welles had ridden (provided it was still standing); and take the same mountainous drive with the hairpin curves that Grace Kelly and Cary Grant had traveled in *To Catch a Thief*. Also visit places that still vaguely remained what they'd once been—Venice, the Ponte Vecchio in Florence, Bruges with its canals and centuries-old buildings, ancient Japanese inns. Throw in a barge trip along the Seine, and since she'd always been crazy about traveling by water, why not take a trip up the Rhine, down the Nile, and on the Volga? Later, she might try the Amazon, or go whole hog and take a Mississippi steamboat.

After all her river and canal trips, she might live on a houseboat in the Boat Basin off West Seventy-ninth Street. Or maybe pick up a yacht, hire a crew, and cruise the Caribbean. "You'll go, too," she promised Colombo.

And then there were the minor indulgences such as the Victorian birdcage she'd seen at the antiques fair at the Armory in June with Adam. The intricate wire structure was as delicate as spiderwebbing. The dealer had named a price that made her wince. Adam had wanted to buy it for her. He'd been disappointed when she'd turned him down. He could give it to her posthumously.

Spending money was fun. Thank you, Adam.

Lydia finished off the dumplings, soup, and shrimp with walnuts. She let Colombo polish off what was left of the seafood deluxe along with a half-empty carton of noodles. She had just put the untouched General Ching's chicken in the refrigerator when the telephone rang.

"Honey, this is your mother," a familiar voice said, as if Lydia would have any doubt about who it was. "We just got back from a long haul to Muncie. Your sister said you'd called. I'm so glad you two patched things up."

"Mom, you must be exhausted."

"Oh no, Carl and Otis did the work. I supervised."

After downing two more bottles of Tsingtao during the hour-and-a-half talk with her mother, Lydia decided to level with her and not lie about her windfall.

"Listen, Mom, I've got something to tell you. Now, don't jump to conclusions. Just hear me out. There wasn't any romance involved. I mean I didn't sleep with him or anything."

"Slow down. Who are you talking about, honey?"

"A man who befriended me while Mark was sick and dying."

"Well, that was nice of him."

"There's more."

Although her mother said nothing, Lydia could hear an unspoken "Uh-oh." She rushed on. "This man felt sorry for me because Mark had died and left me with all those steep hospital bills."

"I worry about that, too, honey. As soon as business picks up, I'll send you something to help out."

"Mom, just listen, okay? Unfortunately, this man died, too." She wasn't going to say how. If Adam's murder had such scant coverage in the New York newspapers that her co-workers had missed it, it wasn't likely to appear in her hometown newspaper.

"Goodness, bad luck just seems to follow you around, honey."

Lydia sighed. "Yeah. But the good news is, this man left me quite a bit of money." (She wouldn't mention the house in Southampton now, maybe later.)

"Why, isn't that lovely? How much?"

Lydia went into shock. Her mother not only hadn't disapproved but sounded downright pleased. "I don't know exactly," she said. "But it's enough to pay off the hospital bills with quite a lot left over." No reason to go into how much. "Anyway, I'd like to help out Chots and the kids, but I don't think she'd accept any money from me. I thought maybe if I sent you a check, you could cash it and give the money to Chots, telling her it was money Dad had left and you were giving it to her because she needed it now."

"Honey, I don't like to lie."

Lydia spent a half hour convincing her mother she was lying for a good cause. Finally her mother agreed. "I think it's wise not to mention to your sister that a man left you money. We'll keep this between us," her mother added.

"Mom, if you need a little something to keep the business afloat, I'd be glad to help out."

Christ, Lydia thought, she was beginning to sound like Adam.

CHAPTER 13

Barolini called her from different phone booths all along the LIE on his way into the city. Her line was always busy. At least he knew she was home. Bragging to her friends about the killing she'd made today. Yeah, the murderer makes a killing. Hey, not a bad title. He'd suggest it to Joe McGinniss. Shit. Dream on, Barolini! But you never knew, McGinniss might be interested. If not him, some other writer. Now, wouldn't that be nice? Get in all the juicy parts, of course. Sex, money, and murder in the Hamptons.

He called Miller one last time from Queens. When she answered he hung up. So far, what he'd expected hadn't happened. She hadn't skipped. Yet.

He guessed he didn't have to worry. She wouldn't head

for Rio de Janeiro or the Caymans until she sold the house and got her hands on Auerbach's money. Still, she might take off if she was running scared.

It wasn't going to be long before she made a move. The question was, what. She might have had an accomplice in Auerbach's murder she'd lead him to. His bet would be that fag Neil Underwood. Maybe they planned to split the loot. He'd like to put a tap on her phone, but he needed something more to go on. And he didn't want to tip his hand to anyone in the department. Just bring her in after the confession. She acted like it wasn't getting to her, but she was feeling the pressure. He could tell by the way she'd gotten defensive. The more nervous she'd become, the more excuses she'd made. Soon she'd start tripping herself up.

When he finally reached Miller's neighborhood, he circled her block looking for a place to park the Toyota. And damned if he wasn't in luck. A white van pulled out just ahead of him, in front of Myrna's Unisex Haircutters, near enough to keep an eye on her building. He cut off a yellow Honda and slid in.

If that asshole partner of his had been along, a spot would never have opened up. It wasn't that he was superstitious, but Kramer was a jinx. And a bleeding heart. Couldn't believe Miller had done it. No reason, just not the type, he'd said. When Barolini pressed harder, all Kramer could come up with was she'd stuck by her dying husband. Shit. She was sleeping with Auerbach. Husband helpless in the hospital, tubes coming out of all his orifices, while she made the move on fat boy.

He adjusted the seat for more leg room and prepared to wait, wondering what Miller was doing up there besides gloating and congratulating herself on getting away with murder. Like Wendy. About six months before she left him, he'd noticed her smiling to herself over nothing—or so he thought. Poor dumb slob that he was, he hadn't caught on. Afternoons, he'd come home and find her gone from the house, out shopping, she'd said, or having lunch with the girls. He'd taken her at her word. Some detective he made. Couldn't even figure out his wife was sneaking around behind his back. Her and Miller, sisters under the skin.

It surprised him the media wasn't giving fat boy's murder a bigger play. Maybe because it looked like a heart attack to begin with. The day forensics pronounced it murder, some nanny in Manhasset had to go and strangle a baby. Got the media all excited. His rotten luck. After that died down, another woman turned up missing, and the media went back to that fucking theory about a serial murderer. All he could hope for now was that he'd nail Miller before they found the women's bodies or, worse yet, the killer.

Keeping an eye on Miller's windows, he played his favorite video in his head. Pictured the three of them—Wendy, Courtney, and Daddy Warbucks—sitting out there in Great Neck around the dinner table under that fancy chandelier. Daddy Warbucks shoveling the food down while they watched the evening news. Suddenly a familiar figure flashes on the screen! Dozens of reporters yell and surge forward, thrusting mikes in the guy's face!

Tell me, Detective, a pretty blond asks breathlessly, *just what made you so suspicious? How did you crack the case when she had everyone else fooled?*

Detective Barolini, a man says, *You did some fancy footwork. Do you see a big promotion in your future?*

Wendy's now-husband punches the remote and cuts off the TV. Courtney yells, "Hey, that's Daddy. I want to watch. Did you see that, Mom? All those reporters crowded around him? Daddy's a hero! He's famous!"

Like he told Kramer, it ain't over till it's over. What the hell, this could still end up a book, a movie, or a miniseries—maybe all three.

Naturally, the actors would look better than real-life people. Except maybe the guy who played him. He wouldn't want to be played by some glamour boy. Just someone who looked seasoned, lean and mean. He'd settle for Clint Eastwood.

CHAPTER 14

Ten feet from Barolini's gray Toyota, a figure crouched in a shadowy well below street level at the bottom of a flight of stairs outside Super Locksmiths, Inc. An iron railing separated the stairs from the sidewalk. Locked to the railing were samples of various kinds of window gates on display. A light over the locksmith's door threw the gates' criss-crossing shadows on what could be seen of the crouching figure. While Barolini kept watch on the fourth-floor window up in Miller's apartment, the figure kept watch on both Barolini and the window.

The wait had been long, starting before the arrival of the Toyota. The observer became restless—shifted positions, stood, crouched, stood again. Considered leaving, giving up. For that night at least. But as long as Barolini remained, leaving was out of the question. Stuck.

Still, Barolini wouldn't hang around forever. Stay and get it over and done with, no?

CHAPTER 15

The metal tip of Colombo's leash tapped the steps as he ran down ahead of her. His final walk for the night, thank God. In the entranceway, Lydia found herself groping for the leash. The light between the front door and the hall door had burned out. It was on earlier around six when she took Colombo for a walk. Better call Sal tomorrow and have him take care of it.

The building was fast going to pot. If the neon light in the hall went out, too, as the flickering threatened it would do any minute, the whole damn downstairs would be dark.

Outside, the night had turned chilly. She should have put a sweater on under her jeans jacket. If it hadn't meant climbing three flights, she would have gone back up and gotten one.

She wanted to make the walk quick, but Colombo needed a longer outing. Adam had acquired him on the advice of one of his numerous doctors who'd said walking a dog would provide him with much-needed exercise. Adam got the dog from the ASPCA. He told Lydia he'd wanted a dog that was all dog, not something pampered, pedigreed, and spoiled. "Not like me," he'd added with a grin.

Of course, Adam rarely walked Colombo. He left that to the doormen.

On the corner of Third, Lydia passed Waterwear, a boutique with swimsuits for poolside posing. At the other end of the block she turned right, not consciously thinking of where she was going until she realized she was on Carolyn's street. It must have been in the back of her mind. She'd barely paid attention to Carolyn's place when Adam had pointed it out from a cab. But that was before she'd met Carolyn. And before Adam was murdered.

The street was prettier, posher, than hers. No tacky Laundromats or locksmiths. But it was also darker and more deserted. Leafy trees obscured the streetlights. She was glad to have Colombo with her.

Carolyn's house was one in a row of brick houses, each with a plaque proclaiming it to be a historical landmark. Colombo obligingly squatted under a nearby tree, giving her an excuse to look over Carolyn's house. Since the town house was in a prime Manhattan location, it was probably worth as much as, if not more than, Adam's house in Southampton, which was on the wrong side of Montauk Highway. This made Lydia feel less guilty.

And what was she going to do with her recent acquisition? Whenever she saw the pool, she'd be plagued by the memory of Adam's half-submerged body. The green room would remind her of Mark's last days. A hospice where people awaited death. She'd put it up for sale.

Anyway, what would she do with herself out there? Milke had a house in East Hampton, and the art director lived in Water Mill. She didn't want to always be running into people she saw at work, even if she no longer worked there. Worse yet, she'd have Alec Urzaga as a next-door neighbor. A man who'd accused her of drowning Adam. Besides, she didn't trust him.

If you weren't a beach person and didn't enjoy the frantic summer social scene, the Hamptons didn't have much to offer. She could visit the Elaine Benson Gallery in Bridgehampton or go to Guild Hall in Southampton. Scarcely worth all that grief on a crowded LIE when there were more and better galleries and museums in Manhattan.

Except Adam had wanted her to have the place. Shouldn't she respect his wishes?

Lydia became aware that Colombo was waiting patiently while she stood around considering options and weighing obligations. She got one of several oversized Baggies from her L. L. Bean bag, and after turning the Baggie inside out so her fingers touched only plastic, scooped up the mess and threw it into a nearby garbage can.

Lydia was about to move on when she noticed that Carolyn Auerbach's light on the first floor was also flickering. The TV? The first floor was a flight up. Too high to see into from street level. She hadn't pictured Carolyn as a couch potato sitting home eating popcorn and watching a sitcom.

She decided to see what Carolyn was up to and took a quick look around to make sure no one would catch her spying. Behind the wall bordering a parking garage driveway she glimpsed an abrupt movement. Or thought she had. She waited, but nothing moved. Imagining things, she guessed.

Colombo in tow, she went up the steps to Carolyn's door, as if she were making a friendly call, which was somewhat improbable since it was after eleven. Standing on tiptoe, she peered in. She didn't see Carolyn. Other than the flickering light, the room was dark. A film projector beamed a track of light onto a screen. Some sitcom. "Cagney & Lacey" was never like this. Two naked women embracing. One blonde, one Asian. The blue channel on cable TV? Wrong. She did see Carolyn, after all. Carolyn was the blonde. What was she doing in there anyway? Playing the film for her own entertainment? That was carrying narcissism to the nth degree.

Lydia looked closer and saw someone sitting in the shadows. A man. Something about the set of his shoulders looked vaguely familiar. She considered hanging around to figure out who the guy was, but some neighbor might spot her and call the police. She didn't want to be accused of voyeurism along with murder.

She resumed walking Colombo. Carolyn had mentioned filmmaking. Maybe this was something she'd directed as well as starred in. Lydia wondered if Carolyn enjoyed playing the part or if it was a matter of economics.

Heading toward First Avenue, she glimpsed an orange moon that was quickly obscured by torn wisps of fast-moving clouds.

Colombo started straining at the leash, suddenly eager to keep going. She knew where. To Adam's co-op on East End Avenue. Now Vanessa's.

"No we don't," she said, and gently but firmly tugged Colombo toward Second Avenue and his new home.

A drunk in a three-piece suit blocked her way in front of the Coconut Grill. "Hey, doggie, nice doggie," he called, reaching out to pet Colombo.

"Back off, he bites," Lydia said. Not true, but what did this guy know?

"Collies don't belong in the city," the man said.

"He's not a collie."

"A whatever. Big dogs belong in the country."

She tugged Colombo away and crossed the street against a light.

"You're gonna get that sweet animal killed," the drunk

called from the other side. A couple just coming out the door of the Antico Caffee gave her a dirty look.

"Neither of us will be killed," she assured Colombo, hoping she was right.

CHAPTER 16

What the hell was Miller up to hanging around that house? Barolini wondered. Taking note of the layout? Planning to do Carolyn Auerbach so she'd get a bigger share of the will?

Nah, Miller was greedy, but she wasn't stupid. She wouldn't murder Auerbach's wife when she was under suspicion for murdering him. And if she was going to kill anyone, why not Vanessa Auerbach? She was the one who got the biggest share of the pot.

While he was thinking this, Miller turned and looked his way. He barely had time to duck behind a parking garage wall. When he looked again, she was up on the front stoop, looking in Carolyn Auerbach's window.

After she finally moved on, Barolini climbed up the front stoop to find out for himself what she'd been looking at. He chuckled. Two lesbies licking each other! Neither was what he'd call appetizing. A flat-chested Chinese girl and a bony blonde. Maybe one of those erotic films Carolyn Auerbach made. Someone was sitting in the chair. Hard to see who. Must be Carolyn Auerbach enjoying the show. He'd been having trouble with his night vision lately, his eyes like his stomach—shot to hell. Funny, he wouldn't have pegged Carolyn Auerbach for a dyke. Could be she swung both ways like Miller claimed her husband did. Except he didn't believe that shit. Either you were queer or you weren't.

He'd have liked to stick around and see more of the movie, but Miller had disappeared. He hurried down the steps of the stoop. Just as he reached the sidewalk, he caught sight of something on the move behind him. He swung around. Nothing. He walked on and swung around again. Still nothing. Shit. He'd have sworn someone was tailing him. Must be nerves. He was falling apart. His digestion, his eyesight, and now his nerves. Got to start getting back in shape.

He caught up with Miller on Second. Some guy in front of the Coconut Grill was making a play for her mutt. The dog didn't appear to mind, but Miller gave him the cold shoulder and headed home. He checked his watch. Nearly eleven-thirty. He might as well head home, too. She wouldn't be going out again at this hour. He watched her pass the café on the corner and climbed into his car.

CHAPTER 17

After she passed the Antico Caffee, Lydia walked quickly toward her building on Seventy-seventh Street, suddenly uneasy. Colombo was also tense. Ears up. Wary. Her edginess was catching, she guessed. Traffic from Second Avenue whisked along behind her. In the distance a car door slammed. Otherwise the street was quiet. The roisterers wouldn't appear until the bars closed.

With the streetlight burned out, the street was completely dark except for what little moonlight filtered through leafy trees. Glaring lights in protective wiring shined above shadowy recessed doorways, making the night more ominous, emphasizing the darkness.

Three black teenage boys came her way. White sneakers, baseball caps, baggy jeans. Laughing and cutting up, hitting one another in rough horseplay. Feeling guilty yet suspicious, Lydia tensed and speeded up, giving them a wide berth as she and Colombo went around them. They kept on walking.

Or so she thought. Hearing footsteps behind her, she nearly broke into a run until she realized the footsteps were hers.

She fished her keys out of her jacket pocket and held them so that they jutted out over her knuckles, a supposedly good way to defend yourself—keys to the eyes and kicks to the crotch.

She had one foot on the doorstep of her building when Colombo gave a low, mean growl. With a sudden pull at the leash that caught her off guard, he broke away, barking. Almost simultaneously an arm shot around her neck, the pressure blocking off her windpipe. She couldn't scream or make any kind of noise. She couldn't think straight, only struggle as hard as she could, wishing she'd worn her cowboy boots with heels instead of her sneakers. The grip tightened and blood roared in her ears. It was happening to her as it happened to so many other women. She was going to be raped. Maybe killed.

Behind her, he breathed heavily, asthmatically. She felt warm, sour-smelling breath on the side of her face, then heard a high-pitched curse and a groan and was released as suddenly as she'd been grabbed.

Lydia screamed and wheeled around in time to see a big, hairy blur leaping at her attacker's back as he ran between two cars, dropping something with a clang onto the street, then charging into oncoming traffic. Colombo was close on his heels, his barking starting up all the dogs in the neighborhood. A man yelled out the window to be quiet or he'd call the cops. Good!

Lydia raced across the street behind Colombo, yelling, "Stop thief!" hoping that someone would grab her attacker. But the sidewalks were suddenly empty. The mugger ran toward the drop-in shelter. For a minute she wondered if he'd turn in there—if that was where he'd come from. One of the homeless. Except the slouch hat he wore pulled down over his face and the trench coat with the collar up wasn't what the homeless wore. In fact, her attacker looked more like a spy in an old-time movie than a modern-day mugger.

She fell behind as he sprinted toward Third Avenue. Colombo, racing after him, was losing ground, too. When she reached the corner of Third, she found Colombo futilely barking. A cab just moving away from the curb held up the black BMW behind it. A woman crossed the street as speedily as she could in high heels and a long, tight skirt. More mugger material than mugger. Probably, she'd just left the cab that Colombo was barking at. The attacker must have jumped into it the moment the woman got out. Lydia ran to get a good look, but it was already moving down Third Avenue.

Colombo stood looking as confused as she felt. He came trotting back to her, the metal tip of his leash clicking on the cement.

"Good dog. Brave dog," she told him.

He wagged his tail and walked tall.

She was surprised that she still had her L. L. Bean bag over her shoulders, and clenched in a fist, her keys. Passing the drop-in center with the clothes piled up on giveaway tables, she started to shake, her knees almost buckling. She put her hand to her neck where it hurt from the pressure of her assailant's grip. She remembered the hammerlock cutting off her breath and her futile kicking and struggling. All of a sudden she thought of Adam. Had this happened to him when he was being drowned? She hoped he was drunk and drugged up.

Again there were people on the street—a yuppie couple and three middle-aged women. A man walking a Doberman. Where had he and that Doberman been a moment ago?

She remembered hearing the clang as an object hit the street and went back to look for it between the two parked cars in front of the dry cleaners. She groped around until she felt metal. A gun! Serious business, this. Gingerly she picked it up with two fingers, trying not to smear any fingerprints. She bagged the gun in a Baggie she carried along for Colombo and put it in her Bean bag. Had her attacker worn gloves? She couldn't remember.

Colombo looked on with interest. She patted his head. The ferocity of his attack was unnerving but reassuring. "To think," she told him, "that I ever considered you a coward."

She thought he smiled. She was getting soft in the head, falling for a dog, and reminded herself it was cats she preferred. Strange that he'd cringed in the tub when someone broke into her apartment but was so gung ho tonight. To protect her? After all, she hadn't been there when the intruder conveniently let himself in with a key. Colombo's attack tonight had been so violent, so . . . almost personal. She had a flash. Maybe it was someone Colombo knew and hated. The person who'd killed Adam and was now after her?

But that seemed far-fetched. Besides, it was just plain dumb to try to kill her so soon after killing Adam. Either dumb or mad. And most of Adam's friends, according to him, weren't mad, just borderline. It had bothered her where she fit in, and she'd asked him. "I need someone sane in my life," he'd said. "I've changed." But he hadn't. Not really. He'd still kept company with his crazy friends. Anyway, she thought, going back to her original argument with herself, killers weren't exactly rational.

Her knees went weak when she saw a figure standing on the steps of her apartment building, until she heard old Mrs. Nagy's baby voice asking if she was hurt. Mrs. Nagy wore a tatty bathrobe and a cardigan sweater draped over her shoulders.

"I call the police," she told Lydia as they went inside. "They say they come right away. But where are they?"

Just as soon as she said it, there was a commotion behind them. Lydia turned to see two men in sneakers and jeans—dressed like the black teenagers and, come to think of it, dressed like her, too. Except the teenagers' jeans were baggy.

The two men coming through the door were the same two cops who'd been there the night when the tape was stolen.

"Well, we meet again," the cute, curly-haired one said.

"Who wasn't it this time?" sandy mustache asked.

"Maybe this will help you find out," Lydia said, reaching into her Bean bag. "I picked it up from the street when Colombo knocked it out of my attacker's hand."

"Colombo?" the cute cop said.

"My dog."

"Jesus, the last time you hid out behind the shower curtain," he told Colombo. "What got into you tonight?" Colombo smiled again. Lydia decided any guy who talked to dogs had to be all right.

"Tonight he was a real hero. Some guy grabbed me by the throat. Colombo went for him and scared him off. My throat still hurts," she said, rubbing it.

"Jesus, lemme see. Looks like he left marks."

Lydia exhibited her throat. She pulled down the folded neck of her sweater for everyone to get a better look.

"I don't see any marks," sandy mustache said.

"She says it hurts," the cute cop reminded him.

"She's not making it up. I heard someone out there, the dog barking and all," Mrs. Nagy confirmed. "That's when I called 911."

"What'd this guy look like?" sandy mustache asked.

"I didn't get a good look. He was standing behind me. And he had *this* pointed at my head. Colombo knocked it out of his hand." That wasn't exactly how it happened, but she got carried away with her story. She brought the gun out of her bag and gingerly removed it from the Baggie, watching for their surprised expressions.

Except cops were used to guns. Only Mrs. Nagy, standing by in her cardigan-draped bathrobe, let out a gasp. All the cute cop said was "Jesus." "You bagged it?" sandy mustache asked. "You expected this to happen?"

"I keep a supply of Baggies handy when I walk Colombo."

"Lemme see that." He was careful about fingerprints when he took the gun.

A voice crackled on the squawk box attached to his belt as he looked the gun over.

"Yeah, well, this isn't a real gun, see." He held it out for his partner. "You can tell by the barrel."

Lydia felt disappointed. Her peril seemed less real. "You mean it's a toy?"

"It's a flare gun," the cute cop said. "You use them to signal for help when your boat—or aircraft—goes down. Dangerous, though, if you point them at somebody."

"What do they do?"

"Kill you up close. They use a propellant—gunpowder charge. Either kill, blind, or scar you for life."

"It was the super," Mrs. Nagy said. "He's trying to get rid of us, so he can raise the rent."

"It wasn't Sal. He's short; this guy was my height. Why use a flare gun when the real thing is so readily available?"

"Good question. You got enemies?"

"Hasn't everyone?"

"What did this guy look like?"

"My height, around five nine. Average weight. White. No Face, like in 'Dick Tracy.' At least since he was wearing his hat pulled down and coat collar up, I didn't see it. A trench coat."

The squawk box was getting noisier. "How about fingerprints?" she shouted above it.

"You gotta match them up. You know how many muggers we got in this city?"

"A lot, if you don't try to catch them," Lydia said.

"What for? We got turnstile justice."

"You mean it's hopeless?"

"I mean hopeless," he answered, sounding weary.

"Can I have my gun back?"

"Yours?"

"I earned it. If the fingerprints aren't important, why not give it to me?" She could show it to Detective Barolini. Or Kramer, since he was nicer. He'd check it out.

"Evidence," sandy mustache said, hanging on to it. Lydia was about to ask him what good evidence was if they weren't going to use it, but he held his hand up to quiet her and listened to the box. He turned to the other cop. "That's us. Let's roll." He started down the hall.

The cute cop hung behind. "Listen, anything happens,

call. Don't worry it turns out to be nothing. That's what we're here for. My name's DeFilippi and my partner's Dougherty. Just call and ask for D and D, like Dean and Deluca. So long, Colombo."

Colombo seemed sorry to see him go. So did she. She consoled herself with the thought that she could always call him the next time someone attacked her or broke into her apartment—until she remembered her resolution not to get involved with any man.

"Mind if I borrow a chair?" she asked Mrs. Nagy.

"What do you want a chair for?"

"I'll show you."

She got a chair from Mrs. Nagy's kitchen and stood it in the entranceway. "Just hold the door open, please, so I can see."

While Mrs. Nagy and Colombo stood by, Lydia climbed up onto the chair and twisted the lightbulb. The entranceway immediately lit up, spotlighting cracked and missing tiles on the floor and damaged mailboxes.

"Why, it was working all the time," Mrs. Nagy said. "Didn't I tell you? It's the super. He'd doing everything he can to get rid of us."

Lydia shook her head. It wasn't the super or your ordinary, run-of-the-mill mugger. This was personal.

CHAPTER 18

Colombo sat in the passenger seat, peering eagerly out the car window as if he could see in the dark. He'd sensed where they were going the minute she'd hit the LIE. "Sorry to squelch your hopes, fellow," Lydia said. "But it won't be the same. Your pal Adam won't be there."

It was three something in the morning, and she was on

her way to Southampton. The Datsun was the only car on the North Sea Road. The moon looked falsely bright, luminescent, as if lit from behind. It soon became obscured by fast-moving clouds, and it was back to country black again.

Lydia began having doubts about whether she would be any safer out here than in town. Especially with a serial murderer at large. She'd heard it on the air. Idiot. She was scaring herself. The police merely suspected a serial killer. A number of women had turned up missing, that was all. Maybe they'd just had enough of suburban living. Besides, the women were from Nassau County, not Suffolk, where she was headed.

It wasn't just nearly being strangled that had convinced her to leave town so suddenly. What had clinched it was discovering that the door to the empty apartment across the hall was unlocked again. This, after she'd had the Israeli locksmith across the street put new locks on the door and the fire escape gate. Tonight, as always before going into her apartment, she'd tried the doorknob just to check. Still shaky from the attack, she'd turned the handle. It had opened onto darkness.

She'd run back across the hall to her apartment and locked her door behind her. After throwing some clothes into her canvas bag, she'd called Colombo and taken off.

Tomorrow she'd phone Detective Kramer at Suffolk Homicide and tell him about the attacker and the flare gun. Maybe he could get the gun from the Nineteenth Precinct and check it out with the lab. No use asking Barolini. He'd only scoff.

She'd call in sick at the office. Too bad if Milke didn't believe her. Better to lose her job than her life. Or be blinded or permanently scarred by a flare gun. Maybe both, if Colombo hadn't fended off her attacker. Where had her assailant disappeared to so quickly? Into the cab that the woman had just vacated? Colombo had been standing at the curb, barking.

Or had it been the BMW behind the cab that Colombo was barking at? She'd thought the car had been slowed by the cab, but it might have been just pulling out. But muggers didn't go around in BMWs. Except this wasn't an ordinary mugging.

Could the attack be connected with her job instead of Adam's murder? At *gazelle*, appearance was all. Someone who didn't know how dangerous a flare gun could be might have wanted to scar her. Absurd. Granted she wasn't universally loved at work, but she was scarcely actively hated. Or was the attack retribution for turning down some writer's article? If the finished piece got rejected, the author was paid only a kill fee—a quarter of the amount. Milke was famous for changing her mind at the last minute and scrapping something a writer had slaved over—while Lydia, not Milke, got the blame. It sounded like too drastic a measure for a writer to take, but even so . . . violence was rampant these days. Look at the people who got fired and went gunning for their boss, killing anyone who got in the way. Or think of all those post office employees seeking retribution and shooting at random.

After the tavern turnoff, the houses became even fewer and farther apart. A pair of yellow eyes glared out of the inky night like eyes in a Stephen King movie. She shivered and rolled up the window on her side, then Colombo's window for good measure. He gave her a puzzled look.

Maybe it was a mistake to leave town. At least in the city there were people around to hear you scream. Never mind they seldom came to your rescue. Someone, like Mrs. Nagy, might just call 911. What this country needed were more Mrs. Nagys. Out here, most of the summer people had gone, the population dwindled. But on the north, less expensive, side of the highway, there were bound to be more locals. Also some retired summer people who stayed the year round. And Alec Urzaga lived right next door.

Small comfort that.

Had Barolini checked out Urzaga's claim that he'd been working at the hospital the night Adam was drowned? Of course, Urzaga could have charmed some susceptible nurse into lying for him. Or if charm hadn't worked, bribed. She put nothing past him. But then she felt an almost equal distrust of Vanessa and Todd. And she wasn't too sure about Carolyn.

She would have missed the mailbox at the turnoff if Colombo hadn't started barking. Excited. Leaping around. Good thing she'd rolled up his window. He was ready to jump out.

As she turned in to the driveway, the car headlights swept across the parking area under the trees where Adam's BMW had been parked on Labor Day weekend, the front wheels run up over the curb. It wasn't there now. Had the police confiscated it? Or had it been stolen? Maybe she should call Vanessa. After all, if Vanessa inherited his personal property, that meant the car should be rightfully hers. Of course, Vanessa would probably either hang up on her, or else claim Lydia was the one who had stolen it. But she should at least give it a try. Attempt to make friends with her. If she was going to find out who'd murdered Adam, sooner or later she'd have to talk to both Todd and Vanessa, along with Carolyn and Urzaga.

Lydia parked at the top of the hill in front of the garage and poked around in the glove compartment until she found her flashlight. Leaving the engine on idle, she got out to move the garbage cans blocking her way. Colombo raced around the side of the house as if he expected to find Adam waiting at the front door. Lydia sighed.

In a few minutes he reappeared, listless and despondent.

"Sorry, but I warned you," she told him.

The garage door opened manually. Also squeakily. She breathed in a dank, musty smell as she entered. She beamed the flashlight into dark, spiderwebby corners, feeling nervous yet foolish. Who did she expect to find lurking behind the barbecue grill—Urzaga or the serial killer? She spotted a coiled garden hose, two bikes, a rolled beach umbrella, collapsed lawn chairs, and extra garbage cans. No one crouched behind them.

She drove the car in and closed the garage doors, not wanting to alert Urzaga to her presence. Besides dropping into Megan's to talk to Bobbie the waitress tomorrow, she'd also pay a call on him. If he didn't know she was here, she might catch him off guard and get him to reveal something crucial. Of course, he could have heard her drive up, but it was getting on to four. Even Urzaga had to sleep sometime.

No lights from his house were visible, but then the woods concealed everything except the top deck. Of course, in the winter when the trees were bare she'd probably be able to see over. Not that she cared to. His house was a bastard mix of materials—stone, concrete, brick, wood, and glass. Three stories high and sitting on the edge of a cliff. A real cliff-hanger, so to speak.

No telling if Urzaga might be on night duty at the hospital. Or he could be in Manhattan, where he had what he referred to as his pied-à-terre. If he was in town, that would be a real break. Then she could snoop around tomorrow to her heart's content.

All summer Adam had complained about the noise Urzaga's construction crew made and about his refusal to let Adam see what he was up to. "He says he wants it to be a big surprise to everyone when he's finished. I think he's just trying to avoid me. Or hiding something. And I'm going to find out what." And he had. Enough to report it to the zoning board and an official at Hamptons Hospital. If he'd lived that long.

Enough to get him murdered?

She'd told Barolini about it on the way to the Nineteenth Precinct to be fingerprinted. Barolini had dismissed it. Treated it as something she'd dreamed up on the spur of the moment, because she was afraid he'd haul her in. He was too determined to pin the murder on her to find the real killer. And Kramer seemed to be in the dark about what was going on. DeFilippi and Dougherty—D & D—just ordinary cops, would make better detectives than those two. Maybe there was some truth to the name New York's Finest.

She inhaled the smells of earth and distant ozone and admired the lacy tree shadows across the sloping lawn. Her trees. Her lawn. Her sky. Her stars. Well, maybe that was going a bit far. Next thing she'd be sounding like Scarlett returned to Tara. Maybe Adam had guessed she'd come to care about the place, which was why he'd left it to her. Or was she crediting him with a wisdom beyond death he hadn't displayed in life? Just because he'd been so goddamned generous. To hell with it. Enjoy.

"I owe you one," she said to Adam. A remark he'd made
often. Colombo, who'd been sticking close to her side, nuz-
zled her hand. A sign of approval?

She started up the flagstone path toward the house. The
moonlight came and went, so she kept the flashlight on as
she climbed the hill on the gray-shingled side of the house
facing the road. The opposite, glassed-in side faced the
woods and beyond, like an extension of its surroundings.
Bobo, the Frank Lloyd Wright student who had designed
the house, had done a good job. Wrong, his name wasn't
Bobo, but that was close. A clown's name. Someone well
known in architectural circles. Probably dead now.

Hearing a rustling in the shrubbery behind her, Lydia
wheeled around. A rabbit hopped across the lawn and disappeared under a bush. Colombo ignored it, too depressed
to give chase.

She found the key under the middle rock beneath a bush
near the door where Adam always kept it. But what if Jared
Evans or Kim or someone else at National Trust had told
Lilco to cut off the electricity? Unlocking the door, she
went in and held her breath as she flicked on the wall
switches, and was relieved to see the hallway and dining
room light up. The chairs were evenly spaced around the
glass dining table—a chair at each end, three on either side.
Everything looked disconcertingly the same. Apparently the
National Trust people had sent someone to clean.

In the kitchen she tried the wall phone, and was com-
forted when she got a dial tone. Adam's house had always
made her feel slightly uneasy. She'd have liked to turn on
all the lights, but she didn't want to attract Urzaga's attention. If he was restless and roaming the top deck he could
see over. Or he might drive by on his way home from night
duty at the hospital. She almost wished she'd kept her
promise to Carolyn and invited her out. Of course, she
couldn't very easily have extended a midnight invitation.

Lydia went from room to room, looking under beds, in
closets, and behind chairs. She carefully checked all the
locks. Colombo padded after her, making her feel somewhat safer. She couldn't bring herself to look out the windows facing the pool and had to force herself to go into the

green room she'd shared with Mark. The worst lay ahead—
Adam's room at the end of the hall.

Colombo had already gone in. Bracing herself, Lydia
entered. The cleaners had been here, too, leaving it as
anonymous and antiseptic as a hotel room. Even the fireplace had been raked clean of ashes and scrubbed down.
No pill bottles on the night table or the bathroom shelf. No
vodka bottle next to a glass. No huaraches, tan slacks, or
blue guayabera shirt lying in a puddle on the floor. The
only hint of Adam's presence was his books on the shelves.

The red eye on the answering machine was steady. She
lifted the plastic lid and saw that Barolini had taken the incoming message cassette. He'd refused to say if there had
been a gap on the cassette between Vanessa's morning call
and hers in the late afternoon. Why? She pushed OGM/Play
and got Adam's voice. Colombo, who lay on the bed in the
spot where Adam had slept, sat up and looked hopeful, then
accusing. As if she were doing this to torment him. "Sorry,
fellow, I know it's tough," she told him, and took the cassette off. Too painful for both of them. Tomorrow she'd
buy new cassettes.

Hearing a noise at the window, she tensed. But it was
only a tree branch scraping the glass. If anyone were lurking nearby, Colombo would not only bark, he'd attack.

The house was freezing. She turned the thermostat in the
hall to seventy, brushed her teeth, and shivered into the
flowered flannel nightgown she'd brought out, sacrificing
sexy for comfort and security. The story of her new life.
She grabbed two blankets from the linen closet, put them
on the bed, and crawled in.

Sleep eluded her. Once again, she wondered where Colombo had been when Adam, drunk and drugged, was being held underwater. After witnessing the way he'd attacked
No Face, she was sure Colombo would have come to Adam's defense. Unless he knew the murderer and thought it
was some kind of horseplay in the water. But he'd been
limping. The vet had said it looked like he'd been kicked.
Kicked out of the way by the murderer. Who? She tried to
remember how Colombo had reacted when Urzaga ap-

peared. But she'd been too intent on her futile rescue effort to notice.

Tomorrow she'd search the house for clues. After all, the cops didn't know Adam as well as she did. Something they wouldn't notice might jump out at her.

Sleep wouldn't come. She closed her eyes and counted backward from one hundred. Tried deep breathing. Finally she reached across Colombo to the bed table and turned on the radio. All she could get was that hyper dj in Bridgeport relating telephone messages between rap and rock, wishing happy birthday to Franco from Sandy, and telling Linda that Gary was sorry and still loved her. She left it on the way Adam used to, when the sound had carried in to her and Mark. Then it had kept them awake. Now it put her to sleep.

CHAPTER 19

The ringing phone woke her.

She recognized Neil's voice before she recognized her surroundings. She was lying in Adam's bed, Colombo beside her.

"How did you know I was out here?"

"Elementary, my dear Miller. You weren't in town, so obviously you'd flown the coop. Inconsiderate of you, sweetie, not to call and let me know."

"I'm not legally awake yet, so don't start bitching please. I'll call you back after I've had coffee."

Neil said he'd be writing later and didn't want to be interrupted. They agreed to go out to dinner. "I'll stop by at Adam's place," he said. "Or rather, yours. Seven-thirty."

The house had warmed up. Still in her flannel nightgown, she went barefoot down the hall to the kitchen, Colombo at her side. What would she feed him? Another thing she should have thought of before making her midnight getaway.

She found more dog food than human—a carton of Alpo in an undercounter cupboard and a box of Wheat Thins. No coffee even. Only a box of black currant tea. Where did that come from? Adam didn't drink tea, and he always mentioned when he was having guests, keeping her informed of his daily activities. Far more than she cared to know. She often tuned out. Maybe she hadn't been listening.

The refrigerator had been cleaned out, and the freezer in the pantry emptied and unplugged. She remembered the flood in the hall when she'd arrived that night. Obviously National Trust had hired someone from a local cleaning service the way Adam had when he came out to the house. He said that Francoise drove him crazy enough in town with her constant chatter. He didn't need her here.

Besides, Vanessa would have raised hell, Adam added. She was jealous of Francoise. Everybody. She'd been furious when she found out that Adam was paying for Francoise's psychiatrist.

Lydia knew little about Francoise, except that she lived in Queens. She had a son in the first grade, a husband who was a waiter at Le Perigord, and made numerous lengthy calls to her relatives in Brittany, sticking Adam with the phone bill. Had Francoise known that Adam was leaving her eighty-five thousand? It struck Lydia that Francoise, like the others, might have resented her inheriting Adam's house and a trust fund. But she doubted that it was Francoise who'd attacked her last night.

Lydia consulted Adam's list of service people while she sipped tea and munched stale Wheat Thins. The list gave names and numbers for repair, cleaning, pool, and lawn people. Also caterers, bartenders, and waiters. She called refrigerator repair and got a woman who said that Larry would be over at eleven-thirty to fix the freezer.

Lydia hung up in shock. In New York you were an optimist if you expected to get a repair made in less than three weeks, and a fool if you took the day off expecting them to be there.

She called Gillian to tell her that she had a rotten cold and wouldn't be in.

"Oh, I'm frightfully sorry," said Gillian Markham-Smith, a British import. "But don't worry, I'll manage."

"You'll do fine. Have a chance to strut your stuff," Lydia told her. After all, if Neil had been supportive of her, she could do the same for Gillian. Had Gillian not been such a big office gossip, Lydia would have given her Adam's phone number to call in case of a crisis. But if her co-workers found out that she'd inherited a house in the Hamptons, besides money, they'd hate her for life.

"Offhand, do you remember who we've paid kill fees to lately?" Lydia asked.

"Easier would be remembering who we haven't."

"If you have a free minute, check the files and get the names of people who got them in the past six months."

"I'll make a free minute."

Lydia said she might be at the doctor's when Gillian called back and to leave the information on the machine.

Of course, the whole idea that some writer might attack her with a flare gun was absurd. Anyone who resorted to such tactics had to be crazy or stupid, and most writers had a modicum of intelligence, and gave the outward appearance of sanity.

Now that she looked back on it, fleeing the city at midnight seemed foolish. Melodramatic. Overreacting. Lydia looked at her watch. Ten-thirty. An hour before Larry the repair person arrived. She'd visit Urzaga later. No telling how long she'd be there.

She pulled on blue jeans and black turtleneck—the only clothes she'd brought with her—and began a methodical search for clues, beginning with the kitchen. A lot of stuff like newspapers, cans, and bottles would already have been deposited in the garbage and carted off. In the living room she peered into the giant jar holding the pampas grass and looked under soft pillows, not sure what she was looking for.

She wasn't cut out for sleuthing and felt foolish searching for clues. What did she expect to find? A signed note saying "I killed Adam Auerbach"? Or Adam's secret diary written in code that only someone with her superior intelligence could decipher? Adam didn't keep a diary. Or records of any kind.

She stood on chairs to inspect top closet shelves, looked in medicine cabinets, under mattresses, and behind pictures. By eleven-thirty she'd covered the house and come up with zilch.

Also, it looked like the repair people in the Hamptons were no more dependable than those in Manhattan. She considered calling on Urzaga but vetoed the idea. No doubt Larry would arrive the minute she left. Better stick nearby just in case.

Draping her jeans jacket over her shoulders, she called Colombo and went out on the deck. Red and yellow leaves splattered the flooring of herringbone slats. The deck collared the thick trunk of a maple tree that someone had the sense to leave standing. All around were trees with autumnal leaves. In Central Park the leaves were just turning. Fall came earlier out here, spring later.

It didn't seem possible that late last spring, less than six months ago, she, Mark, and Adam had sat here on the deck at the white metal table sipping after-breakfast coffee under April-green leaves and reading the *Times*. Each with a copy Adam had brought back from the village.

The peaceful quiet was sometimes interrupted by frantic squeals. Sounds she couldn't bear to hear. She would grab the long-handled retrieval pole that she kept handy, run across the lawn, dip the net into the pool, and rescue some small, panicky animal that had fallen into the water and was unable to climb the smooth, steep sides and save itself.

"Save me," Adam had said after she rescued a squirrel. "Don't let me drown." Eerie. As if he'd predicted his own death. She'd tried to save him, and was now suspected of his murder.

Adam might have been on the road to self-destruction, but he'd wanted to end his pain, not his life. She looked at the dead leaves and shivered. Who had held him under while he'd struggled in the water? And why? Hate? Greed?

Revenge? Fear? With Urzaga it might have been fear that Adam would report him. But report him for what?

She took a deep breath and cut across the lawn to confront the scene where Adam had drowned, hoping it might tell her something. Stir a memory.

The air was chilly and the sky the color of lead. In the nearby trees, birds complained of her presence, while small animals scampered through grass that was fast being overtaken by weeds. All that was left of the geraniums in the urns were stalks with brown leaves. The white paint on the urns was flaking.

Colombo ran ahead to the deep end of the pool, sniffed the cement, and looked up at her, asking what had happened. "You're the one who was there," she reminded him. Or was he? Where had he been? Chased off? Shut up in the house and shut out later?

The pool had been drained and covered with a tarp. She stood looking down at the dead leaves piling up on the gray canvas shroud.

No voice spoke to her.

From the house came the sound of the ringing phone. She sprinted across the lawn, glad to get away, and took the call in the kitchen.

"Hi, this is Larry. I'm running behind schedule. Okay with you if I come over after lunch?"

She said yes. Did she have a choice?

"I'll be there at four."

Larry took long lunch hours. But at least he'd be here today. Or would he?

Okay, what next? Urzaga's place? Or Megan's for lunch? No, tonight she and Neil could go there. If Megan's was good enough for Adam, it was good enough for Neil. And no telling when Bobbie was on duty. Urzaga's, then.

CHAPTER 20

Lydia left Colombo behind in the house, not wanting him to beat her over to Urzaga's to tip him off to her presence. That would defeat her purpose. Instead of going by the gravel road, she took the shortcut through the woods so she'd see his place before he saw her. If he was in Manhattan or on hospital duty, she'd have a good look around. Otherwise she'd just have to settle for surprising him by suddenly appearing on his doorstep.

And it might be better if he was home. Then she could ask him point-blank why he was trying to get her charged with Adam's murder. Not that she expected an honest answer, but she'd like to see him squirm a little. Urzaga squirm? That was an oxymoron. He'd be cool as the proverbial cucumber. Even so, she'd give it a try.

Trampling dry stalks and dead leaves, she followed a well-worn path through the woodsy undergrowth. Who had used it so often? Urzaga? Certainly not Adam, who had no great love of the outdoors or of walking. When he visited Urzaga he drove the quarter of a mile over.

A small animal ran for cover before she could see what it was. She breathed in a mixture of decaying leaves, pine, and the distant smell of ocean, and stopped to admire a fairy ring of mushrooms surrounding a dead tree trunk. Poisonous or edible? Neil would know. He belonged to the mycological society, a group so in love with mushroom hunting that they went on hunts to South America and Asia.

Neil swore that he knew where to find precious morels, but would reveal his source to no one but Steve. Once he and Steve had shared an oyster mushroom with her and

Mark. It had looked like a blond pancake and, sautéed in butter, tasted like heaven.

Lydia glimpsed a walled fortress—the concrete back part of Urzaga's house that slanted forward to wood in front. The few small windows could be holes for cannons. The only thing missing was a moat.

Keeping out of sight, she walked as lightly as she could in her cowboy boots. She should have brought along sneakers. But at least in boots, jeans, and jacket, she was sufficiently covered so that any ticks carrying Lyme disease couldn't get at her.

Nearing the edge of the woods, she slipped behind a tree to see without being seen. A man-made streambed wound its way across the lawn, disappearing under several tarps covering a wide, excavated area that Adam had sworn was going to be another Lake Erie. Large boulders, positioned midpool and at the far end, substituted for diving boards.

"Well, do you approve?" a voice asked from behind. She swung around. Alec Urzaga flashed his TV star smile.

"Oh, hi," she said, nonchalantly. As if people always hid behind tree trunks before approaching someone's house.

Tall, trim, and chiseled, Urzaga wore tan jodhpurs and riding boots. Did he think of himself as Maxime de Winter in *Rebecca* or Rhett Butler? Or maybe he wanted to give the impression that he'd just returned from a polo match and really was, as he claimed, to Argentinean aristocracy born. Ralph Lauren would love him. Including the star-shaped scar between his eyes. Just sinister enough to be intriguing. She wondered if he got it playing polo. A trophy scar, so to speak.

"Shades of the old swimming hole," she said, nodding toward the man-made stream and tarp-covered excavation.

"Glad you like it."

"Did I say that? You do have a tendency to jump to conclusions, like telling people I was trying to drown Adam."

"That's absurd," he said. The scar deepened when he frowned. "I said no such thing."

"What did you tell Barolini, then?"

"There were two who came to see me. Barolini asked the questions and another detective took notes. I said that you were in the pool with Adam and called to me to help save him."

"The way I heard it, you said it looked like I was trying to drown Adam."

"Barolini said that? He's lying. If you don't believe me, you could ask to see the notes."

"If he's lying, he won't let me see them. Was the other detective hefty? A shape sort of like Bill Clinton's? Nice brown eyes."

Urzaga laughed. "I didn't look into his eyes. This guy was husky, not hefty. Short and muscular. Big biceps on him."

That couldn't be Kramer. But Kramer must have seen the notes. Maybe he'd tell her what was in them.

"You don't like my meandering stream?" It wasn't a serious question, just something to change the subject. "I'm aiming for the bucolic. My landscaper is planting weeds for the natural effect. Queen Anne's lace and wild pansies, that sort of thing. Why were you lurking behind a tree?" Urzaga asked abruptly.

"Mushrooming. Looking for fungi. I belong to the mycological society."

"Be careful. The fairy rings in this woods are poisonous."

She took heart that he warned her of poisonous mushrooms. At least he didn't want her dead. In fact, he was sounding downright friendly, offering to show her around. Careful, she told herself.

"I hear you're my neighbor now, thanks to Adam," he said.

"Who told you?"

"I've had bitter complaints from both wives and your friend Neil."

"Neil? You heard from him?"

"He complained the loudest. Said Adam had promised him the place. But they all said that. I could make the same claim, but then I know how often Adam changed his mind. Also, when he told me he planned to make Vanessa and her lover coexecutors, I figured that between them they'd grab everything Adam owned. And who expected Adam to die?"

"The murderer."

"Well, that could be any one of us, couldn't it?"

Lydia was confused. Neil had phoned Urzaga, someone he professed to dislike intensely? And Urzaga's reaction to Adam's announcement that Vanessa and Todd would be co-executors had sounded genuine. Exactly the same as hers. Except Adam had said that Urzaga would be an executor, too. Maybe she was wrong about Urzaga. Maybe Barolini lied about what Urzaga had said in order to nail her. But why? Again she asked herself if Barolini held some special grudge against her.

"Planning on making this your weekend retreat?" Urzaga asked.

"I don't know. I like the place, but I'm not especially wild about the Hamptons."

"If you decide to sell, give me first dibs. I'll make it more than worth your while. You'll do fine as a neighbor, but I don't want to take the chance of anyone cutting down the woods."

"They're yours; how could they do that?"

"The woods belong to Adam, didn't you know? He bought them so no one would interfere with his privacy."

Judging from the well-worn path through the trees, Adam hadn't had as much privacy as he'd thought.

"I don't want some partying jerks blaring rock 'n' roll into the summer night. See this?" Urzaga pointed to some rocks jutting up around what looked like a large sewer pipe leading to the house. "That's going to be a waterfall. The pipe camouflaged, of course. It leads into what will be my indoor pool. I'm also putting in a sauna and an adjoining exercise room with all the latest equipment."

"Can you expand under the house without weakening the foundation?"

"Trust me, I've consulted with experts. I know what I'm doing."

"I never trust anyone who says trust me."

"Smart lady."

They reached the back door. "Come in and have some coffee. You never really got a chance to see the place when you and Adam came over. June, wasn't it? Your husband's birthday. He didn't come along."

"Adam convinced him he couldn't take the climb."

Urzaga laughed. "Neither could Adam. He collapsed on the second-floor deck and refused to go any farther."

"You have a good memory."

"For memorable events. By the way, I haven't had a chance to tell you. I was sorry as hell to hear about Mark."

"Thank you."

Careful, sweetie, don't let him sucker you in, too. He didn't give a damn about Mark. And he isn't interested in anyone other than himself. The man was bilking Adam, remember? And trying to get you sent up the river.

"You've been put through a lot lately."

"Yes, well . . ." She let it hang. Maybe he was being sincere.

The back door led into the garage. She liked the musty, earthy smell of garages. They reminded her of the warehouse that was part of the family moving business. The warehouse was large and made of concrete, half of it underground. Neighbors jokingly called it an air raid shelter. It adjoined the lot beside their house, set back, with a tree-shaded drive so it wouldn't be an eyesore. Lydia often sneaked in and played there when she was little. Chots wouldn't join her because she thought it was scary and because their parents forbade it. Lydia loved the mysterious things concealed under the tarps.

Urzaga's garage also had a lot of hidden mysteries. A rubber-tired monster under a camouflage canvas cover that could have been a Jeep, juggernaut, or armored tank. A sleek silver-gray Jag snubbed a tan VW van beside it. She saw no sign of Adam's blue BMW. Of course, it might be in the hidden new addition, behind the wall with a wide garage-type door. Next to it was a people-sized door that she headed for, as if she thought it led to the kitchen. As soon as her fingers touched the doorknob, his hand clamped over hers.

"Off limits," he said. "That leads to the indoor pool. You have a standing invitation to use it after it's finished."

"Why the big door?"

"That's part of the surprise. For now, no one sees anything. Kitchen's this way," he said, and stepped back to let her precede him up a short flight of stairs.

What was he hiding? Something Adam had found out that had cost him his life? Or maybe it was just Adam's BMW. Maybe this guy wasn't a murderer but only a common thief and a liar.

She stepped into a kitchen suitably equipped to run a small restaurant. Six-burner stove, eye-level oven, and glass double-doored refrigerator.

A hefty red-faced blonde sat at a table polishing silver. Urzaga introduced her as Mrs. Janowsky. "The person responsible for all my superbly cooked dinners. The kitchen is her domain."

Mrs. Janowsky's red face got redder. Although she looked far younger than Urzaga, she beamed upon him as if he were her son.

"Full-time, not live-in," Urzaga announced after closing the kitchen door behind him. "Her husband took off and left her with four little mouths to feed."

The dining room had a chandelier that would have done Louis the Sun King proud. And totally wrong for a summer house. Urzaga, like Barolini, tried too hard. In their striving toward upward mobility, they overdid it. Urzaga was, of course, smoother and more accomplished. And to be fair, this wasn't exactly a summer home since he lived here year-round. She wondered where his pied à terre was in town. Adam hadn't said.

"Come see the view from the top deck," Urzaga said, and bounded up the steps ahead of her, expecting her to follow. Since she wanted to get a picture of the layout, she did.

Urzaga was in good shape, taking the steep, narrow stairs in easy stride.

She was gratified to see his surprise when he found her right behind him. "What? Not winded?"

"I live in a fourth-floor walkup. I'm used to climbs."

"Oh, yes, I forgot."

How did he know? Had it been Urzaga who'd stolen her tape?

"How do you know where I live?" she asked.

"Adam mentioned it."

Maybe. Adam was a gossip. "Great view," she said, keeping to the middle of the deck. It was a large, cement-floored area surrounded by a flimsy railing. Beyond it nothing but thin air.

"Like a drink?" he asked.

"Thanks, I don't drink this early in the day."

"Never touch the stuff myself. Alcohol isn't my thing."

What was? Cocaine? Heroin? Or some drug easily obtainable from the hospital pharmacy?

"Come over here and get a bird's-eye view." He was standing by a revolving telescope on a tripod. She went reluctantly. "Turn it to the left and you see a purple ridge. That's Connecticut. And there's Long Island Sound," he said, hovering over her. He wore some kind of spicy cologne she wasn't sure she liked.

"Oh, yeah, terrific."

Swiveling the telescope around, she aimed it at Adam's house. The trees still had enough leaves to prevent a clear view, but when all the leaves had fallen, it wouldn't be necessary for him to walk through the woods in order to spy. That is, if it was Urzaga who'd worn the path down.

"I use this to study the stars," he said, as if he knew she suspected him of spying. "Fascinating. Come over tonight and I'll show you. Make it dinner. I'll have Mrs. Janowsky cook something special. What would you like?"

"I'm going out," she said, stepping away. He was too damn close. She found it disconcerting.

"Some other night, then. Tonight will be too cloudy to see much anyway. The good view is from here, regardless of the weather," he said, and steered her to the side overlooking the sheer drop where pointy rocks jutted out. Far below were dollhouse rooftops and a church spire to be pinioned on.

It made her nervous having him standing so near with only the flimsy railing dividing her from outer space. "I forgot, I have to get back. The refrigerator repairman's due about now."

"What time is he coming?"

"One-thirty," she said, moving the time up.

"It's only a little after one now. Repairmen are notoriously late."

"In case he isn't, I want to be there."

"Sure, if you're going to worry. Just one thing I want to mention. For the record." He smiled. "I don't know what Adam told you, but I'm not the bastard you think. I didn't fleece him. Or pick his pockets. Adam suggested funding the Institute. I didn't ask him to."

"That was between you two." She wasn't going to get self-righteous so near that damn railing.

"It should have been, but it wasn't. Adam had a way of blaming people for taking him up on his offers. And I wasn't about to pass that one by. Getting funded isn't easy. I'm not a quack, you know. I'm a damn good doctor with credentials to prove it. And I helped Adam. Was helping. But it wasn't just Adam. There are millions of others out there with the same problem."

"Millions?"

"A hell of a lot. Too damn many. Adam was strictly a depressive. But my mother had both her highs and lows. Bipolar. One minute up, the next down. She went through hell. And she had it all—beauty, wit, intelligence, a loving husband, devoted friends. Not to mention a charming genius son." He grinned to show he meant this as a joke, then his eyebrows drew together, deepening the scar. "She killed herself."

"Oh."

"On her down days, she couldn't get out of bed. She suffered. For weeks. Even months." He spoke intensely of his mother's symptoms, his eyes burning with a kind of feverish madness. And he kept moving in closer. In pressing his point, he was pressing her against the goddamned railing.

"I couldn't bear seeing the same sort of thing happen to Adam," he said.

Lydia felt the wooden railing cut into her back, and visualized the long drop down to the rooftops. She was eye level with his chiseled chin. "Hey, goddamn it. Would you please get out of my face?"

"You're not listening."

"How can I up against the railing? Heights make me nervous."

"Sorry." He retreated. She took a deep breath.

Urzaga talked on, defending his actions. "Yes, Adam contributed to the Institute. So what?"

Except it doesn't exist, she didn't say. Now was not the time to argue.

"It's a bona fide institute, not just on paper," he said defensively, as if she'd spoken. "And I'm having an uphill battle getting contributions. Most people consider depressives depressing. Self-pitying. People who lie around feeling sorry for themselves. All they have to do is get ahold of themselves and buck up."

She opened her mouth to speak, but he held up his hand like a stop sign. "Hear me out. I'm competing with AIDS and cancer. No use applying for government funding; nothing comes of it. You have to have the right disease and be affiliated with the right prestigious place—Harvard, UCLA, Johns Hopkins. Granted, the lab Hamptons Hospital is setting up isn't much—but it's something. I've got a lot invested in it. Emotionally and otherwise."

He was beginning to simmer down.

"Oh, I believe you. I didn't realize you were so committed," she told him.

She'd long ago learned that if she said something nice, people got suspicious, but if she was insulting, they seldom caught on. Urzaga gave her a measured look as if weighing the remark, trying to decide if she was being sarcastic. Apparently the decision went in her favor. He relaxed a little, smiled. Recovered his cool. "I am committed. Excuse me. I sometimes get carried away."

Committed or obsessed?

It was windy up on the deck, the sky a lowering gray. She shivered in her jeans jacket and wondered how she could get away from him without provoking another Latin temper tantrum. She realized she wasn't being fair. You don't have to be Latin to have tantrums. Look at Adam.

But Urzaga was unable to drop the subject. Defensive. "So what if I supplied Adam with dope? Admittedly, it's an unorthodox practice highly disapproved of by my medical colleagues. I knew I could lose my license. But I also knew what happened to my mother, and I didn't want to see it happen to him. I loved the man, damn it. Here," he said, "you're shivering." He draped his blazer over her shoulders, letting his hands rest there for a moment. She was almost sorry when he removed them. Her love life had become a sexual Sahara. Also, it was nice to have a man see to her comfort, after all the time she'd spent seeing to Mark's.

"Adam was a rebel," Urzaga said, and proceeded to tell her all about Adam—as if she didn't know. "He had a lot to rebel against. His mother came on alternately hot and cold, seducing him one minute, rebuffing him the next. She married his father for money, and looked to Adam to be the man her husband wasn't. His father wanted Adam to be the jock he never was. But Adam didn't give a damn about sports— completely uncoordinated, poor guy. Both parents wanted him to be the perfect son, making up for their disappointment in his retarded brother, in themselves, and in each other. A big order for a little kid."

"You guys did a lot of talking," she said, surprised he knew so much about Adam's family. Surprised, and maybe jealous?

But Urzaga was so intent on the subject, he didn't notice.

"Rebellion was Adam's only weapon. He got a big kick out of shocking people and going against the status quo. Loved the idea of sniffing H in the men's room at a restaurant."

"Not while I was around, he didn't."

Urzaga held up his hand. "I'm making a point here," he said.

One of those people who loved to lecture. Tolerated no interruptions.

"Pills taken legitimately didn't do it. Hell, he saw two shrinks a week. They put him on lithium, Elavil, Prozac— you name it. Nothing worked until I took over. Adam was my guinea pig."

Yeah.

"But a willing one. And under my strict supervision. It was after he stopped the dosage I was allotting him—

thanks to a so-called helpful friend," Urzaga said, giving her a look, "that he got worse. Feelings of hopelessness and mania. Couldn't concentrate, his mind kept racing. Irritable, impulsive. Got into a hyperactive state that gives someone like him the energy to act on a suicidal impulse.

"And it was suicide, pure and simple. Just like my mother. Only he got someone to do it for him. By making threats. Telling people he was taking them off the dole and out of his will."

You included, Lydia thought.

"He even threatened to expose me to the powers that be. For what, I'm not sure. He was asking to be killed. Begging for it."

Wasn't that what rapists claimed their victims did? She tensed up. Was he going to say next that he saw there was no way out for Adam and obliged him?

Urzaga stepped toward her. She moved back and found herself up against the railing again. Her heart pounded as if it were going to break through the wall of her chest. Was this going to be a confession before he killed her?

He laughed. "Don't look so scared; I won't push you over. Doctors don't have to resort to drowning or pushing over a railing. The right injection will do it."

"Thanks. That's good to know. It makes me feel a hell of a lot better, Alec."

"First time you've called me by my first name."

"I have to get back."

"So go," he said, smiling. "Just give me my jacket." He stood close, removing it from her shoulders. She again smelled the spicy cologne and decided she liked it after all. His breath was warm on her cheek. Was he going to kiss her? "By the way," he said. "If you tell anyone what I just said, I'll deny every word of it. Medicine isn't that advanced in its thinking."

CHAPTER 21

Lydia went away confused. Was Dr. Carlos Fernando Alejandro Urzaga a good guy or a bad guy? Quack or dedicated? Truly wanting to help Adam but using questionable methods out of zeal? Or had he been fattening his wallet by preying on Adam's weaknesses?

No denying the guy had charm. She could see why Adam in his never-ending quest to be entertained had added Urzaga to his list of court jesters.

A thorny branch scratched her face. The undergrowth was so thick, she needed a machete to hack her way through. In her confusion she'd entered the wrong part of the woods, and lost the path. The trees grew closely together, branches twining, obliterating the sky. The ground was damp and mossy with odd-looking gray fungi, something in a sci-fi movie that sprung to life and threatened to take over the planet Earth.

She retraced her steps, or so she thought, until she came face-to-face, or more accurately, nose-to-chimney, with a child's playhouse. Freshly painted white with green trim. Hidden from sight of Urzaga's house, even more so from Adam's. Probably Adam, scarcely the explorer type, had never known it existed. Maybe Urzaga didn't either. Then who had painted it? Was Urzaga wrong about Adam owning the woods? This part must be at the far end bordering someone else's property. Often when she accidentally overshot Adam's place, she glimpsed the shingle roof of a · house down a lane. Maybe a little girl lived in the house and this was her playhouse. But no shingle roof was in sight.

When she was little she'd wanted a hideout, not a playhouse, a secret place to be alone—to read, daydream, or sulk. Her favorite spot had been under a tarp-covered dinner table in the warehouse. Armed with flashlight, book, and a batch of unsuccessful fudge made by Lottie, the woman who helped her mother with chores around the house, she'd camp under the table on rainy afternoons. Lottie's fudge had always "gone to sugar." So runny that it had to be eaten with a spoon—Lydia loved it.

When she got older, around eleven, her parents no longer declared the warehouse off-limits. "Just don't roller-skate on that pool table," her father warned. She often hung out with her father's helpers or visited him in his untidy office. He was easier to talk to than her mother, who would pick a hair off Lydia's shoulder, interrupt to tell her not to talk so fast, stand straight, or sit like a lady.

When her mother told her about menstruation, Lydia was so jolted by the news that she ran to the warehouse and told her father all about it. He listened sympathetically, as if he'd never heard of it before, shaking his head and saying my, my, this must be quite a shock.

She was her daddy's girl, as Chots was her mother's.

Opening the door, Lydia entered the playhouse. She had to bend over since she couldn't stand her full five nine. But the playhouse was surprisingly roomy. Roomy and gloomy. The trees outside cast shadows on two scarf-draped windows. The silk scarves looked expensive. The kid who'd fixed up the place either had an indulgent mother or had filched the scarves when her mother wasn't looking.

About half a dozen Barbie dolls lolled about, dressed for tennis, swimming, skiing, and aerobics. There was even a Barbie doll dressed in a business suit and carrying a briefcase. Barbie turned career woman. A closer look showed that the Barbies were not lolling. Lydia stared, unable to take in what she saw. The dolls were posed in subservient positions, groveling, down on their knees, or arms raised, pleading. Some were missing an arm or a leg. Accidentally or intentionally? A Barbie bride was tied to the canopy bed with a velvet ribbon.

Lydia's stomach lurched. She tasted something sour in her

throat. If she'd had anything to eat, she would have thrown up. She ran out of the playhouse. The scene spooked her.

CHAPTER 22

Emerging from Adam's side of the woods, Lydia felt as gloomy as the day, haunted by the sight of the mutilated Barbies in supplicating positions. She thought again of the shingled house down the lane. Was a child being tortured there, the dolls representing what she was forced to do? Beg for mercy on her knees?

The child-abuse authorities should hear about this. Call the parents in for questioning, take the kid away from them. Or maybe the child was playing out what was happening to her mother. Then again, it might be some adult victimizer who'd arranged the Barbies in those slavish poses. Restricted, she hoped, to dolls. But for how long?

Colombo was waiting for her when she got back, scrabbling at the sliding glass door. She gave him a hurried pat on the head and went to get the phone book. Under Suffolk County she found the number for the Child Protection Agency and punched it out with shaky fingers. When a woman answered, she realized she'd acted too hastily. She had no facts, didn't know the child's name—if it was a child—or even where she lived. "Sorry, wrong number," she said, and hung up.

As soon as Larry left, she'd go to her nearest neighbors and find out what she could. Or maybe Larry would know something. He might be familiar with the neighborhood. Maybe he'd done some refrigerator repair work in the area.

The only way to keep her mind off the playhouse was to keep busy. She'd phone Vanessa and tell her that Adam's car was missing. Also, try to find out where Vanessa was

on the day of Adam's murder. Tricky business that, since
the woman was so hostile. No doubt Vanessa would hang
up as soon as she knew who was calling. After screaming
murderer. Steeling herself, Lydia punched 1-212 and Adam's New York number. She had a hunch Vanessa had already moved into his apartment. The phone rang four times
and an electronic Vanessa answered. Her hunch was right.

"This is Lydia," she said. "There's something you should
know. You can reach me at Adam's number in Southampton."

Just being here would infuriate Vanessa. She could only
hope that she'd be curious enough to call back.

Lydia called herself in Manhattan. Gillian had delivered
what she'd promised. Seven writers had received kill fees.
Fewer than Lydia had thought. All pros, all frequent con-
tributors who hadn't attempted to attack before when their
pieces had been killed.

"Oh, by the by," Gillian added in an accent so emphat-
ically British that Lydia would have thought she was faking
it if she hadn't known better, "a Detective Barolini called
inquiring as to your whereabouts. I told him you were
home with a frightful cold, but he said that was jolly well
impossible. He'd been trying to get you all day. His guess
was you were inspecting your cottage in Southampton. The
police and a cottage? Is there something I don't know? It
all sounds very Agatha Christie." Gillian giggled.

Damn. Trust Barolini to blow her cover. Although they
knew at the office that she'd inherited money, they didn't
know about the house. Or about the murder. She'd fully expected someone at *gazelle* to read about the murder in the
paper or hear it on the air. But so far the subject hadn't
come up.

Neil had said Adam's murder received scant mention in
the Long Island papers, where the big news was a nanny
who'd strangled a baby, the missing women, and a possible
serial murderer. After all, Adam was no celebrity. All he
had was money. And out here lots of people had lots more
of that than Adam.

Why did Barolini want to see her? Maybe he was ready
to haul her in on what he considered surefire evidence. But

if that were the case, he would have been here by now since he'd figured out where she was.

To take her mind off Barolini and the playhouse, she went to Adam's bedroom to give it another try while waiting for Larry to arrive. It was almost four.

This time she opted for the obvious, the purloined letter in mind. She pulled out a drawer containing neat stacks of guayabera shirts, each bound by a blue paper band. Freshly laundered shirts Adam hadn't gotten around to wearing. Guayaberas were his favorite summer shirts since he could wear the shirt tails out and hide his Buddha stomach.

It seemed indecent to pry through his things—the shirts, socks, handkerchiefs, and underwear. And how would she dispose of them?

"What'll it be—the thrift shop or some homeless center?" she asked Colombo, who was back in Adam's place on the bed. He gave her an accusing brown-eyed look. Keep them until he gets back, was the advice.

Lydia's eyes roved over the books in the bookcase between the window and the fireplace. Books with markers sticking up in various places, temporarily put aside for any number of reasons. She'd heard them all—his nervous tension kept him from concentrating, his eyes bothered him, or the book was just plain boring. Books he intended to get back to later.

Her eyes glided over titles and authors. Not what she'd expect Adam to read, but then, unpredictability was part of his charm. There were lots of gory mysteries along with some Simenons in French and numerous books on the French Revolution (in English, and all three revolutions). But there were also books by Barbara Pym, Jane Austen, and Elizabeth Bowen, including *House in Paris*, an Adam Auerbach favorite.

A whole bookshelf was devoted to depression, including *The Rage Within*, by Dr. Alec Urgaza, published by Triton. Triton? She'd never heard of it. Maybe a vanity press. And hadn't that title been used before by someone else? But there was no copyright on titles.

She pulled the book out and looked it over. Beautifully designed and illustrated. Quality paper. Lots of leading between sentences. She remembered that Adam had bought dozens of copies and mailed them to everyone he knew— from old Dartmouth classmates to his manicurist. Lydia had never gotten around to reading the copy he'd sent to her and Mark. Maybe she'd left it behind when she'd moved out of her Tribeca loft. She put the book aside to take with her, just in case. She might learn something about Urzaga as well as about depression. Hadn't someone come up with the theory that you could learn all about the author from the subject index?

Next to *The Rage Within* were *Tom Jones*, *Huckleberry Finn*, and *Pride and Prejudice*. All three the same cobalt blue color with the titles, authors, and Grapham River Press stamped on in gilt lettering. But of course—a birthday gift from her. She was touched that he'd kept her gift, considering how inappropriate it had been. What a potential thief might take for three books was actually a hollow cardboard box divided into three compartments for concealing valuables. Okay for someone like her who needed a hidey-hole to stow away some twenties or costume jewelry, but not for anyone with vast paper holdings. Adam had National Trust to take care of such things.

She'd take the fake books back with her, too. Something rattled inside when she pulled the box down from the shelf. Adam must have found a use for it after all.

Lydia unlatched the box. In the first compartment she found enough keys for a building superintendent. Also, some dated pictures of Vanessa, Neil, and Carolyn, whom she didn't always immediately recognize because of the changes in hairstyle, color, and costume. Obviously to fit her persona for the day. Vanessa might play different roles on the stage, but Carolyn appeared to play them in real life.

Lydia could see why Adam might hide keys, but snapshots? Maybe his intention hadn't been to hide them, merely to use the box for storing personal belongings. She certainly couldn't visualize Adam putting pictures in a photograph album.

She sat on the bed and turned on the light, the better to see the pictures. The gray day was getting grayer. Almost four-thirty. Where was Larry? Maybe, just like any New York service person, he simply wasn't coming.

The first picture was of Carolyn in a short, white, pleated skirt wielding a tennis racket, her platinum hair caught up in a ponytail. She looked about twelve, but she must have been something like seventeen. Was platinum her real color or had she started dying her hair early?

Vanessa's pictures were glossy head and shoulder shots that made her look like she wasn't wearing anything. Glamour photos. Studio poses for her acting portfolio. Although her hair varied in length, it was always the same style and color—black helmet bangs and slightly turned under, draped over one bare voluptuous shoulder. Lots of cleavage. And heavy on the eye makeup.

There was just one snapshot of Adam and Neil, which must have been taken when they were in their mid-teens. They sat on the lawn, both with their knees drawn up, wearing letter sweaters—AP. Probably for Aspinall-Phelps, their prep school, which they invariably referred to as Asshole-Phelps. Neil had stick-out ears and wore a wide grin. Adam, unsmiling, looked young, chubby, and vulnerable. He'd often talked about his miserable childhood—but she'd thought they were just the complaints of a spoiled rich kid. Not until she'd talked to Urzaga today had she realized how traumatic it must have been.

There was just one picture of her. Taken by Mark, she remembered. She wore a white terry cloth coverup over her bikini and was holding out a morsel of food to Colombo, a surprised look on her face as if she'd been caught in the act. Mark had often followed her around with his Nikon. They'd met when she was still modeling. He claimed she was his favorite subject.

Adam hated being photographed and refused to pose for a picture. She had only one snapshot, taken by Mark when Adam was too drunk to mind. Despite the sappy smile, he'd looked unhappy.

The second compartment in the box was empty, but in the third she struck pay dirt—a blue spiral notebook squashed into the compartment. Why would Adam hide a notebook? She hurriedly flicked through the pages of scribbled phone numbers, most unidentified or preceded by a first name. There were also birth dates—just the month and day—for Vanessa, Carolyn, Todd, Neil, Urzaga, Adam's mother and brother, her and Mark, whose birthday he'd gotten wrong. June 12 instead of June 22. There were also some unfamiliar names followed by question marks. First names only. Adam's crabbed handwriting was difficult to decipher. It looked more like the writing of an oral-retentive person than a generous man.

There were a lot of blank pages, and on others no more than a written reminder to call this person or that, mostly doctors—Drs. Frankel, Solerno, Pomeranz, Richards, Ciprano, Hathaway, Friedman, Ross, Berger, Stone.

Two pages were devoted to listings of bimonthly high blood pressure and cholesterol levels, giving the date the tests were made. A real hypochondriac, Adam. Another page duplicated the service people listed in the dish-towel drawer along with service people in Manhattan. It surprised her that Adam was so methodical, so thorough. He'd often complained that he was too depressed to do anything, but he was actually more organized than she was.

A page was devoted to the names and phone numbers of brokers and bank officials, including Jared Evans. She flicked through pages containing more unidentified phone numbers, including the Hospital de la Santa Cruz, Buenos Aires. Argentina? Checking up on Urzaga? A hospital where Urzaga had once worked? She'd been under the impression that Adam broadcast everything he knew, but it looked like she was wrong. He was more secretive than she'd thought. Maybe he'd been quiet about Urzaga to cover up his embarrassment for being so easily suckered in.

Eyeing the hospital phone number, she felt the thrill of the chase. It could be just what she was looking for. She'd call it now! Just as she was headed for the phone, she heard the sound of a car engine. Larry, dammit! Now she'd have to wait until he left.

She waited for Larry's knock at the door. Waited and waited. Where had he gone?

Lydia looked out the window, surprised to see that the gray had deepened into an early twilight. A snappy little red sports car was parked at the bottom of the hill under the oak trees. Nice to tool around in. The sort she might buy for herself when National Trust started sending her checks. Refrigerator repair must be a profitable business. Instead of Larry, a blond woman in a gaucho hat strolled about, looking everything over. Maybe she was an enterprising real estate agent who'd learned of Adam's death and decided to inspect the property in case it was put up for sale.

The woman started up the hill toward the house. A strong gust of wind whipped the jeans skirt above her snakeskin boots, tilted her gaucho hat, and blew blond strands of hair across her face. A face that looked vaguely familiar. Her butter yellow hair was nearly the same color as her expensive, fringed suede jacket. Despite the western garb, she looked delicate. Definitely not a home-on-the-range type. More the dude rancher.

It took Lydia another minute to realize that the last time she'd seen the blond cowgirl, she'd been an auburn-haired lady in Laura Ashley skirt doing the Scarlett O'Hara bit.

CHAPTER 23

Carolyn Auerbach disappeared around the side of the house, apparently headed for the front door. Since the Datsun was out of sight in the garage, Carolyn wouldn't know she was here. Lydia shut Colombo in Adam's bedroom so he wouldn't run out and give her away. She tiptoed down the hall, keeping to the shadows and waiting to see what Carolyn would do next.

What Carolyn did was open the door and come in.

Colombo started barking. Naturally.

Lydia let Colombo out. He raced ahead of her down the hall toward Carolyn and skidded to a stop.

"Oh, hi there, Colombo," Carolyn said airily. She reached out and hugged him, but he wiggled from her grasp.

"What's wrong, don't you love me anymore?" she asked.

"Someone attacked me last night. He's become my protector, and trusts no one," Lydia said, eyeing Carolyn for her reaction, and picturing her in a trench coat and slouch hat. It didn't quite take. Also, her attacker had an iron grip. But then, looks could be deceiving. Carolyn might not be as delicate as she appeared.

"Please explain to him that I'm a friend," Carolyn said.

"It's okay, she's a friend," Lydia told Colombo, and hoped this was true.

"Who attacked you? A mugger?"

"I'm not sure. I didn't see. I was grabbed from behind and nearly choked to death. Colombo chased after him, but he got away. Disappeared. I say him, but it could have been her."

"That's scary. Frightening. Lucky you weren't hurt. I forgive you for leaving in such a hurry. It's a really terrifying experience. Even if you're not hurt physically, it affects you emotionally."

"It happened to you?"

"I was mugged in London. And far, far worse in L.A. It's too, too terrible to even talk about. Don't you think you should shut him up in the bedroom? He might attack me."

"He'll be okay."

"Yes, but what about me? Lydia and I are dear, dear friends," she said sweetly. Colombo gave his tail a half wag. Carolyn took off her suede jacket and handed it to Lydia, demoting her from dear, dear friend to maid.

"I was very upset that you sneaked off in the middle of the night without telling me. Afraid something had happened. So I took the chance that you were out here."

You could have called, Lydia didn't say, wondering how Carolyn knew when she'd left. She put the trench coat and slouch hat back on Carolyn. It almost worked. They were close to the same height. But was a thirties spy outfit Carolyn's style? Closer would be a black bodysuit and mask, like a cat burglar. Cary Grant in *To Catch a Thief.*

The attacker had disappeared on Third Avenue. Making a fast getaway around the corner—and into Carolyn's house? But Colombo would have followed.

"How did you know when I left?"

"Psychic. I got this feeling around midnight. And knew immediately that something had happened. Then I got your machine instead of you."

"You called me at midnight? I could have been asleep."

"Ah, but you weren't. Excuse me, I have to go to the bathroom. Even psychics use the loo." She smiled. "Oh, and I'd dearly love some tea."

Lydia tossed Carolyn's jacket over a chairback. She didn't like being ordered around, and liked even less having uninvited guests. Where was the bewildered, apologetic Carolyn she'd met in Jared Evans's office?

Colombo sat in the kitchen while Lydia put on the tea-kettle. She gave him some dog crunchies, but he ignored them and kept an eye on the bathroom. Was he suspicious, too?

Carolyn emerged freshly made-up. She'd taken off her gaucho hat and put on candy pink lipstick. Her butter yellow hair was brushed to one side so that it fell in a shiny swoop to the shoulder of an exquisite high-necked Irish lace blouse. A brooch was fastened to a black velvet string tie that wove in and out of the lace. The same brooch she'd worn at the reading of the will. It depicted the scene of a lad and lass seated by a wooded stream, the lass in a long, sweeping dress. Obviously Carolyn meant to combine cow-girl with old-fashioned femininity. She must have spent hours putting herself together. Milke Forte would love her, Lydia thought, swirling the tea bag in the water.

Carolyn's nostrils quivered. "Wonderful! Black currant tea. My favorite."

"How did you know it was black currant?" Lydia asked, handing Carolyn a cup. She stood in the kitchen doorway, too far away to be able to read the print on the box.

"Smelled it," Carolyn said, leading the way into the living room as if it were hers.

They bypassed the fat chintz chair where Adam used to

sit, as if his ghost inhabited it, and sat on the couch. Co-lombo jumped up between them.

"He's a dear, dear thing, but doesn't all this doggie de-votion drive you mad?" Carolyn asked.

"I can live with it," she said, not sure whether it was devotion or protection.

Carolyn looked around. "You'll have such fun redoing this tacky place."

"I'm in no big rush."

"No?" Carolyn's eyebrows shot up. Blond now. Either she'd dyed them to match her hair or that was their natural color. "Poor, dear Adam was more concerned with his crea-ture comforts than aesthetics. Goodness, you're missing the wonderful view."

She set her cup and saucer on an elephant tray and pulled back the curtains that Lydia had closed last night.

The deck lay in gray-blue shadow, with the white metal table barely visible. The woods beyond blended into the on-coming night.

"Don't you just love it out here when it starts getting dark?" Carolyn asked.

"No."

"No? Why not?"

"I feel exposed with all this glass. Like a goldfish in a bowl, to use an original turn of phrase," she said, and de-cided she'd been around Neil too long. She was even be-ginning to sound like him.

"But there's no one to see you. Your nearest neighbor is Alejandro, hardly a Peeping Tom."

Lydia wasn't so sure.

Carolyn took a blue pack of cigarettes from a pocket in her jeans skirt and lit up. "You don't mind if I smoke, do you?" she asked after the fact.

Lydia inhaled the smell of cafés and cathedrals. "Not if you let me have one, too. I used to smoke Gauloises."

"I knew it!" Carolyn cried, and leaning over Colombo, took Lydia's hand and held it next to hers. "See? We're twin-souled! Sisters! Just look! I noticed it at National Trust. Both of our right thumbs have identical indentations.

Do you know how rare that is? Maybe you were a courtesan in your past life, too.

"I'm sure we've crossed paths down the centuries. But we've never met here before. This is your first visit. I don't mean when you came out with Adam, of course; that doesn't count. But I was here in another lifetime. I knew it the moment I walked in the door. Before that even. I gave Adam directions on how to get here the first time I came out, and he'd had the house for over two years!"

And this was the lost lady of the National Trust corridors?

"Adam had a poor sense of direction," Lydia said.

"I've always loved this place—the woods, the hills, the poetic solitude. And Adam knew it."

Carolyn left the unfairness of it all unsaid, but Lydia got the drift. "Pretty pin," she said to change the subject.

"Oh, you mean this?" Carolyn's slender fingers went to the brooch. "An heirloom. I always wear it. It brings me luck. I'm dying to know. Did you find it?"

Was there a part of the conversation she'd missed? "What?"

"What you've been looking for today! The big clue."

"Not even a small one," Lydia said to throw her off. Was Carolyn really psychic? This was getting scary.

"I'll find it. It makes me absolutely furious to think someone murdered Adam and is getting away with it. After all, I knew him, and Detective Barolini didn't. I'll be able to tell if something is wrong," Carolyn said, grinding her cigarette into the elephant tray. "And if you'll forgive me for saying so, I also knew him better than you. After all, we *were* married."

The phone rang. Lydia took it in the kitchen. Colombo followed her out. Did he think someone would attack on the phone?

"Hi, this is Larry. I got held up. I'm really sorry, but I won't be able to make it after all. I'll be there first thing tomorrow morning. Eight o'clock sharp."

"Make it nine; I don't get up that early," Lydia said, and hung up. Shit. Stuck out here for another night. But if she was going to find out about the family that was connected to the playhouse, she might as well ask him. If he didn't know, she'd have to visit everyone in the neighborhood.

Lydia lingered in the kitchen, wondering how to get rid of Carolyn without appearing inhospitable. Carolyn was beginning to spook her as much as the place. All that past-life business plus the costume changes made her wonder if Carolyn were hiding her real identity. Or maybe she was trying on different selves to find out who she was. Lydia supposed she should be grateful Carolyn hadn't come dressed as Lizzie Borden.

"Oh, there you are, hiding out!" Carolyn said from the doorway. "I'm going to conjure up my psychic powers and see where I'm led to."

"I've already looked."

"Oh, but you didn't know where to look, did you?"

Lydia thought of the blue notebook. "True," she said amiably. "Go right ahead. I'll just get some stuff together I want to take back to town."

She made a beeline to Adam's bedroom, where she grabbed the blue notebook on top of the bed table and slipped it under her black turtleneck sweater.

But the notebook was too thick. Its spirals poked against her skin and stuck out in peculiar little bumps. She was slipping the notebook into an inner pocket of her jeans jacket when Carolyn came trancelike down the hall.

"Time to take Colombo for a walk," Lydia said to validate her excuse for putting on the jacket.

Colombo trotted happily out the door ahead of her, as if he were glad to get away from Carolyn. But he stuck close to Lydia, and didn't head for the highway, thank God. It had always worried her and Mark that Colombo would get hit by a passing car. He was a city dog, not used to running loose. Adam scoffed at their worries, claiming Colombo knew enough to get out of the path of an oncoming car.

The air had changed from chilly to downright nippy. She shivered and listened to the birds making sleep noises as they settled in for the night.

Inside the house the light was on in the green room. Hers and Mark's. She felt as if her privacy were being invaded. Why did that have to be the first place Carolyn chose to nose around? Why not Adam's bedroom, a more logical place for a clue, especially since that was where she was headed when Lydia was slipping the notebook in her pocket?

Keeping just beyond the pool of light thrown across the grass, Lydia stood under a giant tree and watched Carolyn go about her sleuthing. She'd already torn the room apart—mattress from bed, pillowcases from pillows. Now she tipped precariously forward as she stood on the seat of the wicker rocker in her high-heeled cowboy boots and pulled blankets from the top closet shelf. Then a few minutes later, after leaving everything in total chaos, she went on to make a mess of another room.

Was Carolyn on a search for clues to Adam's murderer or for something she didn't want found? The notebook? She'd check it out more carefully tonight. After Carolyn was in bed.

There was no doubt in her mind that Carolyn intended to stay the night. Probably even longer if Lydia let her get away with it. And, of course, she'd go with her and Neil to Megan's tonight for dinner. Which meant that Lydia wouldn't get a chance to talk things over with Neil.

On the other hand, this would give her a chance to learn more about Carolyn. How she really felt about Adam. All this poor dear Adam stuff was phony, but then, so was Carolyn. Phony but sometimes disarmingly open and honest. Only when was she being what? Or who? She didn't even know where Carolyn had been the night Adam was drowned. Somehow it seemed rude to come right out and ask. If Barolini didn't consider Carolyn a suspect, she must have a witness proving she'd been somewhere other than Southampton. Unless Barolini was so intent on nailing her as Adam's murderer, any alibi Carolyn gave he'd accepted. Maybe he just considered Carolyn a harmless flake. A flake, yes, but harmless? Lydia wasn't so sure.

Despite the fact that she was getting chillier by the second, Lydia lurked in the shadows watching Carolyn as she went from room to room, shaking out pillowcases, stripping beds. Probably if she'd been in the house, Carolyn would have conducted a strip search of her, too.

Hearing a twig snap behind her, Lydia whirled around. Something small and fleet of paw darted into a bush. Probably a rabbit.

The night was eerily quiet as if it were holding its breath. She couldn't shake off the feeling that someone was nearby. What if Urzaga was there in the woods watching her watch Carolyn? After calling Colombo and getting no response, she hurried back inside.

CHAPTER 24

Carolyn was still at her sleuthing when Neil drove up promptly at seven.

"We have company," Carolyn called.

We? Lydia wondered. "It's Neil. We're going out to dinner."

"Oh, what fun!" Carolyn said, and disappeared into the guest bathroom next to the living room. No doubt Carolyn was expecting nouvelle cuisine at the American Hotel in Sag Harbor, not burgers and fries at Megan's in Water Mill. Tough.

Lydia opened the door to Neil, followed by Colombo. "Out there waiting for me," Neil said. "Did you know I was coming, fellow?" Colombo thumped his tail against the door and looked happy to see him. Lydia wondered if that was significant. He hadn't gone after Neil the way he had Carolyn.

Neil looked far better than he had at the memorial service—quite elegant, in fact, wearing his all-purpose beige Armani jacket, a black turtleneck like hers, and beautifully fitting blue jeans. Even his blond hair seemed less wispy.

His greeting to Lydia, although not cool, wasn't as warm

as usual. He was far friendlier to Carolyn, who came out of the bathroom, shining hair draped over a shoulder, pink lipstick gleaming.

"Well, look who's here," he said, planting a kiss on her cheek. Holding Carolyn's hands in his, he swung her arms and eyed her admiringly. "And don't you look fabulous in your cowgirl togs? I'm glad you've gone back to blond. It's far more becoming."

"Blond is my natural color, in case you've forgotten. Actually, I should have a pipe and a plaid sleuthing cap. I came out to play Sherlock Holmes."

"Find anything?"

"Not yet, but I've got the whole weekend."

Neil questioned Lydia with a raised eyebrow. She answered with a shrug. "Anyone for a drink?"

Neil said he was off the hard stuff. "But I'll accept a glass of wine." Carolyn said she would, too. Lydia searched the cupboard under the sink in the wet bar hoping she'd find some. She found enough to last into the year 2000, including the two bottles of Sancerre she and Mark had brought out last spring.

While Lydia took charge of the wine, Carolyn took charge of the living room, turning off lamps Lydia had switched on and rearranging chairs. Except for the fat chintz one by the window. Neil sat in it, displacing Adam's ghost.

"I've switched from sex therapy to filmmaking," Carolyn announced in her airy voice as she finally settled down on the sofa. She kicked off her cowboy boots and sat with her feet tucked under her ruffled jeans skirt.

Lydia handed Neil his glass of wine and joined her. Colombo jumped up between them.

"I'm taking a wonderful hands-on course in filmmaking," Carolyn continued. "If we're not behind the camera, we're in front of it. A small, select group. Incredibly expensive. But worth it. Our instructor, Amy Akito, is absolutely marvelous."

"Who writes the script?" Neil asked.

"We don't use scripts. We start with a premise and let our imaginations take over. Cinema verité. Some of the stuff is quite raunchy," she said, giggling. "Amy has a laissez-faire attitude. So adorable."

The movie last night certainly could be called hands-on—although hands all over would be more accurate. Maybe Carolyn's costar was Amy Akito.

"I have some scripts you might like to take a look at," Neil told Carolyn. "Just in case you decide to do something besides cinema verité."

Carolyn said she'd love to see them, but as he knew, filmmaking cost money, and backers were hard to come by. Did he know of any?

"If I did, I'd have grabbed them up long ago."

"Adam backed those total disasters Vanessa put on," Carolyn said. "She got terrible reviews, even from Clive Barnes, who's famous for liking everything. But when I asked Adam for money to make something serious and artistic—he wouldn't give me a centavo. And Amy is very enthusiastic about my work. She knows some cable TV producer who might be interested."

"I didn't know cable TV wanted anything but commercial," Neil said.

Neil and Carolyn talked shop, bemoaning the fact that Hollywood and Broadway produced third-rate stuff while first-rate artists such as they were ignored.

"What's needed is another Hitchcock," Lydia put in.

"It's the self-promoters who get the backers," Neil said, ignoring her remark. Probably considered Hitchcock beneath him. "Their talent is selling themselves. The really talented get lost in their dust. Then the critics complain that once again Broadway's boring and all Hollywood can come up with is schlock."

Lydia tuned out, but Colombo sat with his ears up, listening. A better sleuth than she was. Living up to his name. If only he could talk. How had the killer lured Adam from the house to the pool on a stormy night? He'd been wearing his swimming trunks, which meant he'd intended to go in. Had the murderer convinced him he should take a dip to sober up? Or had the idea been his, and he'd been too drunk to notice anything as trivial as lightning?

Lydia mentally shook her head, wondering if she would

ever know the answers to her questions. By changing the lighting and moving the furniture, Carolyn had managed to make the room even more stagily dramatic. No wonder Adam had been miserable out here. It was all wrong for someone whose big desire was to hole up—return to the womb. Okay for his show-offy friends like Urzaga, Vanessa, and Carolyn. Even Neil. Movements choreographed, as if thousands watched.

Which was just how Lydia felt all of a sudden. As if beyond the glass someone was looking in—a serial murderer on the loose or just some freelance killer. Or at best Urzaga.

Neil noticed her shiver. "Cold?"

"I've been shivering all day. Maybe I'm coming down with something."

"I'd think you'd be warm with that jacket on."

She'd kept her jeans jacket draped over her shoulders, not risking the chance of Carolyn's rifling through it and finding the notebook.

"You're chilly because it's chilly in here," Carolyn announced. "I'll turn up the thermostat."

"Leave it, we're going out," Lydia said. She was tired of Carolyn's take-charge ways. She wasn't the one who'd be paying the bills. Even Adam, who scarcely noticed the cost of anything, had complained about Lilco.

"Where are we going to eat, gang?" Neil asked.

"Megan's," Lydia said.

"Any place but," Carolyn said. "Let's go to Feminina's. They have yummy food there."

"I'm on a budget," Neil told her.

"All right, the American Hotel in Sag Harbor."

"That's not cheap either," Neil protested.

"How about Osborn's?" said Carolyn, who seemed very well acquainted with the area. "We can still sit out on the terrace. And it won't be so mobbed now that summer's over."

"They're all too expensive. I'm with Lydia. We go to Megan's."

"What's Megan's like?" Carolyn asked.

Why did she ask? A moment ago she'd said any place but Megan's, so she must know.

"You must have gone there with Adam," Lydia said. "It was his favorite haunt." Carolyn shook her head. Maybe she'd just put one foot inside and demanded that Adam take her to a tonier restaurant.

"What's so special about it?" Carolyn asked, slipping her feet into her snakeskin boots.

"What's so special about it is, it isn't special," Neil said. "That's rare for out here. They leave you to your beer 'n' burgers. No waiters hovering around waiting to pour wine every time you take a sip. And they have good hamburgers."

"I'm not allowed to eat hamburger. I have Epstein-Barr and I'm on a very strict diet."

"They have seafood sandwiches," Lydia said. "What does Epstein-Barr have to do with hamburger? I thought it was something that had to do with low energy."

"Well, obviously you just don't know. Diet is extremely important. I've been thoroughly examined by specialists in New York, Boston, and Philadelphia, and they should know. Certain seafoods are allowed. Also, Chinese. But meat and dairy products are out. I can eat whole wheat bread but nothing made with white flour. We'll take my car and decide where to go on the way."

Carolyn donned her gaucho hat and, old-fashioned cowgirl that she was, handed her jacket to Neil. Ever the gentleman, he held it out for her to put on.

By the time Lydia had turned on the outside lights, Carolyn had disappeared through the door. Neil waited on the doorstep. When he reached out a hand to Colombo, who tried to follow Lydia out, Colombo backed away.

"Hey, what's got into you, pal?" Neil asked.

"He's become wary after the attack."

"You were attacked? Out here?"

"In town. I'll give you the details later. There's some other stuff I want to mention that I can't with Carolyn along."

Lydia was having a hard time getting Colombo back inside the house. He wanted to go along with them. "It's okay. You keep watch here. I'm among friends," she told him. Colombo looked as if he wasn't so sure. Neither was she.

"Give me the details now," Neil said. "You can't leave it like that."

She gave him a quick summary of events as they walked down the hill where Carolyn leaned against her snappy little red sports car, exaggeratedly patient to get across the message that she'd been waiting long enough. Lydia deliberately slowed up. Let Carolyn wait. Who invited her along?

"He disappeared on Third Avenue," Lydia said, finishing up her story. "Or she. Totally vanished into thin air."

"You don't think it could have been just an ordinary mugger?"

"What do you think?"

"I don't think so either. At least you're safe out here."

But was she?

CHAPTER 25

Carolyn honked the horn. "Come on, let's go," she called. And honked the horn again.

"I don't think she should drive," Neil said.

"Why not? She only had one glass of wine."

"She's too vague and otherworldly to keep her mind on the road."

"Don't fool yourself. She's not the fluff-head she'd like people to think," Lydia said.

But Neil wasn't convinced. "Maybe you should sit in back and I'll take the death seat."

"I refuse such a noble gesture." Lydia got in the front with Carolyn, who'd already started the car.

"What noble gesture? Are you noble, Neil? And what have you two been whispering about? That's very rude," Carolyn said.

"Lydia was telling me about the attack. You haven't noticed how noble I am?" he asked from the back.

"Well, if you're so noble, you'll agree to another restaurant. They have some inexpensive Chinese restaurants out here."

"I'm sick of moo shu pork."

"We're going to Megan's," Lydia said firmly.

Carolyn lit a Gauloise and didn't argue. She just drove fast and wildly. Lydia guessed it had nothing to do with being vague and everything to do with not getting her own way. Ignoring the stop sign, Carolyn shot out onto the highway, not bothering to see if any car was coming.

Neil volunteered to drive.

"No one touches this car."

After that they drove in silence and suspense. Since Lydia couldn't bear to look where they were going, it was a while before she realized it wasn't to Water Mill. "You're on the wrong road," she said.

"Oh, gosh, I guess I got lost."

It occurred to Lydia that she'd have a hard time questioning Bobbie with two other people along. Leave it for tomorrow. That is, if she lived so long with Carolyn behind the wheel.

"There's that wonderful seafood place up ahead!" Carolyn called. "Let's go there. My treat, Neil, okay?"

"I'll pay my own way, thank you."

"I got seafood poisoning here," Lydia said as Carolyn turned in to the sandy driveway. "Either that or an anxiety attack. The doctor at Southampton Hospital wasn't sure."

"If you were with Adam, it was an anxiety attack. I used to get them all the time when we were married. That's how I ended up at the funny farm. He literally drove me crazy." Carolyn pulled neatly into a tight space between two cars. Now that she was where she wanted to go, she drove skillfully.

They walked across the mix of sand and gravel toward the restaurant, white with blue trim. Inside, gaslights glowed above rows of empty white tables. The few diners looked beyond middle-aged. Some glass-eyed fish were mounted on the walls, but there were no hanging nets with bobbing corks or life preservers.

"It's hokey, but not too," Lydia said.

"Hokey's fun," Carolyn said. "If you grew up where everything had to be in perfect taste, you'd understand. Stultifying. That's why I married so young. To get away from it. My parents still haven't forgiven me. I rarely see them. Where's the maître d'?"

She'd no sooner asked than he appeared. He wore a red bow tie and a tux and looked to be a spritely eighty, older than the diners, who were far from young. They were led to a table overlooking the water. Outside, lanterns threw a flickering glow on inky wavelets.

Neil politely sat with his back to the view while Lydia and Carolyn sat side by side. Each ordered the combination seafood platter. Lydia and Neil drank Michelob. Carolyn, white wine.

"I can't have anything with yeast in it. Or malt. Or even a high alcohol content," the poor little waif said. But her diet didn't stop her from nibbling at Italian bread set out in a basket. Bread, Lydia noted, made with white flour.

"I grew up in Boston," Carolyn said, taking up where she'd left off. "In a coven of Boston Brahmins. I deliberately took Adam's name. Mine is immediately recognizable, and I prefer anomynity."

"You mean like the Mayflower Madam?" Lydia asked.

"Naughty, naughty," Neil scolded, smiling.

"Who's she?" Carolyn asked.

"Never mind."

When the seafood platter arrived, Lydia disregarded polite conversation and dug into lobster, shrimp, and scallops, hoping they didn't come from polluted waters. Carolyn took dainty bites and chattered airily, often touching Neil's hand or stroking his arm. She also vamped the waiter. Apparently playing up to men, gay or not, came second nature. On the other hand, she'd appeared to be enjoying herself cavorting with Amy Akito in that movie last night. Maybe besides being a courtesan in her past life, she'd also been a court cavalier. Why restrict her to gender?

After they finished eating, Lydia asked for brandy with her coffee.

"Good idea," Neil said. "I'll have some, too."

"I suppose it will be fatal," Carolyn said, but if you're drinking so will I."

Lydia inhaled the rich, golden fumes and watched the lanterns sway in the ocean breeze. An occasional gust sprang up, whipping the flames into a yellow frenzy. She gave a shudder of pleasure. She liked scary when she felt safe. And she didn't feel threatened at the moment.

"I hate to admit it, but you chose the right place," Neil told Carolyn. "Adam would have enjoyed it." He raised his drink. "Here's to Adam."

They swapped Adam stories. The nice ones.

"When I was a kid I climbed up a tree and was afraid to come down," Neil said. "Petrified. All the kids were laughing at me, calling names. You can imagine what. Kids can be cruel. Not Adam. He shut them up. Even at the age of ten that little guy had a wicked tongue. They backed off. Then this fat, clumsy kid climbed up, took my hand, and led me down. From that moment on, I was his devoted servant."

"He bought me my house when I'd only remarked in passing that I liked it," Carolyn said. "We were in a cab coming back from a Gurney play. He dearly loved Gurney, and was in a good mood. He said, 'Don't you have a birthday coming up?' That was all. And the next thing I knew, the house was mine. This was after our divorce when he'd given me a very generous settlement."

"He went to visit Mark at St. Vincent's when most of Mark's so-called good friends no longer showed up, and Adam scarcely knew him. Except Mark didn't want to see Adam."

"Wonder why," Neil said.

"Adam was genuinely fond of Mark. Anyway, Adam would be waiting for me after my visit when I was feeling close to suicidal. He'd take me to a fancy restaurant and be at his most charming."

"Which could be very very," Carolyn said. "That was sweet of him."

"I enjoyed the dinners, but I felt horribly guilty," Lydia confessed.

"Wonder why," Neil said again.

"Don't mind him, he's just a man," Carolyn said, taking Lydia's hand. "You shouldn't have felt guilty at all. You deserved something nice after what you'd been through."

"Looks like we're holding our own memorial service for Adam," Neil put in. "This calls for another brandy. I'm paying." He signaled the waiter.

"Vanessa should be here," Lydia said, feeling mellow and forgiving. "After all, she loved Adam, too."

"Loved him? Vanessa?" Carolyn said. "Bullshit."

Lydia was shocked, not at the word but at Carolyn's using it.

So was Neil. "Watch your language, lady. Need I remind you there's a gentleman present?"

Carolyn ignored his bid for humor. "She murdered him. She and that awful, awful Todd."

The waiter arrived with their brandies, and stood nearby, apparently interested in their conversation.

Lydia ignored him. "Where's your proof?" she asked Carolyn.

"It's here somewhere," Carolyn said, peering into her brandy as if she meant in her glass.

"You spent hours searching the house and came up with zilch," Lydia reminded her. "I guess the Barolini bunch was more thorough than we gave them credit for."

Lydia felt only slightly guilty about lying. The notebook was burning a hole in her jacket pocket. She couldn't wait to get back and go through it. Except she didn't want to find anything that incriminated Carolyn or Neil.

"But they didn't find anything either, did they?" Neil asked.

"I'd be the last to know. Unless it was incontrovertible evidence that I'd murdered Adam. Or not even that much. Just enough so Barolini can nail me."

"Your paranoia is showing again. Do you think Barolini's really out to get you?"

"Yeah."

"Why?" Carolyn asked.

"You tell me."

At a nearby table, four women burst into laughter.

"See, those ladies think that's crazy, too," Carolyn said to Lydia, as if she were reasoning with a child.

"What were you doing Sunday night?" Lydia asked her.

"You mean the night Adam was murdered?" Carolyn gave a merry Tinkerbell laugh. "Goodness, you think I did it?"

"Merely asking; no offense intended."

"I was home alone, editing my film for Amy Akito."

"Urzaga did it," Neil insisted. "He had the most to gain—or to lose if Adam cut off money for his Institute. The sleazebag called me the other night—out of the blue." He aimed a finger at Lydia. "He was furious that you got Adam's house. Wants to buy it. Whatever you do, don't sell it to him."

"He told me you called him."

"A bold-faced lie," Neil said, and took a sip of brandy.

"Alejandro doesn't lie," Carolyn told him. "He's a darling, sweet man. Why don't you like him?"

"Yeah, poor guy, all he did was swindle Adam out of hundreds of thousands," Neil said.

"It wasn't that much, and it went to the Institute," Carolyn said, bristling, eyes narrowing and lips tightening. "Adam believed in what he was doing. He gave willingly. Alejandro is a very dedicated man."

"Dedicated to fleecing Adam," Neil said grimly, setting his brandy glass down. "When it came to picking Adam's pocket, Carlos Alejandro Fernando Urzaga made Bonnie and Clyde look like Dick and Jane."

"Well, you're wrong about Alejandro and I refuse to argue."

"Fine with me. Let's go. I'm driving. You two are drunk."

"No one touches my car. You're the one who's drunk," Carolyn said.

Lydia had to agree. The brandy seemed not to have affected Carolyn, who appeared quite sober, driving far less recklessly than on their way over. Neil sat silently in back. Pouting.

"Is Todd from California?" Lydia asked Carolyn. "He looks like an aging beach boy."

"He's from hunger, as we used to say at Asshole-Phelps," Neil said, coming to life. "Ask him where he's from and you never get the same story. Drinks. Gambles. Lived off women before Adam. He has all the vices. But I still can't like him."

"Todd Bigelow is tacky, cheap, and not worth discussing," Carolyn said, and proceeded to do just that. "He stole things from Adam's house that Adam hadn't noticed were missing. Unless Francoise took them, and I very much doubt that. Of course, she could wind Adam around her little finger. I've often wondered if there was more there than met the eye."

"That's absurd. Her French was abominable," Neil said. "Adam was a stickler for good grammar—English, German, Italian, and French."

"He didn't know German or Italian," Carolyn said, skillfully turning in to Adam's driveway.

"But he would have if he had," Neil insisted.

"He's really smashed. Do you think I should drive him home?" Carolyn whispered.

Lydia nodded.

"What are you whispering about?" Neil said.

"I'm driving you home. You can pick up your car tomorrow."

Neil jumped out of the car and headed for his.

"If he wants to kill himself, let him," Carolyn said. "I'll get my bag."

Lydia worried. She walked over to Neil's car. He already had the motor running. She tapped on his window. He rolled it down. "You could stay here tonight. There are all those empty guest rooms."

"I have to get home. Steve will be worried."

"You could call."

"I'm not as drunk as it looks."

"Okay, be careful."

"You're the one who should watch out. The lady's dangerous."

He gunned the motor and took off.

"Really, really drunk," Carolyn said, coming up from behind.

CHAPTER 26

Colombo greeted them as they entered the house. Carolyn put down her Mark Cross overnight bag to give him a hug.

"Shades of Grace Kelly in *Rear Window*," Lydia said.

"I always keep it packed for emergencies. Since you're ensconced in Adam's room, I'll take the green one."

Lydia was beginning to think Carolyn might be psychic, after all. How else to explain her uncanny ability to figure out what upset her the most and act on it, choosing the room she'd shared with Mark? There were four other rooms. Why that one?

"It's kind of a mess after this afternoon," Lydia told her.

"They're all a mess," Carolyn said, as if she hadn't created the chaos. She paused. "That's my fault. I've been a real pain in the neck, wrecking your place and inviting myself to dinner with you and Neil. You're really very sweet to put up with me."

Damn. Carolyn wouldn't even let Lydia stay mad at her.

"That's okay, glad to have the company. This place is practically all glass. So easy to break into."

"Well, we've got Colombo to scare anyone off."

Colombo swaggered up to Carolyn and licked her hand. Lydia guessed she could write Carolyn off as Adam's murderer. Otherwise, he wouldn't be so friendly.

Playing Faithful Dog to the hilt, he followed Lydia into Adam's bedroom.

"Sweet dreams," Carolyn called, as Lydia closed the door.

She hauled the mattress from the floor back onto the bed and set about remaking it. The minute she'd finished, there was a knock at the door.

"Me," Carolyn called. "Brought you something soothing." She carried a tray with a white cup and saucer decorated with blue flowers. Lydia immediately thought of the glass of milk in Hitchcock's *Suspicion*.

"It's got rum and honey in it," Carolyn said, handing her the tea.

"Thanks, but it will keep me awake."

"No it won't. It's decaffeinated. Now, sit down and drink. I'll keep you company."

Carolyn patted a place beside her on the newly made bed.

Lydia remembered Neil's "watch out," and warily sniffed the tea, but smelled only a hot, spicy fragrance. The tea was strong and dark. Too strong to detect any strychnine or whatever Carolyn might have laced it with. That is, if strychnine had a taste.

Colombo jumped up on the bed between her and Carolyn, wanting to be part of the family. He'd come to her rescue if she were attacked, but not if she were given a so-called harmless cup of tea.

Carolyn stole sideways glances as Lydia raised the cup to her lips. Or did she just imagine it? Maybe not. "Hot," Lydia said, and put the cup back on the saucer without taking a sip.

"That's when it's good," Carolyn told her, but didn't press the issue. She poked a strand of blond hair behind an ear, and spoke almost diffidently. "Remember when I told you that something worse than being mugged had happened to me in California?"

Lydia nodded.

"I was raped. He came in through a back window when I was sleeping." Carolyn shuddered. "I was still asleep while he tied me up. Isn't that incredible? I woke up with this heavy weight on top of me. I was sure he was going to kill me afterward. It was my worst nightmare come true.

I've always had a fear of being raped and killed afterward. And of serial killers. When I was married to Adam I kept imagining Ted Bundy was stalking me, but I thought they'd cured me of it at Oak Grove. After I left Adam, I went to California to start a new life. And then this happened. It sent me right back."

"To New York, Oak Grove, or Adam?"

"Oak Grove." She glanced out the window and abruptly switched topics. "I need some towels and things for tonight," she said airily.

Maybe she didn't want to dwell on the subject.

Lydia set her tea on the bed table.

"You didn't drink it."

"It cooled off while we were talking."

"First it was too hot, then too cold," Carolyn complained.

"Call me Goldilocks."

"I'll get you another cup."

"Don't bother. This way to the linen closet."

"I know where it is. I've been here more often than you," Carolyn said reproachfully.

Lydia slid open the closet door wondering why, when Carolyn claimed she hadn't cared for Adam, she sometimes sounded as possessive of him as Vanessa? What were those two trying to prove? That he cared for one more than the other, or for both of them more than her? What did it matter now that he was dead?

Carolyn spent nearly a half hour going through the closet to select the perfect towels and bath mat.

Lydia plied her with Kleenex, toilet paper, and soap. She didn't want Carolyn to come barging in for something she'd forgotten and catch her with the blue notebook.

She'd felt itchy ever since her walk through the woods to Urzaga's. She locked the bathroom door and left Colombo to stand guard outside, not sure who to be wary of. After peeling off her clothes, she stepped into the shower, enjoying the hot water pelting her skin. That is, she enjoyed it until she remembered the shower scene in *Psycho*, and quickly jumped out.

Toweling off quickly, she slipped into her flannel nightgown. It was then that she noticed that the teacup and saucer were missing from the night table where she'd put them. Carolyn must have come in and taken them while she was in the shower. Wanting to get rid of something lethal?

Lydia tiptoed down the hall to the kitchen, passing Carolyn's bedroom, where a light showed under the door. Colombo padded after her. She checked out the sink— nothing in it. No cup and saucer in the dishwasher either. Carolyn must have washed them and put them back in the cupboard.

Lydia padded back to Adam's bedroom and locked the door. If Carolyn interpreted this as a hostile act, so be it. She disliked having her privacy invaded, even if Carolyn thought she was being nice and thoughtful in removing the cup and saucer.

Before getting out the notebook, Lydia crossed the room to close the Levolor blinds. Beyond the yellow light from her and Carolyn's windows, the night was pitch black. After triple-checking the lock on the deck door, Lydia drew the blinds and made sure there were no cracks between the vertical flaps. The windows flanking the bedroom fireplace were no problem since they were too high for anyone to see into.

Lydia filched the blue notebook from her jeans jacket pocket and crawled into bed. Colombo jumped up beside her and looked over her shoulder. "Okay, let's see what we've got here," she said. He gave her cheek a congratulatory lick for discovering the notebook. If only she could discover some giveaway clue in it.

Just to be sure she hadn't missed anything, Lydia flicked through the pages she'd looked at earlier to the telephone number of the Hospital de la Santa Cruz. Tomorrow she'd call the number. She just hoped someone there spoke English since she couldn't get much beyond *buenos días*. Next came a page headed "Small Loans," which, she guessed, was wishful thinking on Adam's part, since only one was marked "pd."

Adam had said he considered loans as gifts, so he wouldn't have been too surprised that Gloria, Jason, Jane, Don, Rita, Ronnie, Kathy, Dave, Kim, and Curtis hadn't paid back the money varying in amounts from $175 to $2,500. Since only first names were listed, his notes weren't very helpful. The amount marked "pd." was next to Charles—$1,500. Didn't Adam have a cousin by that name?

Also, Rita sounded familiar. Adam's manicurist? None of the other names meant anything. No doubt people he'd met at bars, formed a drinking friendship with, and dropped. Or they'd dropped him after "borrowing" the money. Poor Adam. Ever cynical and ever hopeful.

A kind of *thwack* sounded on the deck, setting Colombo to barking. Hearing running footsteps, Lydia slid the notebook under her pillow and switched off the light, the better to see who was out there, and at the same time not be a target.

CHAPTER 27

Colombo hurled himself at the door, alternately snarling and barking. Lydia made her way across the room in the dark, weak-kneed, dry-mouthed. Something sharp nicked her shinbone. When she reached the window she groped for the Levolor blind. Separating the cloth slats, she peered out and saw a slight movement beyond the deck near the woods. Or were her eyes playing tricks on her? It was too dark to be sure.

Colombo still barked but less ferociously. Maybe it wasn't a person out there but an animal. She might have imagined she'd heard running footsteps. Or maybe hooves. She'd heard reports of deer in the area. There were always a lot of baffling night noises. Probably during the day, too, but the night was when she noticed them. If she let Colombo out, he might take it into his head to give chase to whatever it was and she'd lose her bodyguard.

"Carolyn, did you hear a noise?" she called, and got no answer. If Colombo's barking hadn't wakened Carolyn, her yelling should have.

Lydia hurried down the hall and pounded on the door to the green room. What good was a houseguest who didn't help scare off intruders?

"Hey, wake up," she yelled. "I think someone's outside." Again no answer. She opened the door and peered in. The dim light in the hall showed an empty bed. Neatly made, unslept-in.

Lydia switched on the light and entered, getting a whiff of sexy-flowery perfume. The room was tidy, untouched. Carolyn had put things in order quickly. Lydia went out into the hall and called Carolyn's name again. Where in the hell was she?

Turning on each light switch she passed, Lydia walked to the living room. Looking around, she had an eerie sense of déjà vu. It was like the night she'd gone looking for Adam. All that was missing was the cigar butt in the elephant tray. She checked out the dining room, the guest rooms, and all three bathrooms, then turned on the yard lights and looked outside. Carolyn's car was still parked at the bottom of the hill under the trees.

Lydia returned to the green room as if it might tell her where Carolyn had gone. Spying the overnight bag on the wicker rocker, she was tempted to rummage through it, but Carolyn might walk in on her. Maybe Carolyn had become restless and gone for a stroll. But if she had, it wasn't within range of the yard lights, and it was highly unlikely that at this hour she'd go for a walk in the woods or along the road. A chill went up Lydia's spine at the idea that it might have been Carolyn out on the deck tonight spying on her. Was she lurking somewhere in the shadows watching? Why?

Lydia returned to her bedroom, got the iron poker from the fireplace, and placed it on the bedside table. So what if she was overreacting?

Feeling uneasy, she returned to the Small Loans page in

the notebook and tried to concentrate. Unfortunately, there were no dates given, so she couldn't tell how long ago the loans had been made. Would someone have drowned Adam for not coming across with another loan? Possibly. But there wasn't much to go on without any last names. They might be in his address book, which was in the hands of either Barolini or Vanessa.

On the last few pages she struck pay dirt. Adam had drawn up a chart with twelve initials across the top, beginning with J and ending with D. Aha! Elementary, Miller, as Neil would say. January to December.

Adam a chart maker? This was a side to him she'd never known. Hadn't even guessed at. But what else did he have to do with all his time? To the left of the initialed months were the initials FFOAA. She knew that one—the Friendly Freeloaders of Adam Auerbach. But the names underneath weren't quite what she expected.

The phone rang, sounding loud in the silent house, startling Colombo. She glanced at her travel alarm clock. Almost two. Who would be calling now?

"He's out there with you," a woman said, voice low and poisonous.

No mistaking who.

"Could you be more specific?" Lydia asked. Maybe Vanessa had flipped out and meant Adam.

"You know who I mean. Don't act dumb. The initials are TB."

Jesus! First she had to figure out J to D; now it was TB.

"Vanessa, why would Todd Bigelow be here?"

"He got your message."

"The message was to you, not him."

"You knew he'd be here. You wanted him to know where you were so he'd come and see you."

That's crazy, Lydia almost said, but caught herself. You didn't call a crazy person crazy. "Vanessa, I wanted to let *you* know that Adam's car wasn't here. I don't know what happened to it, but I didn't steal it, okay?"

"It's my car. I brought it back from Southampton. Todd stole it from me and drove out to see you."

"Vanessa, the only person here besides me is Carolyn."

"You invited that nutcase?"

"She invited herself."

"Let me speak to her."

"She's asleep. I'm not waking her."

"You're lying."

"Call her here tomorrow morning if you don't believe me."

And if Carolyn didn't show up, Lydia would have more to worry about than Vanessa's accusations.

"Where else would that fuck go? I've a good mind to report him to the police for car theft."

"That was a rotten thing for him to do, steal your car."

"You don't know the half of it. After all I've done for that shit."

"You'd think he'd be grateful."

"Without me, that fuckup would be dead or in prison."

Prison? She'd like to know more about that. Apparently sympathy was the way to get Vanessa to talk. "He's lucky to have someone like you."

"You said it! I even lied to Barolini for that scumbag. He's nothing but poor white trash. Common. Adam was a true aristocrat. To the manor born. But Todd Bigelow is slime."

"You'd think he'd show more appreciation after you lied to Barolini for him. What about?" She held her breath. Vanessa wasn't going to tell her that. But she did. When Vanessa hated, she hated. Bless her.

"This is *entre nous*," Vanessa whispered, as if Barolini were listening in. "Todd didn't come to rehearsal that Sunday. Just Kevin and me. Kevin Drake. You've heard of him, of course. 'Day After Tomorrow'?"

"Oh, the big soap star," Lydia said, hoping she'd guessed right and sounded properly impressed.

"Exactly. Everyone who watches it is going to be flocking to the Auerbach Theater. He's a draw. An adorable man, a real love. I got Kevin to lie, too. He's so crazy about me, he'd do anything. Besides, he wants to be in the play. Todd is violently jealous of him. Almost as jealous as he was of Adam. He always sticks around when Kevin's there, but he didn't that Sunday."

"Where'd he go?" Lydia whispered.

"Who knows? Too chickenshit to come to rehearsal. Hiding out from an enforcer. You know what an enforcer is?"

Lydia knew, but thought it would be wiser to let Vanessa explain and feel superior. "No, what?"

"He's a hired thug who does the dirty work for a bookie. He breaks knees as a sample of what's to come later if you don't pay up now. Todd owed twenty-seven K—that's twenty-seven thousand to the uninitiated—and this time Adam refused to come across with the money. He said Todd deserved to be taught a lesson. Of course, he always said that, but this time he meant it. Todd was scared shitless."

"Maybe he hid out of town," Lydia said. Like Southampton?

"He wouldn't say. To protect me, in case the enforcer tried pressure. I told Todd to go out to Adam's. No one would come looking for him there. If he'd gone, Adam would be alive today."

Vanessa couldn't be so naive as to think Lydia would believe that. Was she deliberately trying to implicate Todd?

"Adam would have let Todd stay with him for my sake. He'd do anything for me," Vanessa said belligerently, as if Lydia would dispute it.

"He adored you. You were always on his mind. He often called me by your name."

"That means nothing. He called me by yours, too. He was just too drunk to keep his women straight. Of course, I was the one he loved. He only saw other women when I refused to see him. To make me jealous. It didn't work."

Oh no?

Lydia wasn't sure how she should play this. Agree or disagree? To agree so readily might make Vanessa suspicious. But if she didn't, Vanessa might get mad and hang up. There were still things she needed to know. She decided to play it both ways. "I kind of suspected that, but I wasn't sure. I guess you're right."

"Is there any doubt? I knew just how Adam's mind worked. I knew that man like a book."

"What did you mean when you said Todd would be in prison if it weren't for you?"

"I said no such thing."

Lydia could have kicked herself. She'd pushed too far.

"If he comes out there, call me," Vanessa ordered.

"I certainly will." Also Kramer and Barolini.

"I'm giving him until tomorrow morning. If he's not back with the car then, I'm calling the police."

"Has he done this before?"

"Thursday night, but that was with my permission. If he's with some woman, they're both going to pay," Vanessa said, and hung up.

Lydia got a flash. Thursday night when Todd had the BMW was the same night she'd been attacked. And a BMW had been behind the cab. She'd thought it was black, but maybe it was blue. Colombo must have been barking at the BMW, not the taxi.

Had Todd attacked her at Vanessa's instigation? Maybe Vanessa didn't want her dead but scarred for life. Maybe dead was too soon after Adam; scarred would have to do until later. It must have been Vanessa's plan, and Todd was only too happy to carry it out. Todd and Lydia were about the same height, and he was muscular. Her attacker had an iron grip. Todd also might go in for a slouch hat and trench coat, thinking of himself as a tough guy like Bogey. That fit in with being an actor. Or maybe Todd had acted independently, mad because she got the money he thought was due him. Getting even for being cheated out of what he considered his fair share.

She'd have a lot to tell Barolini and Kramer tomorrow.

CHAPTER 28

Lydia returned to the chart in the notebook.

	J	F	M	A	M	J	J	A	S	O	N	D
Vanessa ($15K)	√		30K	√	√	√						
Todd ($7K)	√	√	√	√		10K						
Carolyn ($5K)	√	√	√		10K		√					
Neil ($5K)	√	√	√	√	√	√						
Francoise ($1K)	√	√	√	√	√	√	√	√				
BP ($20K)	√	√	√	√	√	√						

What jumped out at her was the presence of Neil's name and the absence of Urzaga's. And who was BP to rate twenty thousand? Someone Adam was smitten with and hadn't mentioned? It didn't sound like Adam, who wore his heart on his sleeve. She'd come back to BP later. Now she just wanted to get an overall picture.

Missing check marks must mean that the cash flow was cut off. Punishment for bad behavior. Of course, Adam doubled the amount the following month to make up for the money missed out on. Great disciplinarian.

But after June, everyone except Francoise had been cut off without a cent. No check marks. This time Papa meant business.

In May, Todd's allowance was cut off. And apparently he hadn't completely restored himself to Adam's good graces, since he'd received just 10K in June when, if the 7K had been doubled, it should have been 14K. Todd had been reduced 2K a month to 5K, the same amount as Carolyn. Still, it didn't seem fair that before then he had raked in more money than Carolyn. After all, she'd been Adam's wife. Furthermore, Adam had called Todd a thug, a drunk, and a pain in the ass. Apparently Vanessa was right. Adam had doled out money to Todd as a favor to her. Adam had told Lydia that Vanessa had said Todd's liver was shot from drinking and he'd be dead in a year. It was important to make Todd's last days happy. But at the memorial service Todd had looked far healthier than Adam ever had. At least while she'd known him.

But Adam wasn't a pushover. If he gave Todd money, he got something out of it. He enjoyed relating Todd's latest outrageous behavior that got him tossed out of bars and told never to come back. Todd amused Adam and was paid for it. Another court jester. Someone who momentarily took Adam's mind off his depression.

Lydia turned her attention to Neil. Surprising that he was still on the list after his big blowup with Adam. Surprising that he was on the list to begin with. Neil had ridiculed those who were, never mentioning that he was on it, too. Neither had Adam. Maybe both were embarrassed to. Neil because he accepted Adam's charity, and Adam because he offered it to someone he wouldn't even speak to.

At least getting the monthly stipend knocked out any motivation Neil might have had for murdering Adam. He benefited more from Adam's being alive than dead. Or did Neil think that if Adam sent him checks, he'd remember him in the will despite everything? No, she didn't want to think of it. If only she could banish thoughts like banning smoking. A no-thinking section in her brain.

Next to her, Colombo gave a deep growl, alarming Lydia. Quickly she slid the notebook under the pillow. But he slept on, apparently warning villains in his dreams. She knew just how he felt. A creaking sound came from the deck. She doused the light and groped her way in the dark to the door again. Parting the vertical slats of the blinds, she peered out. Nothing but blackness. Nothing stirred. Another stray animal. She'd have to get used to the night noises out here or end up at Oak Grove like Carolyn with her fear of being pursued by Ted Bundy.

Returning to the notebook, Lydia went on to Francoise. The only one not cut off after June. Probably the thousand a month was for her shrink and not included in her regular salary. Did Francoise's husband know Adam had paid for her shrink?

Little wonder Francoise was so devoted to Adam. The few times Lydia had visited him, Francoise's hostile looks had rivaled Vanessa's. Adam said Francoise was deranged—probably why he was so fond of her. Of course, Adam went in for hyperbole. Still, Lydia had run into Francoise on Seventy-ninth and York, arguing heatedly in French with the air. So intently she hadn't noticed Lydia.

Francoise might have interpreted Adam's generosity as more than concern for her welfare. Maybe it was to a certain extent. Francoise was an attractive woman. Also, Adam was no Simon Legree who'd reprimand Francoise for leaving surfaces dusty or occasionally neglecting to vacuum. Was the extra thousand for the shrink and Adam's indulgence enough to encourage someone a bit unhinged to believe that this meant far more than it did? And misinterpreting Adam's friendship with her or learning of the mysterious BP, had Francoise drowned Adam in a fit of jealousy?

No, that was reaching.

On the other hand, her husband, suspecting that something was going on between his wife and her employer, might have harbored murderous feelings toward Adam. Also far-fetched.

More incriminating was Vanessa's lying for Todd, who no longer had a valid alibi. For that matter, neither did Vanessa. If Kevin Drake had covered for Todd, he could just as easily have covered for Vanessa. Kramer and Barolini should know this, too. She'd tell Kramer, who could relay the information.

Colombo stirred beside her. She gave him a pat on his orange rump and tried to figure out why BP rated a cool $20K a month. Blackmail instead of a secret lover? But blackmailers usually got paid off in lump sums, not monthly allowances. They'd increase the amount when they came back for more money. Besides, how could you blackmail someone like Adam, who was ready to spill his guts about what a rotten person he was to anyone who'd listen?

Had Adam ever mentioned a Betsy, Beth, Brooke, Bonnie, Beatrice, Beverly, Barbara . . . ? Barbara! Barbara-Bobbie! Bobbie the waitress? Who might have deliberately thrown Barolini off her trail by saying she'd seen Lydia fighting with Adam? No, she was clutching at straws again. And BP wasn't necessarily a woman. Why not a man? More reason to keep it secret. As with Mark, so with Adam. Beginning maybe with Neil back in their teens. Perhaps Neil was lying, and it was a lovers' quarrel between him and Adam, not Neil calling Urzaga evil, that had ended their friendship.

She immediately knew who BP was. How could she have been so dumb as to not figure it out sooner? BP stood for bipolar. Under the guise of the Institute for Bipolar Research, Urzaga was getting $240,000 a year from Adam. Not bad!

And not good for Adam when he stopped paying.

Adam had complained numerous times to Lydia about having to send his checks a week in advance. No check marks—or checks—in July meant nothing for August, and in August, nothing for September. In not writing checks, Adam had written his death warrant.

The killer was someone who had counted on getting money from Adam—if not alive, then dead. Someone in the will—or who had expected to be. Todd had hyperventilated when he discovered he wasn't, and Neil had been bitterly disappointed.

Lydia looked up from the lined pages to the ceiling as if she'd find the name of Adam's murderer written there. She suddenly became aware of the eerie quiet. Once in a while a branch scraped the window or some animal scampered across the deck. Otherwise the silence was intense, disturbing. And where was Carolyn?

Still Colombo slept serenely, breathing evenly, orange and white sides rising and falling, rippling the soft fur.

The travel alarm said four-twenty. Certainly Carolyn must be in bed now. Lydia just hadn't heard her come in. She got up to take a look. Her bodyguard immediately woke up and trotted after her. A light at the far end of the hall supplied enough light to see by. She turned the doorknob softly and waited for her eyes to adjust to the darkness. The bed was still empty.

Carolyn must be with her darling Alejandro. Where else would she go in the night on foot? But if Carolyn and Urzaga were lovers, why keep it a secret? Why wait until after midnight and sneak over? Were they in on Adam's murder together? Had they agreed that it was smarter to keep apart and play it cool? Maybe that was why Carolyn was out here. To see Urzaga, not her.

Questions, questions, questions. And she was getting no damn answers.

Lydia returned to bed. Colombo leaped up beside her, circled around several times before settling down, taking up more than his share of space. A shaggy orange and white blanket. Woman's best friend. "How did I ever live without you?" she asked. He thumped his tail and went back to sleep.

And she went back to the notebook, hoping to find some kind of revelation. The next page showed detailed theater expenses. Amounts paid for salaries to the cast, technicians, and stagehands. Also expenses for lighting, sets, props, publicity, and programs. Included in the cost was a rehearsal dinner for the cast at Mortimer's for $931.07. All costs were listed to the last penny. Apparently Adam had demanded receipts. Which must have been humiliating to someone like Vanessa. As if Adam hadn't trusted her. He hadn't. Probably with reason for a free spender like Vanessa.

But each expense was checked off. Meaning paid. Meaning Vanessa had no reason for holding Adam's head underwater. At least where theater expenses were concerned.

The breakdown of expenses given for BP on the next page made Vanessa's theater expenses look paltry by comparison. The combined amounts for public relations, equipment, and miscellaneous expenses came to over four hundred thousand dollars.

The twenty thousand a month from Adam had been merely the beginning. Urzaga had even conned Adam into spending money for public relations when the Institute was still on paper. Or nothing more than a lab at Hamptons

Hospital. All expenses were rounded off to zeros, not detailed as they'd been for the Auerbach Theater. Adam hadn't asked Urzaga for receipts, trusting him more than Vanessa. Foolish man.

Urzaga—the Houdini of con men. He'd almost won her over. Convinced her of what a dedicated doctor he was. She pictured him again on the roof deck earnestly proclaiming what he'd done was for the love of Adam. How he'd monitored Adam's heroin dosages. Poor Adam. It would have been cheaper for him to have gone to Washington Heights for his fixes.

It hurt to see how much Adam had been duped by Urzaga. Little wonder Adam was depressed. Urzaga called it clinical when it was his own behavior that brought it on. Lydia remembered how Adam had sobbed and ranted about Urzaga that Sunday. His last Sunday. His last day on earth. Two days before he'd threatened to expose Urzaga.

On the next page she found three entries under the initials TB and expenses listed under Dragonfly for CA. TB for Todd Bigelow, CA for Carolyn Auerbach, and *Dragonfly* must be the name of her movie. It sounded Japanese. Maybe that was Amy Akito's influence. Was Todd Bigelow going to act in Carolyn's movie?

No. TB was separate from CA, with the amounts of $6K for February and $12K for April crossed off, but the $27K for August was left as it was. The amounts crossed off must mean Adam had paid up so some enforcer wouldn't come after Todd, who, confident that Adam would pay off whatever losses he incurred, had become more and more reckless, upping the stakes. But in August Adam hadn't come through with the twenty-seven thousand. And perhaps by September Todd could stall no longer. Had Todd paid a visit to Adam figuring it was better to off Adam than to be offed himself? Believed that he'd be left enough money to go on gambling the rest of his life? He'd certainly been desperate to get his hands on that eighty-five thousand Adam had left him.

It looked like CA had lied, too. Although if you judged the lie by the amount Carolyn got, the lie was a small one. Dragonfly rated a measly sixty-five thousand, a fraction of

the amount Adam had given Vanessa for her play and
Urzaga for his Institute.

Tomorrow she'd turn the notebook over to Kramer, who
could pass it on to Barolini, even though it named Neil. She
felt like a traitor, but she could be charged with withholding
key information if she withheld the notebook. Anyway, if
Barolini didn't consider being cut off from lying-around
money sufficient motivation for the others to kill, why
would he think it of Neil? The important thing was that
Todd Bigelow no longer had an alibi.

She put the notebook under her pillow and closed her
eyes.

CHAPTER 29

A gray light pressed against her eyelids. Opening her eyes,
Lydia saw light seeping in under the Levolor blinds.

She got up and peeked out at a silvery morning. Ragged
bits of mist floated up from the lawn. She stood soaking up
the scene when she saw a ghostlike creature come running
out of the woods as if pursued by some mythological demon. Carolyn!

Her clothes were rumpled and her blond hair tangled. As
Carolyn neared the house, Lydia saw a frozen look of terror
on her face, like Munch's screaming woman. Why so terrified? What had happened at Urzaga's?

Lydia tried to be rational. Maybe Carolyn had scared herself when she'd startled a deer that had ended up running
the other way, more frightened than she. Or the woods
might have spooked her with all those mysterious noises,
the thick underbrush, the thorny bushes and deep tree shadows. She might have lost her way as Lydia had yesterday.

Carolyn ran up the steps to the front deck and disappeared from view. A few minutes later, Lydia heard footsteps tiptoeing down the hall, a door opening and closing. And then silence. Colombo slept through it all.

Glancing at her travel alarm, Lydia saw that it was seven minutes after five. She'd been awake almost all night and needed some sleep with all the things she had planned for the day. Besides, being overtired and edgy, she might have just imagined Carolyn's terror. Not even Urzaga could have been that bad in bed, she told herself sleepily.

She woke up at nine-thirty and got out of bed quickly and quietly so that she wouldn't wake Carolyn. She didn't want Carolyn hanging around when she called the Hospital de la Santa Cruz and Kramer. She didn't want Carolyn hanging around, period.

The phone rang just as she passed Carolyn's door. Damn. If she answered from the bedroom, Carolyn might hear. The house was far from soundproof. She and Mark had overheard Adam's conversations from the green room. Adam had had a voice that carried, but she didn't want to take any chances.

Lydia sprinted down the hall to the kitchen and grabbed up the phone in the middle of the fourth ring.

"Thank God, I was worried." Neil.

"Worried? Why?"

"I shouldn't have left you alone with that woman last night. You okay?"

"I'm fine. Well, not really, but I'm okay. What about you? You were flying."

"I was depressed, drunk, and querulous. I apologize, and I'm delighted you're alive. Although I'm just barely with this hangover. Serves me right."

Lydia reassured him that she was fine and said she wanted to talk to him later. "Things I couldn't mention last night."

"You can't give me a hint?"

"Not now."

"Come over any time, love, and meanwhile be on your guard."

"Okay, I'll be over before twelve."

"Great, stay for lunch. And don't bring *her*."

Lydia hung up feeling rotten for suspecting Neil, her very best friend, who worried about her. Had she worried about his driving when he was drunk last night? No, not as soon as he'd driven off. But she didn't really suspect him, she assured herself. It was just getting everything straight and up front, so they could once again be open with one another. The way friends ought to be.

The phone rang again.

"Hello," she said. Silence at the other end. Or almost. Heavy breathing. She said "hello" again. The breathing continued.

"Who is this?" she asked. No answer. She hung up. A heavy breather so early in the morning?

She'd just fixed herself tea and fed Colombo when the doorbell rang. Lydia opened the door to a tall, fat man with long hair and a friendly smile. He wore work clothes and carried a toolbox. "Hi, I'm Larry. Sorry to be late again."

He hadn't sounded fat on the phone.

"Freezer's in the pantry. In the hall on the left."

"I know where it is," Larry said. "I've been here before. That freezer was always giving Mr. Auerbach trouble. Sure was shocked to hear about him. You his wife?"

"A friend."

His blue eyes looked her over as if he were remembering details to repeat to his bar buddies.

She was about to leave him to his work when she remembered the playhouse. "Do you know who lives at the left turnoff going toward the highway?"

"The Ellmans. Nice people."

"Are they here now?"

"Nah, they always leave after Labor Day. Visit their daughter and grandchildren in Seattle, then head south for the winter."

"Grandchildren?"

"Yeah. Older couple. Friendly. Lonely. They say they don't know many people out here anymore. Everything's changed."

"Did their daughter and grandchildren visit them here?"

"Not that I know of. Why are you so curious?"

"Oh, I just like to know my neighbors."

"Your neighbors?"

"Yeah. Who else lives nearby?"

"Mr. Holzman. He lives a quarter of a mile down the road. To the right."

"Married with children?"

"Not him. He comes out with his boyfriend."

"Are there many people living around here with children? I have a ten-year-old niece I've invited out, and I thought it would be nice if she had some playmates."

Larry scratched his wavy head. "Hey, yeah, I forgot, the Janowskys. Live behind the Ellmans. Lots of kids. One ought to be your niece's age. Course, they're locals."

"You mean they don't associate with summer people?"

"Well, not exactly. Sort of the other way around. Mrs. Janowsky, she works for Dr. Urzaga. Husband comes and goes. Stays just long enough to make another baby. Now, Dr. Urzaga. He's a guy you wanna meet—single, rich, and good-looking."

"Uh-huh," Lydia said.

"Well, I guess I'd better get to work."

She'd pay a visit to Urzaga later, and find out more about the Janowskys. She'd talk to Mrs. Janowsky, that pleasant red-faced, beefy blonde who adored her boss. The kind of masochistic, worshipful woman who considered abuse from a man as a sign of affection—something she might have learned from her mother and passed on to her own daugher as a family tradition. A visit to Urzaga was definitely in order.

In less than a half hour Larry had the freezer running again.

"Gives you any trouble, I'll come back and fix it gratis," he said on his way out, and winked. Friendly, not flirtatious.

For breakfast she had more tea and Wheat Thins. There were only seven left. She took four for herself and left three for Carolyn. Standing at the living room window, she sipped her tea and chewed the crackers slowly to get what taste she could out of the small bits. Outside, Colombo interrupted his bush-sniffing to give her a look, then went back to what he was doing. The sky was gray again. A wind sprung up, shaking a shower of yellow and red maple leaves onto the deck.

Time to get busy. Make some calls. The first to the Hospital de la Santa Cruz in Argentina. She'd never called outside the country before and wasn't sure how to go about doing it. Gillian put through the overseas calls at the office. Consulting a Manhattan phone book Adam had brought out, she found a chart giving international country and city codes that conveniently used Buenos Aires as an example. Argentina's code was 54, Buenos Aires 1. Since they were two hours ahead of EST, she estimated it was close to noon down there.

"*Yo habla seulement* English," she said when she got through to the hospital, mixing French and Spanish. Then gave up on both languages. "Could I speak to someone in Administration who understands English?"

"*Un momento,*" a woman said.

There was a lot of switching, clicking, exclaiming, and explaining. She could understand Spanish better than she could speak it. Lydia leaned against the kitchen counter wondering how much this call was going to cost her while idly eyeing the glasses on the shelves across from her. She'd left the cupboard door open. All the glasses were sparkling clean except for a highball glass, dull and cloudy, as if someone had dunked it under tap water and put it back with the others.

"Dr. Guzmann," a man's voice said. "May I help you?" Not a trace of an accent. It didn't seem like a doctor would be answering a phone in Administration, but maybe they did things differently in Argentina.

"This is Detective Miller from New York Homicide."

"Who?" Dr. Guzmann asked, as if he didn't quite believe her.

"Detective Miller," she said crisply, sounding her most official. "New York Homicide." How many years did you get sent up for impersonating a police officer?

"I'm calling for information on Dr. Carlos Fernando Alejandro Urzaga," she said, hoping all three first names made it sound more authentic.

"Him again!"

"Has someone else called about him?"

"Yes, someone up your way. Just last month. Finally caught up with him, have you?" Guzmann asked.

Lydia's pulse speeded up. "Was the call from a Mr. Auerbach?"

"Could have been. Don't remember. But I'll tell you the same thing I told him. Urzaga was dismissed from this hospital for questionable practices over five years ago. I have no idea where he's gone since then."

It wasn't difficult for Lydia to coax the reason for dismissal from Dr. Guzmann. "Too many of his patients died. We couldn't prove anything more than carelessness, but we didn't want him here. Some people referred to him as el Doctor Muerte."

"Doctor Death," she said. A chill ran up her spine.

"That's right."

So this was what Adam had learned.

"Was there some kind of pattern?" she asked. "Did the victims have something in common—hopelessly ill people he thought deserved to die? Or were the deaths random?"

There was a pause. "I don't recall. Nothing was proven."

"Well, what did they die of? Neglect?"

"I can't say anything more. We get sued down here for slander, too, you know. Sorry." Dr. Guzmann hung up.

Lydia put the phone down feeling troubled and distressed. Not happy as she would have expected in getting the information she was after. Urzaga was beginning to look worse than she'd imagined. What was his record like at Hamptons Hospital? Maybe he was watching his step. They not only hadn't dismissed him but were also sponsoring his project. Or so he said.

Had Urzaga killed Adam for cutting off his funds or for finding out what she'd just learned? Maybe for both reasons. Poor Adam, probably fully intending to keep quiet until Tuesday when he exposed Urzaga to hospital authorities, couldn't keep from letting Urzaga know he knew. He'd said Urzaga refused to answer the phone that Sunday. She pictured Urzaga standing by his answering machine, listening as a drunken Adam called, demanding to speak to el Doctor Muerte.

This should shake up Barolini when Kramer relayed the information.

But how about that cloudy highball glass in the cupboard? What if Urzaga had been on hospital duty as he claimed and hadn't gotten Adam's message until later? Someone had joined Adam in a drink the night he was murdered, washed off the fingerprints, and put the glass back. But who among his friends drank? Urzaga claimed he didn't, while Neil said he was off the hard stuff. Carolyn made a big production of not drinking anything but wine, although she'd had a brandy last night. Vanessa was AA, which didn't mean she couldn't have had tonic. Todd hung out in bars. And had no alibi. But then, neither did Carolyn or Vanessa. Although Steve said Neil was in all day, Steve often got so drunk, he blanked out. Or he might lie to protect Neil. Any one of the FFOAA could have done it.

Carolyn had taken the cup and saucer from her room last night, washed them off, and put them back. Which maybe meant only that Carolyn was tidy. She'd put everything back in place before calling on her lover. If *lover* was the word.

CHAPTER 30

Lydia phoned Megan's to make sure Bobbie would be on duty at lunchtime and found out that she was. First she'd drop in on Neil and casually bring up the subject of the notebook to gauge his reaction. No. First she'd deliver the notebook to Kramer.

She called Suffolk Homicide. Kramer wasn't on duty. Lydia bit the bullet. "May I speak to Detective Barolini?" she asked.

"He's off today, too. Can I help you?"

Well, she'd tried. She asked for Kramer's home phone number and got it.

"I was just on my way out," Kramer said, picking up before she had as much as said hello.

Lowering her voice, Lydia told him about finding the notebook. "Also, I've discovered other incriminating information."

"Incriminating information on whom?" Kramer asked. "I mean who?" Maybe it was against the rules for cops to use good grammar.

"Urzaga, for one, but also Todd Bigelow. That's the trouble. Everyone looks guilty. Except me, of course."

Kramer laughed. "Miller, I like you. Can I level?"

"Try me."

"Give that notebook and your information to Barolini. He's not going to be happy with me if I get it, and even less happy with you. After all, it's only fair. He's the one heading the investigation."

"He's not on duty either. Besides, I don't want to deal with that bully. I'm out here at Adam's place in Southampton. It won't take me long to get the notebook to you."

"Tell you what. I'm going over to Sag Harbor, and Auerbach's place is on my way. I'll stop off for the notebook, look it over, and give it to Barolini as soon as I get back. Tell him you want to talk to him. Okay?"

Hearing a noise, she looked out in the hall, trailing the phone cord after her. Carolyn had just emerged from her room, wraithlike in a filmy white negligee—the kind Lydia thought women wore only on their honeymoons, if then. "Not okay," she said. "What time will you be home?"

"I'm not sure. I'm taking my kid to the whaling museum and going to look around for Steinbeck landmarks. He used to live in Sag Harbor. His widow still does. Want to come along?"

Steinbeck again. Lydia remembered Kramer's excitement when he'd found one of his books at her place. "I'd like to," she said, and surprised herself by actually meaning it. "But I can't. I've got a lot of errands to do."

Carolyn came into the kitchen. She shook the teakettle to

see if there was enough water in it, and turned on the burner.

"It's already hot," Lydia told her. "I'm speaking to Carolyn Auerbach," she explained to Kramer.

"Who are you talking to?" Carolyn asked her.

"She's with you?" Kramer asked, sounding surprised.

"I'll explain later," Lydia said to both of them.

"Is that why you'd rather come over here and talk?" Kramer asked.

"You guessed."

"Come at five. I'll be back by then."

He gave her his address. Lydia memorized it. She didn't want to write it down with Carolyn watching. It was in the village of Southampton, but on a street she hadn't heard of. Probably not in a part of town that summer people knew. Presumably he was divorced if he'd invited her along to Sag Harbor. Not that you're out looking, she reminded herself. But he was a nice guy. And she liked his looks. She'd always liked cuddly, teddy-bear men. It was in spite of Mark's good looks, not because of them, that she'd ended up with him. Handsome men generally had monster egos and minimal brains.

"Who was that?" Carolyn asked, swirling the tea bag in her cup.

"I left you some Wheat Thins," Lydia said, dodging the question. "Only three. There were hardly any left."

"Thanks, but I'm not hungry." Carolyn lit a Gauloise with a shaky hand.

"Have a good night's sleep?" Lydia asked, doubting Carolyn would admit to where she'd been, but interested in hearing her answer.

"A horrible nightmare. Horrible."

A nightmarish experience at Urzaga's? Maybe it wasn't just the woods that had frightened her. Carolyn looked awful. Worse than a just-got-up look. Her face was drawn and pale, eyes deep-circled. It bothered Lydia to see Carolyn looking so shitty. For all her annoying little ways, Carolyn had a lot of spirit, and Lydia hated seeing spirits squelched.

"Excuse me, but I'm not my usual sunny self this morning," Carolyn said. "I have a frightful migraine. I'm sorry to be such a poor guest, but I'll just take my tea and go back to my room."

Guest? Who invited her? "That's okay. In my book the best guests are those who aren't constantly underfoot," Lydia said, hoping Carolyn would take the hint. "I like people who can entertain themselves," she added, as if she were an experienced hostess who entertained weekly. "Anyway, I've got a lot of stuff to do."

Carolyn paused in the kitchen doorway. "What? Would you like me to help?"

"Thanks, no; my chores are boring."

"I'll be glad to keep you company. My migraine just gets worse if I stay in bed. I'll be ready in a few minutes," Carolyn said, and marched into her bedroom before Lydia could stop her.

Lydia went outside and called Colombo, in a hurry to take off for Neil's before Carolyn appeared. She didn't want to leave Colombo behind and chance his straying onto the road.

Unfortunately, Carolyn showed up before Colombo did. She'd put herself together fast and done a good job. Lydia had to admire Carolyn's skill with a makeup brush. She thought she'd learned all the makeup tricks of the trade back in her runway days, but here was Carolyn completely transformed and looking perfectly natural. As if she'd done no more than put on a dash of lipstick. And in just a few minutes.

Carolyn could give the beauty editor at *gazelle* some tips. Black circles and little lines had disappeared. Lashes were longer, eyes and hair shiny. And it wasn't just her makeup, but also her clothes. The ruffled jeans skirt and white lace blouse she'd worn yesterday looked as fresh as if she'd donned them this morning. Lydia remembered how bedraggled her clothes had looked when she'd emerged from the woods. If Lydia hadn't felt sorry for Carolyn, she'd hate her.

"Colombo has taken off again, damn it," Lydia said.

"Let him have some fun. He's been penned up too long in the city. He'll be back when he's hungry."

The drunk in front of the Coconut Grill the other night

had scolded her for keeping a country dog in the city. Maybe she should let Colombo have some freedom to roam, Lydia thought.

"Don't bother with your car. We'll take mine," Carolyn said, sounding cheerful once again. It was as if she'd put on a happy mood with her makeup.

"Thanks, but I'm taking mine." Damned if she'd let Carolyn boss her around. She got in her Datsun and slammed the door, leaving no argument. Carolyn sat gingerly in the passenger seat as if she risked contamination.

"Sure you want to come along?" Lydia asked. "It's not going to be exciting. I'm going to Caldor's and the supermarket at the Bridgehampton mall."

She hadn't planned to go there, but she couldn't very well take Carolyn to Neil's, and she had to get supplies sometime.

"I don't want to be a bad guest," Carolyn said primly.

"Come off it. Since when do guests have to tag after their host?"

"You don't want me?" she asked, sounding hurt.

Shit. The lady was as hypersensitive as a teenager. Upset at the merest hint of criticism. How could she have stood up to Adam's insults?

"Suit yourself," Lydia said, backing the car down the hill and onto the gravel drive.

"Your radio doesn't work," Carolyn complained.

"No, and I don't have an ashtray, either." Lydia nodded toward the hole in the dashboard where the ashtray had once been.

"I always play the radio in a car."

Carolyn was uncharacteristically silent on the drive to the shopping mall, cigarette trembling between her fingers. No longer attempting to be cheerful. Lydia liked her better that way.

Now that most of the summer people had gone, the roads were gratifyingly deserted. The trees were solid masses of coppers, reds, and gold.

Carolyn chain-smoked, ignoring the scenery and sprinkling ashes on the floorboard. Lydia began to find her silence unsettling. Several times Carolyn looked her way as if she were about to say something, then clammed up.

"Want to talk about it?" Lydia asked.

"Talk about what?"

"Whatever is bothering you."

"Nothing's wrong. It's just my dreadful migraine."

Uh-huh. It suddenly struck Lydia that Carolyn might have come along because she was scared to stay at the house alone. But if she was so frightened, why didn't she just jump into that nifty little red sports car and head home?

Even on a Saturday, the parking lot at the shopping mall was only halfway full without the summer people. Lydia told Carolyn that if she didn't feel well, she might prefer to stay in the car.

"I would, if we'd taken my car and I could play the radio."

Carolyn tagged along with Lydia into Caldor's, where Lydia bought several flashlights for various parts of the house, a powerful flashlight for the garage, a penlight, and plenty of batteries. She considered buying a Swiss knife for protection, but she'd probably be the one who ended up getting hurt.

After Caldor's, she went next door to the supermarket. Carolyn followed.

"Which do you like?" Lydia asked slowly pushing the cart past the long row of cereals. Getting no answer, she turned and saw that Carolyn was missing.

Curious, Lydia abandoned her cart and went looking. She found Carolyn two aisles over, brushing past women with de rigueur toddlers and babies in carts, intently searching the shelves. Keeping her distance, Lydia watched. Toward the end of the aisle, Carolyn paused, reached out for something on a shelf, and casually slipped it into the pocket of her butter yellow suede jacket.

As soon as she moved on, Lydia went to take a look. She found an array of boxes, bottles, and cans containing insecticides and rodent poisons. She couldn't tell what Carolyn had pocketed—roach or rat poison. The big question was why. And why shoplift something so inexpensive? She could picture Carolyn shoplifting at Bergdorf's or Bloomie's—but a household poison? Maybe Carolyn was one of those compulsive shoplifters who replaced lack of love with little gifts to herself. But insect poison? Maybe it was against Carolyn's principles to pay for what she could steal. Or just possibly she might have stuffed the object in her pocket, intending to pay on the way out.

Sure.

Lydia grabbed a box of pasta before returning to her cart where Carolyn stood waiting.

"Forgot the fettucine," she called, waving the box.

Carolyn didn't take the poison from her pocket at the checkout counter. Because she didn't want to be identified for buying some lethal substance that showed up in a dead body? Her body, for instance. But millions of people bought insect poison. Who would notice? Still, if you were planning such a thing, you wouldn't want to take chances.

When they got back to the car, Lydia put the groceries in the trunk instead of the backseat, just in case Carolyn tried sprinkling something deadly in the Total.

CHAPTER 31

Lydia took Route 27 west to Water Mill. She found a parking place directly across the highway from Megan's and pulled in. Her watch said twelve-thirty. Busy hour at the pub, but then, it usually was crowded. She hoped Bobbie had time to answer questions.

"Why are we stopping here?" Carolyn asked.

"Lunch at Megan's." She had no choice but to take Carolyn along.

"I told you, the doctors have forbidden me to eat hamburgers."

"They have seafood."

"I had seafood last night," Carolyn said in a sinned-against voice.

"Sorry, but I have my reasons for eating here."

"What are they?"

"Come along and see." Which should have gotten any-one as nosy as Carolyn into the restaurant. But she stayed put.

"It would be just too embarrassing going in there."

"Embarrassing? Why?"

"I . . ." She hesitated, looked at the end of her cigarette instead of at Lydia. "Adam was in one of his foul moods and said some terrible things to me. I couldn't face anyone who heard. The Fourth of July weekend. I'll never forget it."

Lydia remembered that Adam had asked her to join him and Carolyn that weekend on what he said was Carolyn's once-a-summer visit to his place. He'd told Lydia that if she came along, it would make Carolyn's visit more bear-able and give him something to look forward to. "You don't have to worry," he'd said. "Carolyn can play chaper-one." She'd been tempted by Adam's invitation, but she'd turned it down. Instead, she'd sat at Mark's bedside, hold-ing his hand while he drifted in and out of consciousness.

"Carolyn, that's too far back for anyone at Megan's to remember. A lot of summer people pass through that screen door."

"But Adam came here more often than most. If you're so determined to go in, please do. I'll just get some ice cream next door. It's a bit chilly for ice cream, but then, I don't have a choice, do I? Anyway, I doubt I could actually eat anything with my migraine."

"Okay, sit out here and suffer, if that's what you prefer."

Pissed at Carolyn's pity-poor-me act, Lydia got out of the car, slamming the door behind her.

Carolyn, saying nothing, meekly followed her across the highway.

Christ, now I've done it, she's tagging along, Lydia thought, but Carolyn veered right toward the ice cream store, whose window displayed boxes of candy and stuffed toys.

As soon as Lydia stepped into Megan's, she became nervous. What if for some crazy reason Bobbie really thought she was the woman who'd been with Adam that Sunday? She could see Bobbie pointing at her from the witness chair in court. "She's the one. She did it. She even came to my place of business and tried to bribe me to lie for her."

Megan's smelled of smoke, beer, and frying food. Men in T-shirts and jeans packed the bar. Only a few tables were taken. Megan's and the Madison Pub had certain things in common. Their jukebox selections were better than most, and wood won out over plastic, splintered and rough-hewn though it might be.

Lydia thought she remembered what Bobbie looked like. A chunky brunette in her thirties. The only waitress in sight was a thin redhead with disproportionately large breasts. Implants?

She wanted to sit at the table in back where she and Adam usually ate, but it was a table for four. She settled on a table for two overlooking the street.

Lydia worried that the redheaded waitress would wait on her instead of Bobbie. But a woman with bouncy brown curls, brown eyes, and apple cheeks bopped up to her table, menu in hand. Lydia immediately recognized her. A nice, friendly person like Bobbie wouldn't frame her, would she?

"Hi, what'll it be?" Bobbie asked. No spark of recognition.

Lydia ordered a cheeseburger, fries, and a bottle of Rolling Rock. Then, "You don't remember me, do you?" she asked, holding her breath.

"Oh, like, you know. People come and go. Walking in and staggering out," Bobbie said with a friendly wink.

"Do you remember a big, noisy man who used to come here in the summer? Gray-blond beard? Broad-shouldered?" Should she do this? Wasn't she asking for trouble, putting ideas in Bobbie's head?

"Oh, yeah, sure, *him*! The guy with the gut. I liked him! A real piece of work. He got murdered, you know. He could be a royal pain in the ass, but boy oh boy, he wasn't cheap."

A fitting epitaph, Lydia thought, and was vastly relieved

that Bobbie hadn't recognized her. She wished Barolini were here. But maybe he still wouldn't believe she wasn't guilty. He'd probably accuse her of showing up in a disguise so Bobbie wouldn't recognize her. A wig. Or even a mustache.

"I was real shocked when I heard," Bobbie continued. "Jeez, how many people you know get murdered?"

Brown eyes focused on Lydia. "Oh, yeah, now I remember you."

Lydia tensed. She'd asked for it.

"You two guys came strolling in here in T-shirts and bathing suits. Barefoot. That's not allowed. Lucky I didn't throw you out. That was way last June."

"You're sure of that?"

"What do you mean? Sure I'm sure."

"You're Bobbie, aren't you?"

"How'd you know?"

"I'm Lydia," she said for future identification.

Bobbie gave her a so-what look. "Cheeseburger and fries coming up," she said, snatched up the menu, and bounced off.

She was prompt with the beer, slamming the bottle of Rolling Rock down on the table along with a glass. Sipping the beer, Lydia again tried to think who could have been with Adam that fatal Sunday. Around six. The time the ME had set. She didn't recall any tall, skinny blondes at Adam's memorial service. What did Rita, the manicurist, look like? The name Rita didn't sound like a blonde, but . . . There was Kim Lapinna, Jared Evans's assistant. Too far-fetched. She idly looked out the window and saw Carolyn cross the highway, daintily licking a pistachio ice cream cone. She had tucked some magazines under the elbow of her suede jacket, which was nearly the same color as her butter yellow hair. Wait a minute. Butter yellow equaled blond. And Carolyn was tall and skinny. Well, thin. Lydia's heart skipped a couple of beats. Why hadn't she thought of it before? That one was easy. At the memorial service Carolyn had raven hair, and at the reading of the will, auburn. Bobbie appeared with the rest of her order.

"See that woman getting into the car across the street?" Lydia asked Bobbie nervously. "Does she look familiar?"

Instead of looking at Carolyn, Bobbie looked at her. "Huh?" she asked.

Luckily, Carolyn was having trouble getting the car door open because of the ice cream and magazines. "That blonde climbing into the Datsun," she said. "Have you seen her before?"

Bobbie looked. "Jeez, that's her!" she cried, nearly dumping the cheeseburger and fries in Lydia's lap. "The woman who was here with the fat guy who was killed. That cop came in with a picture of him and asked me was he with anybody. I told him yeah. Boy, the fat guy was calling her every name in the book. He sure had a dirty mouth. And loud! Everyone was staring. She ran out crying. Me, I'd have killed him myself. Is she the one who did it?" She eyed Lydia. "You know her?"

"The cop who showed you the picture thinks you meant me," Lydia said, avoiding her questions.

"No shit! Why does he think that?"

"From your description. But it isn't your fault. He jumps to conclusions."

"Hey, you two do look alike, now you mention it. Except . . ." Bobbie paused, catching herself before she added that Carolyn was prettier. "Except her hair is blonder and longer," she said diplomatically. "And now there she is, big as life, sitting in that car. Guess she didn't do it or she'd be behind bars."

Lydia was about to march Bobbie to the phone to tell Barolini who she'd seen with Adam, then remembered he was off duty. May as well wait until she saw Kramer and tell him.

"Listen, that cop gave me his phone number just in case. I better call him. Only I don't know where I put his card."

It wouldn't hurt to have Bobbie back her up. "His name is Barolini. Call him tomorrow. He's off duty today. But maybe tomorrow, too. Anyway, ask for him. If he's out, just tell whoever answers that it wasn't Lydia Miller you saw Adam Auerbach with—that's me," she reminded her, "but

Carolyn Auerbach. She's his first wife and staying out here with me at Adam's place."

She hoped Bobbie didn't ask what she was doing there so she wouldn't have to explain. Bobbie didn't. Her mind was on something else. "Jeez, you're staying with a murderer?"

"Well, there's no real proof. Just because she was with him at six doesn't mean she killed him two hours later at eight."

"You ask me, she did it. Boy, I wouldn't be in the same house with that woman. You'd better report her, not just sit on your ass and wait to talk to that Barolini."

"Don't worry, I'm meeting with his sidekick later."

"So if you're seeing him, why'd you want me to call Barolini?" Bobbie demanded, hands on ample hips.

"Because you're the one who saw Adam with her. I may not be believed, but you would."

"You mean I'll be put on the witness stand in court? Oh boy." Bobbie's eyes sparkled. She was obviously thrilled with the idea of being center stage and fingering a possible murderer. Thank God it wasn't her.

Lydia asked for the check. She was getting nervous thinking of Carolyn unguarded in her car. As if Carolyn might guess what was going on in here and take off.

"You're getting into the car with a killer? Boy, not me. I wouldn't do it. What if she tries to kill you?"

"Why would she? I won't let on I know. Besides, there's no proof she did it. I'll be okay. Anyway, Barolini's sidekick can take over. Where's the check?"

"This is on the house," Bobbie said, and glanced at her plate. "Anyway, you didn't eat."

Bobbie accompanied her to the door and peeked out at Carolyn. "Be careful," she whispered. "You could be next!"

Thanks. That's all she needed to hear.

CHAPTER 32

Bobbie might have been an alarmist, but her words spooked Lydia. Before crossing the highway, Lydia waited for a slow-moving car a quarter of a mile away to pass. She was in no hurry to join Carolyn, who sat in the car reading a magazine, blond hair curtaining her face, only her nose visible. There were a lot of questions she'd like to ask her, but Lydia decided it was less hazardous to her health if she didn't arouse Carolyn's suspicions.

"I'm reading your column," Carolyn said, holding up the magazine for Lydia to see when she got in the car. Cissie Gaier, the supermodel, was on the cover. She was twenty-two but looked thirteen—like an anorexic Lolita.

Carolyn dropped the magazine into the lap of her jeans skirt. "You didn't stay long," she said as Lydia pulled out on the highway.

"You were right, the food was pretty bad." But Lydia's stomach chose that moment to rumble, giving away the fact she hadn't eaten. "So bad, I couldn't eat it," she said to cover.

"Why did you go to that awful place anyway?"

Lydia shrugged.

"You said you had a reason for going there," Carolyn reminded her.

"Sentimental reason. I used to go there with Adam."

"I can't imagine being sentimental about that place."

Lydia could see why she wouldn't be.

"Where are we off to now?"

What was all this "we" stuff? Did she consider them a team? "Back to Adam's," Lydia said. She'd call Neil and

186

ask him over. She didn't want to be in the house alone with Carolyn.

"Oh, God, it's so horrible," Carolyn said. "My migraine. It hurts for me to talk."

"So shut up," Lydia said.

Carolyn closed her eyes and shut up. Her face looked white and strained. Lydia almost felt sorry for Carolyn, but not quite. The most she could say for Carolyn was that she was kind to animals. Adam had told Lydia that Carolyn had rescued drowning animals from the pool, just like her. Which had prompted Lydia to say she'd like to meet her.

Suddenly it clicked. It was Carolyn Adam had expected the night of the murder. His words on her answering machine had been someone she'll like was joining them, not someone she liked.

Probably Carolyn had come out to charm Adam into resuming her monthly checks. On her best behavior, she'd agreed to go to Megan's even though she didn't like the place. Adam had known what Carolyn was up to. Drunk and mean, at his most venomous, he'd launched his attack. Lydia pictured Carolyn running from Megan's, crying after Adam's verbal zapping.

Then what? Had Carolyn waited for Adam in the car, silently plotting her revenge as he covered the miles driving back, answering him sweetly as if nothing had happened, choking on her hurt pride? Or had she gone to the nearby candy store and called Urzaga to come and get her? Did the two of them wait at Adam's place for his return and lure him into the pool? Or had Adam, drunk, jumped in the pool to cool off, and seeing their chance, one or both dragged him under? Or had Carolyn managed it alone? Barolini had said that an anorexic seven-year-old could have drowned Adam in his drunken and drugged condition.

Carolyn sat beside her, eyes still closed, taking deep, audible breaths, arms tight to her sides, clenching and unclenching her fists. Was she practicing a form of relaxation? If so, it wasn't working. Her lips moved slightly, as if she were talking to herself—or praying.

Suddenly Carolyn clapped her hands over her ears and began whimpering. Her ashen face wore the same terrified expression as when she'd emerged from the woods early this morning. "Shut up, shut up, shut up!" she screamed, and reaching out, turned the radio knobs up, one after the other.

Lydia slowed down for the tavern turnoff. Thank God they'd soon be back. "Carolyn, I told you, the radio isn't working."

"Shut up!" she yelled, but Lydia had a feeling she wasn't yelling at her. "I can't stand it any longer!" she screamed in a strangled voice, and flung herself out of the car. She momentarily lost her footing in her cowboy boots, then regained it and started running down the middle of the road, waving her arms and screaming.

Remembering Adam's story about Carolyn freaking out in the car, it hit Lydia what was happening—Carolyn was trying to escape the demon voice of Ted Bundy, probably brought on by the news that a serial murderer was rumored to be at large on the Island.

Lydia drove slowly alongside Carolyn, trying to coax her back inside, telling her she was safer in the car than out on the road. Finally, exhausted, Carolyn got in. She cringed over by the door, as if scared of an unseen presence. Traces of black mascara marked her pale cheeks.

Lydia wanted to ask if it was Ted Bundy's voice she'd heard or just some anonymous serial murderer, but she didn't think now was the time to inquire. Of course, Ted Bundy had been dead for a long time, but she supposed if you heard voices, they could come as easily from the beyond as elsewhere. On the other hand, if it was Ted Bundy's voice Carolyn heard, maybe she'd be doing Carolyn a favor by telling her he wasn't around anymore.

"Carolyn, Ted Bundy's dead, you know. He can't harm you."

"Don't you think I know his voice by now? This was someone else."

"Who?"

Carolyn shook her head hard, to imply she either didn't know or wasn't telling. Or was she trying to get rid of the demon voice lodged there? Then, almost as suddenly as she'd flipped out, Carolyn was back to so-called normal, her eyes in focus. She lit a cigarette and gave a small, embarrassed laugh. "I'm okay now. Sorry. I guess I had one of my minor episodes. I get them when something upsets me."

If this was minor, what was major like? "What upset you?"

"I can drown voices out with the radio. Otherwise I pick up people's thought waves."

Lydia hoped Carolyn hadn't picked up hers. Looking over, she saw that Carolyn was silently crying, smoking while her eyes flooded with tears.

"Carolyn, what is it? What's wrong?"

"Last night," she whispered.

"Last night?"

"Alejandro was with another woman." Barely audible. "I guess you don't know we're lovers. It's a secret."

"Why a secret?"

"He wants it that way."

To keep the cops from guessing they'd murdered Adam together?

"Alejandro is a very private person," Carolyn said, dabbing a tissue at a tear. "You can't imagine what it's like for someone who was a courtesan in her past life to be dumped for some tacky woman. I've always thought Alejandro liked women with style, intelligence, and sensitivity."

Carolyn paused for a breath. "He's a genius, you know. Brilliant. Geniuses aren't like other people. He can be very tender and loving—when he wants to be."

"When he isn't cheating on you with another woman."

Carolyn's answer was more tears.

Lydia was sorry she'd mentioned it, but now that she had, she may as well learn the sordid details. "So how did you catch him up?"

A pause that lasted a quarter of a mile. "After midnight, last night, I went over. I knew he'd be off duty. He wasn't home, so I waited. I thought maybe there'd been some emergency at the hospital. I couldn't get into the house. I tried all the doors. They were locked. I broke a nail trying to pry a window open."

She held out the finger with the broken nail as evidence.

"I waited in the van in his garage to keep warm. Foolish

me, I wanted to surprise him. We hadn't seen each other since Adam's memorial service, and then we didn't get a chance to talk. I fell asleep in the van. When a door slammed I woke up. And there he was with a woman. Tacky—plaid suit and striped scarf, can you imagine? Such a dreadful combination. Totally out of it. Either drunk or high on something. She couldn't even stand up. She slid to the floor when he propped her against the wall so he could open the door. And that was what crushed me. It was the door to the new addition. Never has he let me in there. Never. He keeps saying it isn't ready yet."

"It's off-limits to everyone."

"It wasn't to her. He carried her in as if he were carrying his bride over a threshold. She wasn't even aware of the honor. Too damn high on something."

"Alec high, too?"

"You ask? Foolish woman. He'd never take anything himself. Alejandro always has to be in control."

"And you just sat quietly by watching?"

Carolyn nodded, flooding tears again. "He'd have been furious if he'd known I was there. Accuse me of spying. He gets angry when I phone him, claims I'm checking up. Actually, I am," she said, sniffling. "He's right about that."

"You're not going to mention any of this?"

Carolyn gave a sudden silvery Tinkerbell laugh. "I have my own subtle methods of striking back."

Drowning or poisoning? "Such as?" Lydia said.

Carolyn laughed her tinkly laugh again. It gave Lydia the creeps. She passed the tipsy mailbox and turned in, wondering if she was making a grave mistake to risk even a half hour alone with Carolyn. Maybe she should go straight to Neil's. Except she had to put the milk and eggs in the refrigerator or they'd spoil. She hoped she wasn't being stupid putting groceries ahead of her life.

CHAPTER 33

"Tell you more later," Lydia whispered into the phone. She'd put away the groceries and was calling Neil from the kitchen. Carolyn was in bed with her migraine. Lydia had already told Neil about Bobbie fingering her.

"The sooner you get here, the better," Neil said. "Didn't I tell you she was dangerous? Now, hurry over. I'll worry about you until I see that green junk heap pull into my driveway."

"Yeah, okay, you're right."

"Damn straight, sweetie."

"Mind if I bring Colombo?"

"Sorry, love. Colombo is persona non grata. He'll worry the rabbits and squirrels."

"Not so loud, he's listening. You'll hurt his feelings."

"Better his feelings than my furry friends. Don't worry about him, he can fend for himself. His bite is worse than his bark. Now, get your tail over here. Immediately."

Lydia tiptoed into her bedroom, Colombo tagging along. She packed an overnight bag and picked up the books she intended to take with her. "That's okay, I won't leave without you; I'll be back to pick you up," she promised Colombo, but he didn't look convinced. She debated about shutting him up in the house or letting him roam outside, and decided to let him run free since no harm had come to him earlier.

In the kitchen she wrote a note telling Carolyn she'd gone out and no telling when she'd be back, and fastened it to the refrigerator with one of Adam's Donald Duck magnets. Maybe Carolyn would take the hint and go back to town now that her darling Alejandro was two-timing her with another woman.

Colombo followed her to the car and watched as she flung the bag in the backseat beside the books. Damn. Neil could have let him come along. She considered taking him along and leaving him in the car. But then she was going on to see Kramer, and he might not want Colombo running loose either. It would be cruel leaving him in the car for such a long time.

"Sorry, sweetheart, you're persona non grata," she said, and jumped into the car, feeling like a traitor as she drove off.

She lost her way several times before she found the turn-off to Skink Road. (Neil called it Shrink Road because of the many psychiatrists who lived there in the summer.) Trees and shrubbery shielded the houses from view. The only indication of habitation was the occasional mailbox at the end of a lane, each name preceded by "Dr."

Above the gold and scarlet trees, Lydia spied the gray roof of the converted potato barn lent to Neil by his designer friend Gabriella. Neil had a way of getting people to offer him what he wanted, thinking nothing of it as if it were his due. Maybe it had to do with growing up rich—getting what you wanted was the expected thing. Entitlement.

But how to explain Adam's freeloading friends who hadn't grown up in luxury—although they might pretend they had—who also considered themselves something special? Entitled to Adam's money, the best seats in the house, and flying first-class.

And entitled to kill?

She'd also been Adam's friend. What made her think she was so different? Something to mull over later, she told herself as she brought the car to a stop in Gabriella's circular driveway.

Neil came out to greet her, wearing blue jeans, a black turtleneck, and a smile—the same thing she was wearing, except for the smile. The notebook in her jeans jacket pocket was an unpleasant reminder. Would he still be her friend after she told him what she'd found out, and asked all her questions? Wasn't friendship supposed to be based on trust?

"Dressed like twins. We share the same unerring good taste," Neil said, kissing her on both cheeks, European style.

"Where's Steve?" she asked, as he ushered her into the house.

"Off and away. Today is one of his good days. Knock wood," Neil said, knocking the side of his head. "He didn't have his usual Bloody Marys for breakfast or vodka martinis for lunch. He and a friend went to Bridgehampton to an opening at the Benson Gallery. I bowed out. I like the artist's work, but he's a bore. You ever notice that? Bores have the talent, while the ones with charisma get there on their charm and little else."

"Neil, I'm sure that doesn't apply to you."

"Of course not, darling, I'm an exception to all rules."

She bypassed two mile-long black leather sofas and sat in a big cane chair. There were four cane chairs, all painted a beautiful cranberry and grouped with calculated carelessness around an oval glass coffee table. The enormous living room could have swallowed her and Mark's loft in Tribeca. Except for bedrooms and baths, the house was without walls. Next to the open kitchen with its hanging plants and copper pots, a dining area overlooked a brick patio and a golf-course-size lawn, green as Astroturf. The dining table was cluttered with a computer, printer, typewriter, and mountains of paper. A wastebasket overflowed with wadded paper.

"Where the genius works," Neil explained, following her glance. "I should empty the wastebasket—what Isaac Bashevis Singer called the writer's best friend. Get you something to drink?"

"Am I interfering?"

"I usually break in the afternoon. Three hours in the morning, three at night. Actually, today I knocked off early and began cleaning Gabriella's cellar. Hauling out tons of junk. Beer okay?"

"Beer's fine."

Neil handed her a glass of Michelob and put the bottle on the table. "Have some," he said, holding out a bowl of macadamia nuts. "I'm afraid they're a trifle stale. They've been on the table for weeks." He took a nut and changed the subject. "So Bobbie fingered Carolyn as being the blonde with Adam? Sounds like your sleuthing is paying off. Now tell me what you learned about Dr. Sleaze."

"He's known as el Doctor Muerte at the hospital where he worked in Buenos Aires."

"No kidding!" said Neil, who seldom used such an inelegant phrase. "How'd you find that out?"

She told him. She helped herself to a fistful of nuts and didn't notice whether they were stale or not as she told him about everything else she'd found out. Everything, that is, except the blue notebook.

"Christ, they all look guilty," Neil said. "If that actor alibied for Todd, he could have done the same for Vanessa."

"Exactly."

"Listen, whether you like the man or not, you've got to report all this to Barolini."

"I'm meeting Kramer at his home after I leave here. He's off duty today. So is Barolini, but I didn't try to reach him at home. Bobbie's calling him to back me up, so Barolini won't think I'm lying.

"I know Carolyn looks suspicious, and I'm also positive she was outside on the deck spying on me last night, but I'm still having a hard time believing she killed Adam. And this morning when I saw her coming out of the woods, she looked spooked. As if she were being pursued by demons. When I mentioned this later—"

"You told her you'd seen her?"

"She'd already told me she'd been over to see Urzaga."

"You do have a way of getting people to admit things. Ever think of being a cop?"

Lydia laughed off the suggestion. "Carolyn said the animal noises scared her, but I'm not so sure. I don't think she scares easily, despite her helpless-female act."

"Agreed, she's tough. So is Vanessa. All three of you women."

"Thanks for lumping us together."

"Come on, love, you're being supersensitive. Adam was married to those two and would have married you if he could."

"He proposed right after Mark died. I was offended. But he kept at it."

"That was Adam's MO. Get them at their most vulnerable. Carolyn was just a kid when he proposed to her."

"She freaked out in the car today. Heard the demon voice of a serial killer saying he was coming to get her. She heard it on the radio even though it wasn't working."

"I need a drink. This is getting too fucking spooky."

He got beers for both of them.

"If you think that's spooky, wait until I tell you about the playhouse."

"I'm not sure I want to hear."

She told him anyway. "I found out from the refrigerator repair guy that the woman who works for Urzaga lives nearby and has kids. Maybe it's her little girl who plays there. I'll tell Kramer about it. See what he thinks."

Lydia checked her watch. It was later than she thought. She was meeting Kramer at five, in less than an hour. Time to bite the bullet and query Neil. God, he was going to hate her, and she couldn't blame him for it.

"I found a notebook of Adam's that Barolini missed," she said.

"A notebook? Anything important?"

"A list of the names and amounts of money he gave to people each month."

"So?" Neil said, in his usual voice. But he spilled some of the beer he was pouring into his glass. "You knew all that."

"Not all."

"Anyone I know?" he asked archly.

"Neil, he was sending you checks, too. Even after your fight."

"I considered it my MacArthur Genius Award," he said, laughing, but the laughter sounded false.

Lydia said nothing.

"Of course, one might quibble with the fact that I haven't yet proved my genius status. God, these are awful.

And I keep eating them." He picked up the bowl of mac-adamia nuts, took them to the kitchen, and dumped them into the garbage.

"Why bring this up? It's my business," he called as he opened and closed cupboard doors. "Looks like Steve's wolfed down all the goodies. He exists on junk food. If I fix him a nutritious meal chock-full of vitamins and pro-tein, he just picks at it.

"You want to know about my monthly stipend? All right, I'll tell you how it happened. To make a short story long, three months after the big blowup, I got a check from Adam for fifteen thousand dollars, covering the five thou-sand I would have gotten for the two previous months. I fully intended to tear the check into shreds, put it into an envelope, and return it without comment."

Neil came in from the kitchen with a bowl of Wheat Thins in one hand. In the other his fingers gripped the necks of two more Michelobs.

Great. Wheat Thins were fast becoming her diet.

"But," he said, setting down her beer with a wry smile, "I was three months behind Lilco, MasterCard, American Express, and my Blue Cross was due. Also, the phone com-pany was threatening to cut me—or rather Gabriella—off. And you can imagine with her Latin temperament how ex-cited she'd be about that. She calls at least once a week from Milan to make sure I haven't burned her house to the ground. I had no money in my checking account, and was down to—can you believe this?—my last twenty-seven cents.

"The money I'd squirreled away from my job at *gazelle* had long since been spent. I'd already blown the twenty thousand I got this year from a trust fund my beloved grandmother set up when twenty thousand meant some-thing. Steve contributes nothing, and in his drunken state, couldn't get a job even if he wanted to.

"My dear mother and my siblings think I should be out there in the real world earning a living instead of frivo-lously wasting my time writing a play. I wasted all those years at *gazelle* not writing, and I wasn't about to waste any more. So I kept Adam's check. And the next. And the next after that.

"When I said Adam called crying, begging my forgiveness, I lied. He didn't. He called to say he was cutting me off permanently. But I assure you, I was not the murderer. Yes, love, you caught me out. I was on the take just like the rest of the white trash he supports."

"Adam encouraged dependency, Neil. It made him feel stronger if he considered others weak."

"But you didn't weaken."

"I didn't know him that long. I might have in time."

"So what else was in Adam's golden notebook?"

"Blue. Nothing much."

"Golden, dear, as in Doris Lessing's book by the same name. Let me see it."

"I don't have it with me."

"Why is it I don't believe you? I bet you've got it with you to show to Detective Kramer. You can prove to him and Barolini that Adam cut us all off and the only one not suspect is you."

Neil stood up, bottle in hand. "Look behind you. You're missing a wonderful sight."

For a split second she wondered if it was a ruse so he could hit her over the head with the Michelob and grab the notebook. Or was this a test of trust? She turned her back. A flock of birds flew in formation.

"Canada geese heading south for the winter," Neil said. "Now that I've shown you my geese, you can show me Adam's notebook."

"I mailed it to myself in town." She could feel the outlines of the notebook in the inner pocket of her jacket.

She stood up, too. "Time to be off."

Neil took her firmly by the arm. "First come down and see the fascinating junk I found in Gabriella's cellar."

And what happened once he got her down there? She jerked her arm away. "I'd love to, but I'm already late." A lie.

From outside came the sound of a car driving up. A few seconds later a car door slammed.

"That must be Steve back from the opening," Neil said.
"Oh, I'll be so glad to see him," Lydia said. And meant it.

CHAPTER 34

Andy and her friend Chloe sat in the backseat of the Plymouth, whispering and giggling. Kramer wondered what kind of secrets eight-year-old girls shared. He looked into the rearview mirror and saw two heads together—Chloe's copper Orphan Annie curls next to Andy's stick-straight brown hair, glasses sliding down her nose.

They were on the back road, driving home from Sag Harbor. Driving in traffic made him nervous. Especially with two kids on board. He'd insisted they strap on seat belts and was glad they'd wanted to sit in the back. Safer than sitting up front in the death seat.

He liked this route, fields and woods. It reminded him of how it used to be in the Hamptons when he was Andy's age, before the bulldozers took over. Back when there were potato fields and duck farms. But there were still enough woods to make the search for the missing women difficult. And there was a report of another woman missing that came in just last night. Not long enough to be sure she was really missing. She could have taken off, but her husband and co-workers swore she wasn't the type. It was the second one from Suffolk County. The other five were from Nassau County. That made seven.

Three abandoned cars had been found near various wooded areas and identified as belonging to the missing women. Although the woods had been fine-combed, no bodies were found. As the list of missing women grew longer, the time between disappearances grew shorter.

In the backseat Andy and Chloe had abandoned secret

sharing for an exchange of knock, knock jokes. If only their innocence could be preserved. But even at their tender age, they had to be warned of the evil out there.

Kramer checked his watch. Getting close to five and time for Lydia Miller. Just as well she hadn't taken him up on his invitation to go with him to Sag Harbor. No doubt she had more exciting things to do than view whale tusks with a cop and two kids. Also, he'd have been tempted to warn her about Barolini. But then, she already knew.

It bothered Kramer that Barolini wouldn't produce Auerbach's incoming tape whose messages Miller claimed had been erased. When he'd asked Barolini to listen to the tape, Barolini had said he'd left the tape at home and would bring it in the next day. That was two weeks ago, and Barolini kept saying he forgot.

Well, hell, he thought, forget Barolini. Don't let him spoil your day off. Not that the day had been that great. Kramer had been disappointed to find that Steinbeck had received no more notice than a plaque on the windmill at Long Wharf. Maybe he hadn't been dead long enough. How long did you have to be dead to gain recognition?

These days fame came quicker if you just went out and killed enough people—the more bodies, the more famous. Except no bodies had been found in the case of the serial killer—that is, if there was one, and Kramer was pretty sure there was.

The workings of the criminal mind intrigued him, but otherwise he wasn't cut out to be a detective. He didn't have the stomach for murder, and wanted to look the other way when he saw a dead body.

A black Lexus darted around him, pulling in too soon. Kramer hit the brake. Christ, didn't people know they were driving death tanks? In the backseat, Chloe and Andy went on serenely with their game.

His mind went back to the serial killer. There was a pattern to it somewhere. There always was. He'd gone over it dozens of times in his head. The missing women had led similar lives. They had families, good jobs, and were active in school and community affairs. In fact, it was always some social function that the women hadn't returned from. Kramer had asked Barolini if Nassau Homicide had checked out the people who frequented these groups. Barolini had advised him to worry about Auerbach's murder and let Nassau take care of their own. Kramer was worried about Barolini, who was going after this like the Lone Ranger, obsessed with Miller, who he seemed to confuse with his ex-wife.

His car hit the pothole it always hit on his street. The one he reminded himself to avoid and never remembered.

"We're back," he said.

"There's a car in our driveway. And some lady at the door," Andy told him.

"Yes, she's come to see me."

"Do you have a girlfriend?" Chloe asked.

"No, this is business." Kramer checked his watch. Five-seven. He pulled into the drive, hoping that Miller hadn't arrived early and had to stand around waiting.

Hands jammed into jeans pockets, head tilted, Lydia Miller studied the house as if it were of great architectural interest. It was, in a way—a nice, old, run-down Victorian with a porch, lacy woodwork, and curlicues.

"I have to go home," Chloe said, popping out of the car as soon as he stopped. " 'Bye," she called over her shoulder.

Andy took no notice of Chloe's departure. She stared at Miller intently through her glasses. "What does that lady want to see you for?" she asked.

"Something about a case I'm working on."

"The serial murderer?"

"I told you I wasn't on that one."

"I thought you just didn't want me to know."

"Do you think I'd lie to you, honey?"

"Yeah, if you thought it was for my own good."

"Well, I might leave out something now and then, but I wouldn't lie deliberately," he said, smiling.

He got out of the car, and Andy followed, suddenly shy, taking his hand. "Better go and tend to Jessica and Roger," he told her gently. "You've been neglecting them lately."

He noticed that Lydia was staring at Andy and was suddenly embarrassed. In a blue net tutu over polka-dot tights and a green top, Andy looked like a pint-sized circus performer in glasses.

"This is Andy. She chooses her own wardrobe," Kramer told her.

Lydia smiled. "You certainly are creative," she said to Andy, who looked like she wasn't sure she'd been complimented. But apparently she decided Lydia was okay. "Want to meet Roger and Jessica?" she asked her.

"Andy, Ms. Miller is here on business."

"Who are Roger and Jessica?" Lydia asked as Andy headed for the garage.

"Her rabbits."

"Oh, I get it. Jessica and Roger Rabbit. That's clever. Did she think of those names by herself?"

"Yep. She was wild about the movie. Laura's parents got the rabbits for her. I couldn't very well refuse."

"Laura?"

"Andy's mother."

"Oh."

Too polite to ask or uninterested? "She was killed in an automobile accident when Andy was only two years old."

"How awful."

"Yeah."

Kramer saw the curtains twitching at Mrs. Emerick's window. The only women she'd seen here before were his mother-in-law and teenaged sitters. "Let's go inside."

"How was the whaling museum?" she asked as they walked to the door.

"Andy and I liked it, but I don't think Chloe did. She's Andy's friend who went along."

"I always intended to go there. Did you find out much about Steinbeck in his Sag Harbor days?"

He was impressed. She'd remembered the whaling museum and Steinbeck. "A plaque on a windmill. His widow still lives at their place in Sag Harbor. I drove by. It wasn't easy to find. On a dead-end street between two coves. I thought of calling her, but she's only there in the summer. Probably left by now, although some people stay on for awhile."

"You should have tried at least."

"I thought it would be an intrusion."

"I bet she'd love it. She probably thinks the world has forgotten all about him."

"Yeah, well, I think it has, too. But I hear the Japanese are crazy about him. Now tell me what you've found out. Did you bring the notebook?"

"It's here." She patted her jeans-jacket pocket.

CHAPTER 35

"How about a drink before we get rolling on this?" Kramer asked. "Coffee, tea, wine, or beer. What's your pleasure?"

"Wine's fine," she said, and shrugged off the rhyme. "But I don't want to take up your time when you're off duty."

"That's okay. I've got a night with nothing in front of me."

Kramer didn't seem to be playing for sympathy, she thought, as he left the room to get the wine. In fact, he sounded rather cheerful about it. He had a quirky smile that didn't go with the sad brown eyes, and was wearing jeans and a green crew-neck sweater showing the rim of a white T-shirt. An improvement over the maroon jogging outfit he'd worn before.

Looking around the room, Lydia decided that Kramer would make some woman a wonderful wife. The rose-patterned rug looked freshly vacuumed, the furniture dusted, with only a few of Andy's toys scattered around—board games, a catcher's mitt, and a Barbie doll in a deep-sea diving outfit. It reminded her of the Barbie dolls in the playhouse and she felt immediately depressed.

Kramer returned with two glasses of wine. "I'm out of white," he said. "Red okay?"

She nodded, handing him the notebook in exchange for her glass. Thank God she no longer had to hide it. "I found it in the bookcase."

"Looks like Barolini wasn't too thorough."

"Well, to be fair—and I don't know why I should be since he doesn't play fair with me—it was in a false book set I gave Adam as a present. I guess Barolini didn't guess that it was hollow, something to hide things in."

"Still, you found it, and he didn't. And finding clues goes with the job. Let me take a glance at this."

He sat down on the sofa beside her and flicked through the pages. "You've looked through it." A statement, not a question, but she nodded anyway.

"He gave a good deal of money to some people I've never heard of. Less money than his monthly regulars, but not bad. No last names. I think Charles, the only one who paid him back, is a cousin. And Rita might have been his manicurist. The FFOAAs, I've already mentioned. The Friendly Freeloaders of Adam Auerbach, I mean."

"Except some weren't so friendly."

"Right." She explained the other initials in the chart.

He looked it over. "Barolini wondered why you didn't mention that Neil Underwood was getting money, too."

"I didn't know. How did he find out?"

"Auerbach's checkbook."

Of course.

She was about to tell Kramer about Bobbie the waitress when a small voice interrupted. "This is Roger and Jessica."

Andy stood in the doorway struggling to keep a hold on two squirmy, floppy-eared, nose-twitching white rabbits.

"Andy, what did I tell you about—" Kramer broke off when the rabbits jumped from Andy's grasp and went in different directions. One ran into another room with Kramer in pursuit. The other disappeared under the sofa.

Lydia pulled the sofa out to get at it. Andy, trying to be helpful, squeezed behind the sofa, scaring the rabbit out and under an end table, where it sat frozen. Lydia made a dive for it. Her hands closed on a furry body just as she heard a crash behind her.

"That's okay, you didn't break it," Andy assured her, setting a lamp with a crooked shade back on the table.

She was clutching Jessica—or was it Roger?—when Kramer appeared in the doorway holding the other.

"You'll have to excuse us," he said, relieving Lydia of the rabbit, "while we return these guys to their proper living quarters."

Lydia checked her watch. Almost a quarter to six. As soon as she left here, she'd collect Colombo and head straight back to New York.

She turned on the table lamp she'd knocked over, glad to see it still worked. Like her, Kramer also had a wall-to-wall, floor-to-ceiling bookcase. You could learn about people from their bookshelves and medicine closets. There were books on criminal behavior, the psychological makeup of murderers, and six volumes of the Encyclopedia of Crime. Also three volumes of the Complete Works of Shakespeare. Wrong. Volume II was missing. Next to Freud were a number of books by feminists from de Beauvoir to Gloria Steinem, as if to contradict Freud's findings. Lydia wondered if the books had belonged to Kramer's wife.

Steinbeck took up another shelf: *Sweet Thursday, Tortilla Flat, The Wayward Bus, Travels with Charlie, The Long Valley, The Moon Is Down, The Pearl, Burning Bright, Cannery Row, Sir Thomas Mallory—King Arthur, Bombs Away, Cup of Gold—A life of Sir Henry Morgan, In Dubious Battle,* and more well-known books like *Grapes of Wrath, East of Eden,* and *Of Mice and Men.* It looked like he had everything but *The Winter of Our Discontent,* the book she'd been ready to lend him before Barolini vetoed it.

There was another bookcase devoted to videocassettes—chiefly Disney. *One Hundred and One Dalmations, Sleeping Beauty,* and so on. Obviously Andy's. On top of the bookcase was a picture of a pretty brunette. Lydia picked it up and inspected it. Kramer's wife, no doubt. She had huge eyes like the wistful waif in the *Les Misérables* poster.

"Sorry I took so long," a voice said behind her.

Guiltily she set the picture down. "Do you still want to borrow *The Winter of Our Discontent?*" she asked, as if she'd been inspecting Steinbeck's books instead of his dead wife.

"Love it," he said. "Listen, I'm sorry, but I'm taking Andy to her grandmother's. She lives several blocks over. Pour yourself some more wine if you like. It's in the kitchen."

A second later she heard a door slam.

Lydia considered leaving. But he wasn't being deliberately rude. He had to look after his kid, after all. Only she was in a hurry to get Colombo and get back to town. No doubt Carolyn would want to stay on to be near Urzaga. Okay by her. She just didn't want to be around if Carolyn freaked out again. Let Urzaga handle it—it was more up his alley. Trouble was, Carolyn's demon voice had been brought on by his two-timing her. According to Carolyn, that is. But was there more to it than she claimed?

Lydia was sure Carolyn had left details out when she described that moment in the garage. Or maybe she was still sleepy and confused about the events. The woman with Urzaga had been too high on something to navigate. Had he brought her back to his place to sober her up or to get laid while she was drunk? But since Urzaga had charm and looks to spare, she wouldn't have thought he'd stoop so low as to resort to liquor.

"Raining out."

Kramer stood in the doorway, his hair and sweater wet. "I have to pick Andy up in a half hour. Her grandmother's going out with what she calls 'the girls.' "

Kramer flopped down beside her. "Sorry about the interruption. Now, where were we?"

"The notebook, but there's a lot more."

"Shoot."

"Well, for one thing Bobbie, that waitress at Megan's, identified Carolyn as the woman with Adam the night of the murder."

"Wait a minute. According to Barolini, Bobbie said the woman was a blonde. Carolyn isn't."

"She was on Labor Day weekend. This weekend, too. She's back to blond again. That's just for starters. I have more to tell you."

"Fine, just hold on a minute. I want Barolini to hear this." He picked up the phone and punched out a number, then hung up a minute later. "Line's busy. Okay, what else?"

She told him about Vanessa and the actor alibiing for Todd Bigelow, and, keeping the best for last, her attacker with the flare gun and Urzaga's dismissal from the hospital. "They called him el Doctor Muerte."

Kramer shook his head. "Jesus." He reached for the phone. "Let me try Barolini again." Then, "Damn it. Before the line was busy. Now he's gone out already."

He spoke to Barolini's machine. "This is Kramer. Lydia Miller's here. She brought a notebook of Auerbach's and some disquieting information. She tried to reach you first, but you were out. Call as soon as you get in."

He turned to Lydia. "Thought it wouldn't hurt to lie a bit about your trying to reach him. He's very sensitive about such things."

"So you said."

"Listen, I don't want you going back to that place alone. Is there someone you can stay with?"

"That's okay, I'm going back to town as soon as I collect Colombo."

"I don't want you going back there even for that. I'd go with you, but it's time to pick up Andy. And we don't have a man to spare in the department. Not with the serial murderer around. There's been a report of another missing woman."

"Another? When?"

"Just last night. That makes seven. Of course, she might have taken off."

"But you don't believe that, do you?"

"It's too soon to know." He paused. "You're right, I don't."

A door slammed and Andy appeared in the doorway. "Grandma dropped me off," she said. "She's going out to dinner with the girls."

If it hadn't been for the tutu, she'd have looked like a miniature scholar in her glasses. Damp straight hair, stick legs, tall for her age. Weedy, not chubby like her dad. Or cute by the criteria set for kids, but Lydia found her immensely appealing.

"I'm hungry," Andy announced.

So was she. She'd eaten nothing but Wheat Thins all day.

"Okay, we'll eat soon. Now, run along and give me a few more minutes with Ms. Miller."

Andy dragged her sneakered feet leaving the room.

"Want to join us for dinner? Such as it is," Kramer said.

She was tempted. Besides the fact that she was hungry, it was cozy here. And secure. Nothing threatening. No footsteps out on the deck, and if she drank tea, she wouldn't have to worry about being poisoned. Raindrops slid down the window glass, catching light from the floor lamps. But it was a hell of a night for driving. She realized she should get started before it got worse. "Thanks, but I'm leaving as soon as I collect Colombo."

"I don't like your going back there," he repeated.

"Me either, but I can't leave woman's best friend behind."

"No, but he can wait a little. Better for you to stick around here and tell Barolini everything you told me. That is, if he ever returns home." Then Kramer snapped his fingers. "I just remembered. His daughter's visiting him today. He's probably driving her back to Great Neck now. That shouldn't take long."

"Daddy . . . !" a reproachful voice called.

"Just a minute," Kramer said.

There were details she hadn't mentioned, such as Carolyn's shoplifting the rat poison. Or the playhouse. But it was scarcely a thing to bring up when his kid was here, possibly eavesdropping just outside the door. At least that was the sort of thing she did when she was little, especially if the subject happened to be discussed in hushed tones.

The sound of the rain on the window was getting to Lydia, reminding her of the night she'd found Adam dead in the pool.

"If Barolini wants to talk to me, he can call me in Manhattan," she told Kramer. "It's already seven. It should take me about three hours to get back. I'll be there sometime around ten."

"Do me a favor. Call me as soon as you leave Adam's place. Use a pay phone."

"Yeah, okay, I'll call you from that tavern at the turnoff. Don't worry, I'll be fine," she said, hoping she was right.

CHAPTER 36

Lydia leaned over the steering wheel in an effort to see through the blurry windshield. It wasn't raining hard, just relentlessly. Nothing like the theatrical effects that night Adam was murdered. There was very little traffic for a Saturday night in the Hamptons, but then, this wasn't the high season.

When she reached the fork at Bridie's Lane, she was forced to a crawl by a rain-shiny black car ahead of her whose driver didn't seem to know which way to turn. She gave an impatient honk of the horn, ordinarily something she tried to refrain from, but she was in a hurry to get Colombo and be on her way back to town. The car turned right, finally. Lydia made a left and drove on, hoping that Carolyn would still be in bed, sleeping off her migraine. Chances were she'd be up by now. With luck, though, Colombo would be outside, and she could grab him and take off before Carolyn realized she'd come and gone.

She thought about Kramer. It would have been nice to stay for dinner. Besides being hungry, she liked Kramer and daughter. Interesting to see what he'd cook up. Probably veggies chock-full of vitamins for his kid and some high-caloric rich, chocolaty dessert for himself. Her stomach rumbled. Nothing like worrying about being bumped off to keep your weight down.

She caught sight of headlights in the rearview mirror. A few minutes later a car, brights on, rocketed by, then braked so suddenly that she almost rammed into it. The car turned in to a driveway. It looked like the same one she was stuck behind before—hard to tell in the rain. If she knew the territory better, she'd offer help to the idiot driver—for her own safety. Bad enough trying to see to drive in this weather, much less dealing with some nut who didn't know where he was going on a slippery road.

The car shot out of the drive. She had to swerve in order not to hit it. A half mile later she came upon the same car, zigzagging, taillights wavering in the rain. Was the driver drunk? High on something? She kept a safe distance behind. No telling what the idiot would do next. And the car was blue, not black as she'd thought. A dark blue BMW—like Adam's.

Like Adam's? Maybe it was his. That could be Bigelow ahead. Last night Vanessa had said he'd stolen her car and was coming out to see her. But maybe he was paying a visit tonight instead. Despite Vanessa's paranoid suspicions, she was damn sure it wouldn't be friendly. Was he here to finish up what he'd set out to do with the flare gun? Or instead of finishing up, finish her off? Or was she overreacting? Todd must know where Adam lived. Even so, finding it was a different matter. Especially if he'd been drinking.

She'd be able to tell if the BMW was Adam's since she'd committed his license number to memory. She'd done it because Adam never remembered where he parked, and Mark had been too weak to walk far. There were a lot of BMWs in the summer in the Hamptons. The license initials began with an AGA—for Adam Gaines Auerbach. AGA something something one. Dammit, what was it? Well, AGA was enough.

She sped up, drawing closer. AGA two five one! Todd Bigelow, then. Vanessa, too? They could have made up, and both come gunning for her. Come to think of it, Vanessa hadn't called Carolyn this morning to make sure Lydia hadn't lied about her visit. Also, there was the matter of the breather. Todd might have been checking to be sure she was still out here. Throwing in the heavy breathing for added entertainment.

Whoever was in the car was practically on top of Adam's house now. If it were a game of hot and cold, the driver would be on fire. The car slowed and pulled into Adam's driveway, dousing its headlights as Lydia passed by.

Damn! She should have taken Colombo along with her earlier. Now what? Outwait her visitor—or visitors—who might stay the night? No. Neither Todd nor Vanessa was the patient type. Instant-gratification people. Too jittery to wait. Besides, they'd see Carolyn's car parked under the trees. Two materialists like Todd and Vanessa would know the car didn't belong to her.

Lydia pulled into the drive of the first house she came to. Luckily, the house was dark. It had an abandoned air about it, looking closed for the winter. The house belonged to either the Ellmens, who were visiting their daughter in Seattle, or the two gay men.

After making a U-turn in the drive so she could face the road, she cut off her lights. Although the rain limited her vision, she was able to see as far as Adam's house. But it was too damn black to make out anything much. The sound of rain drumming on the car roof was deceptively comforting. She wasn't in a nice, dry, cozy cocoon, but in danger. The trick was figuring out who she was in danger from— Todd, Vanessa, Carolyn, Urzaga, and maybe even Neil. Was Todd Vanessa's hit man? Vanessa might have pretended to be mad at him for taking the car. According to Adam, Vanessa was a better actress offstage than on. But if this was Vanessa's plan, why call and ask if Todd was out here? And more important, why blow his alibi—and hers?

Thirty-five minutes later, the BMW pulled out of the driveway, took a right turn, and went back the way it had come. Thank God!

Lydia waited until the taillights topped the hill and disappeared before heading to Adam's. She pulled into the drive. Opening the car door, she called Colombo—keeping her voice down so Carolyn wouldn't hear.

No big furry animal came bounding up to shake water over her. All she heard was the rain falling with a steady plop, plop, plop. Where was he? She called louder, expecting to see the lights go on in the house when Carolyn heard her calling. But the place remained dark.

Maybe Colombo was inside. Damn! She'd have to go in and get him.

Lydia drove to the top of the hill and parked in front of the garage so she wouldn't have so far to go in the rain. Shining the flashlight on the flagstone steps, she made her way up the path, rain trickling under the collar of her jeans jacket. By the time she reached the door, her hair was plastered to her head, and her jeans plastered to her skin.

The door was unlocked. She could have sworn she'd locked it behind her when she left. Great! What if Todd and/or Vanessa had sneaked in and prowled around while Carolyn lay in her bedroom suffering from her migraine? Better watch out for booby traps. She locked the door behind her—like locking the barn after the horse was stolen.

No welcoming bark greeted her. She flipped all three switches by the door. The silence spooked her.

"Carolyn, you here?" she called. "Colombo, where are you, sweetie? Hey! Yoo-hoo! Anyone home?"

Silence reigned, except for the hum of the refrigerator and freezer.

She went down the hall to Carolyn's room, flicking on every light switch she came to. The door was shut. "Carolyn?" Lydia called and knocked. No answer. Lydia's heart beat faster as she pictured a bloody room with everything torn apart. Telling herself she'd seen too many scary movies, Lydia turned the doorknob and walked in. Everything was in place. No body in the bed, bloody or otherwise. And no Mark Cross bag open on the wicker rocking chair. Carolyn's gaucho hat was missing.

Lydia looked in the bathroom, cautiously searching behind the shower curtain first. Makeup gone. Also toothbrush. But Carolyn's car was still here, meaning she must have packed and gone over to stay with Urzaga. Obviously she'd patched things up with darling Alejandro.

Lydia breathed a giant sigh of relief. She didn't have to go back to town, after all. In fact, now that Todd and/or Vanessa hadn't found her here, they might go looking for her on East Seventy-seventh Street. She was safer out here. Except the place spooked her. She'd track down Colombo and take off as she'd planned.

In the kitchen she found Colombo's yellow plastic food dish empty. But it hadn't been before she'd gone to Neil's. He'd been in the house some time or other. Then where the hell was he?

Remembering all the places she hadn't eaten—Megan's, Neil's, and Kramer's—Lydia grabbed an apple from the refrigerator, and noticed that the note under the Donald Duck magnet wasn't hers.

"If I'm not back in an hour, come and get me. C"

No time and place given. But Carolyn had to mean Urzaga's. Except if she were so afraid of going over, why would she take her overnight bag? Maybe Carolyn had done as she'd done—packed and thrown the suitcase in the backseat of the car, planning to take off after she'd paid a good-bye visit. She didn't feel like going out again in the rain to see if the bag was in the car. More likely the note was a ruse Carolyn and Urzaga had dreamed up to get her over to Urzaga's house. Carolyn might not be psychic, but she had her antenna up. She could have guessed that Bobbie had fingered her as being with Adam that night, and told Urzaga, who was in on the murder, too.

What the hell, now was not the time to try to figure it out. And it might not be a good idea to advertise that she was here now. After turning off all the lights, she walked from room to room with a flashlight, futilely calling for Colombo. What if the rat poison had been intended for Colombo—to get him out of the way so Carolyn could more easily get to her?

Don't think about it, she told herself. If Colombo wasn't in the house, he had to be outside, that's all. She'd give it another try, not exactly sure what she'd do if she didn't find him.

And that was when she heard the scratching sound at the door in the living room. Colombo! Thank God!

At almost the same moment the phone rang. Lydia stopped in her tracks, torn between letting Colombo in and finding out who was calling. Todd and/or Vanessa checking to see if she'd come back? She'd listen to the answering machine. If there was no message, it would be one or both. Good thing she'd taken time out this morning to record her voice on the machine. Lydia walked halfway down the hall to hear the machine more clearly and heard her electronic self say she was unavailable at the moment and to please leave a message.

"Hi, it's Kramer. You didn't call back. Are you okay?"

She picked up and told Kramer she was fine. "I was delayed because I couldn't find Colombo. But he's scratching at the door now. Thanks for calling," she said, hung up, and rushed back down the hall to the living room.

"Coming," she yelled. Colombo cooperatively stopped pawing and scratching. Which wasn't like him. He didn't even bark a greeting. Suddenly it was very quiet. Lydia stood in the living room doorway, wondering if it was Colombo or someone else. Should she call out or keep quiet? After a long silence she heard the sound of breaking glass.

A hand reached through the jagged edges and turned the doorknob. A flashlight jumped around the room. She couldn't see who was behind it.

"Get moving," she told herself. "You can get scared later."

CHAPTER 37

Slowly, softly, she stepped back, then ran like hell down the hall to the bedroom.

She strained her ears to hear footsteps above the sound of the rain out on the deck but heard nothing. Stretching out her arms and feeling around to avoid stumbling into something, she crossed the bedroom that was suddenly three times as large as before. At long last her fingers touched the cloth of the Levolor blinds. Without risking a look behind and losing time, she turned the door handle. The click magnified into an explosion. Only her heart slamming in her ears was louder.

Once outside on the deck, she looked back and saw a light bouncing about the bedroom, but still couldn't see who was behind it. Or waste any time trying to find out. She had to get to the car and away from here. Rescue Colombo tomorrow. If she stuck around now, there might not be one.

Lydia ducked around the corner of the house, made a beeline for her Datsun, and jumped in. Luckily, she'd put the car keys in her jeans jacket pocket. In her hurry to get started, she nearly dropped the keys. Her hands shook so much, she could barely get the key in the ignition. And when she gunned the motor, the car wouldn't budge. Stuck! Shit! What was wrong? She wasted precious minutes before figuring out that someone must have done something to her tires.

All of a sudden a powerful light yellowed the slanting rain, skipped over trees and bushes, and came to rest on the car. Lydia threw herself out the door on the passenger side and ran to the bushes for cover. The light jogged toward her. Which way to go? She might make it to the road, but there was scarcely any traffic. She could be easily spotted by her pursuer.

Darting from tree to tree to evade the beam, bright as a searchlight, she circled the house and headed for the woods. She'd almost made it when she tripped. Gunshots, muted by the dampness, thudded into the earth around her, some going wild into the air. She'd just scrambled up on all fours when a bullet whizzed by her ear. She hit the ground. Crawling and rolling, keeping on the move the way she'd seen in war movies, she made it to the woods.

As soon as she reached tree cover, she got to her feet and started running, crashing through the underbrush, unable to tell if she was being followed. The rain rattling on leaves drowned out all sounds except her pounding heart. But when she stumbled over exposed roots, all hell broke loose. It was as if she'd awakened the whole woods, setting off alarmed bird cries, panicking animals who scurried this way and that. She had to choose between fast or silent. She opted for fast.

Her legs propelled her forward, while her mind ran in circles as she tried to think of where to go and what to do. All the nearby houses—except Urzaga's—were deserted. Then she thought of one. Larry had said Mrs. Janowsky lived at the far end of the woods. But Mrs. Janowsky was devoted to her employer, who might be Lydia's pursuer. It could very well be Urzaga. After seeing that the note left by Carolyn hadn't gotten her over to his place, he—or Carolyn, or both—had come over to hers. After all, she hadn't heard a car drive up or seen one in the driveway. But then, she'd been in too much of a hurry to escape to get a good look. For now, all she knew was that someone was trying to gun her down.

Damn! She'd told Kramer she was heading back to town at the very moment someone was breaking in. Stupid! Stupid! Stupid!

Lydia was tiring, flagging. Her legs grew heavy. She could scarcely lift one foot after the other. Her water-logged cowboy boots sank into the sodden earth. She listened hard for footsteps behind her, but heard only her own labored breathing and the never-ending rain. Maybe her pursuer had given up. She slowed, looked around, and saw nothing but unrelieved blackness.

After collapsing against a tree trunk, she wiped her wet face with her equally wet sleeve. Exhausted, she sank onto the ground, into what felt like a puddle. Little matter. She'd already taken a mud bath rolling across the ground to escape the gunshots.

She sat quietly, trying to control her breathing. The frightened birds and animals had quieted down. She heard nothing but the rain rattling on leaves. Inhaling the smell of rich, loamy earth and leaf mold, she considered her next move.

Kramer wouldn't check on her until tomorrow—provided he checked at all—and then he'd call her in town, not here. When she didn't answer, he'd assume she was out on an errand.

Lydia sat up and listened, hearing what sounded like branches cracking in the distance. It could be some animal fleeing, a deer perhaps. A minute later, a powerful light flashed on, sweeping the woods, lighting up trees and underbrush. Her pursuer had crept up on her in the dark. Behind the light was a dark figure of average height. In one hand the flashlight, and in the other a handgun.

Heart smashing against her chest, Lydia tried to think clearly. Figure out what to do, before doing the wrong thing. She couldn't use her flashlight. If she tried running, she'd be running blind, and if she stumbled, she'd wake up the woods the way she had before, tipping off her pursuer. None of the trees looked climbable, so forget hiding out in branches.

The light arced out again, nearly catching her before she ducked behind her tree. The pursuer was getting close. She felt around beneath her, found a stone, and threw it as far as she could. Good shot. It landed on the far side of the stalker, who played the flashlight around the area where the stone had hit, then took off in that direction, flashlight bobbing. Lydia congratulated herself. She'd always had a good aim. Deadly. When she was a kid shooting a BB gun at tin cans, her father had called her Annie Oakley. Maybe she should have aimed the stone at the stalker.

As the flashlight beam grew fainter, she breathed easier. After a good half hour of waiting, she ventured out. Maybe the stalker meant to give up the hunt, head back to Adam's house—and what? Hang around until she came back? Play it safe and stay the hell away.

The rain was getting to her. She didn't so much mind being cold, hungry, and bone-weary, as she minded getting wet. She thought of taking shelter in the playhouse. But the sight of the tortured Barbies would make her ill. Except it was dark now, and she wouldn't have to look.

Or she could take cover in Urzaga's van, the way Carolyn had last night. Risky. He might find her. Besides, being in the vicinity of Dr. Death was even less appealing than being in the playhouse. In fact, the wetter she got, the more the playhouse appealed. To hell with it, she'd rearrange the Barbie dolls' stances. Pose them fists up and ready to deliver karate kicks. At the crack of dawn when she could see where she was going, she'd be out of there, making her way to some house where she'd call 911 and be home free.

She set off in what she hoped was the right direction. If she went toward Urzaga's place and turned right toward the far end of the woods, she should find the playhouse.

After tramping around for another half hour in what she began to fear was circles, Lydia spied a darting light. Damn! She'd stumbled onto her pursuer again. She picked a stone up from the ground and waited. Gradually she became aware that the light was too faint to be the stalker's searchlight. Cautiously she moved closer. The light came from the playhouse behind the scarf-draped windows.

CHAPTER 38

It could be a kid in there, but she doubted it. Not at this hour. Granted, the child had the worst kind of parents (or her mother, the worst kind of husband); it still wasn't likely she'd be allowed out at this hour. Lydia was sure that whoever was in there wasn't her pursuer. For one thing, he—or she—had been going in the opposite direction, and for another, her pursuer would scarcely be messing around in a playhouse with the flashlight on announcing his or her presence.

She crept forward warily, placing one soggy boot before the other in order to avoid any giveaway noise. A few feet from a window she stopped, stooped, and looked in. Behind the scarf curtains a shadowy figure moved about. She couldn't make out who it was. The figure was tall, bent nearly double.

She tried the other window and had better luck. A gap in

the scarf curtain revealed a man in a white medical jacket.
A man with a perfect profile and a scar between the eyebrows. Urzaga!

The mutilated Barbies in their slavish attitudes must be
his creation. Sick. A really sick man. He was talking to
someone. Carolyn? She couldn't see who it was, since the
person was out of her line of vision. Judging from the
movements of his lips, Urzaga was babbling, talking constantly in an uncontrolled way, while his hands made precise, controlled movements as he draped a blue and white
striped scarf over the bedside table.

*A plaid suit and striped scarf. Such a dreadful combina-
tion,* Carolyn had said.

Lydia shivered and wanted to run, but where would she
run except possibly into the arms of her pursuer?

And then she heard him clearly. "If you don't shut up,
you're dead," he screamed. No one answered. Out of fear, or
because no one was there? Raving to himself? Wrong.
Someone answered. An inhuman wail. Muffled. Distant. Or
did it just sound distant because of a handkerchief-stuffed
mouth?

Urzaga picked up a hammer. Lydia shuddered. He
directed the flashlight toward the wall. Then, with immense
relief, she saw him pound a nail into the wood. She
couldn't make out what he did next since his body blocked
her view. In a few minutes he stood back—or rather
stooped back—for perspective, and she saw what he'd hung
on the nail. His latest acquisition—a gaucho hat. Carolyn's!

Her mind was so busy trying to process this information
that she didn't take in what was happening until too late.
Urzaga was already going out the door, giving her no
chance to hide. Light played among the trees, and then
there was nothing but total darkness. Had he seen her
watching? She ducked behind the playhouse, trembling. His
footsteps sounded loud in her ears. She couldn't be sure if
the footsteps were coming or going. After an eternity, when
nothing happened, she tiptoed around the playhouse and
risked a look, seeing only dark trees against a darker sky.
In the distance, lights blazed from Urzaga's house.

The muffled inhuman cries persisted. Lydia wished the

rain would drown them out, but the rain had dwindled to a drizzle. Who was in there needing her help? A striped scarf and a gaucho hat—Carolyn or the woman Carolyn had seen him with last night? She imagined a woman with a handkerchief stuck in her mouth, trussed up like the Barbie bride except with a rope instead of a velvet ribbon, waiting in terror for Urzaga's return. Or maybe dying. But what good could she do? Lydia asked herself. If she tried to make a rescue, Urzaga could come back and grab her, too. And who would rescue her?

But the muffled sounds of panic, pain, or both, got to her. Shivering in the rainy darkness, stalling, she knew she had to act.

She entered the playhouse, keeping the pocket flashlight pointed toward the floor, shielding it with her palm, in case her pursuer, who was very likely out there still, saw a light through the scarf-draped windows. Cautiously she shined the light into all four corners.

No one.

No one but the Barbie dolls down on their perfect little knees or with their rosy, unflawed arms upraised, pleading. That is, the Barbies whose knees and arms were still intact. The Barbie bride was still tied to the bed. But something new had been added. A nude, broken Barbie lay on the floor, a heel mark ground into her smashed face. Seven dolls in all. Seven? The same number as the missing women!

She froze in shock, feeling as incapable of moving as she did in her nightmares. Until she heard a muffled, protesting bark. Colombo? Alive! But where? She lifted her head, nearly bumping it on the ceiling, and listened. The sound came from below, as if she were standing on him. Lydia shined the light down on a maroon and tan oval rag rug. Beneath it the barking continued, now sounding joyful. He knew she was here!

She kicked the rug aside and found a square-cut piece of wood with an iron ring embedded in the center. When she pulled the ring, a thick trapdoor lifted up. She got a whiff of stale, damp air as she shined the flashlight down. Below, at the bottom of a flight of stairs, Colombo leaped as far as a rope would allow, barking wildly.

Lydia started down the stairs. After descending several steps, she reached up and tried to draw the rug over the trapdoor before letting it fall. The thud sounded final. Had she trapped herself in? At least this way, her stalker wouldn't find her. But she might not have managed to cover the trapdoor with the rug. If Urzaga came back, he'd notice, and when he didn't hear Colombo, he'd know something was wrong.

Down below, Colombo leaped about frantically. When Lydia reached him, she had a hard time holding him still long enough to untie the rope looped to his collar and attached to a stair post. His fur was dry. He must have been tied up for a long time. Between gleeful barks, Colombo kissed her with his cold corduroy tongue. The moment he was free, he raced ahead as if he knew exactly where he was going.

The pocket light was just bright enough for her to make out a long cement tunnel. Narrow, high-ceilinged—high enough to accommodate a tall man. She shuddered at the thought that Urzaga could seal the trapdoor and bury her and Colombo alive. Who would guess, after all?

Her steps echoed as she ran after Colombo, who seemed to be leading her in the direction of Urzaga's house. To the secret addition? That way was dangerous. All the same, she was curious. Remembering Urzaga's hand clamping down on her wrist when she reached for the door, she wondered what he was hiding there. He'd forbidden entrance to everyone, including Adam and Carolyn. But not to the woman in the striped scarf. What did that mean?

Colombo ran back and forth urging her to hurry. Up ahead she saw a door with an iron ring like the one on the trapdoor. From behind the door came a faint sound. And this time there was no doubt that it was human. Someone—a woman—was whimpering and moaning.

The sounds became louder as she drew closer, droning monotonously as if they'd been going on for a long time at the same decibel level.

Lydia pulled at the iron ring with sweaty fingers. The

thick wooden door appeared stuck. Locked? She gave a strong shove. It opened slowly, creaking. Colombo charged through the door, barking. Someone screamed out in the darkness.

CHAPTER 39

"Please, please don't hurt me," a woman begged. Then she saw the dog. "Colombo," she screamed. "Oh God, oh God, oh God."

In the slender light of her flashlight, Lydia made out what looked like a do-it-yourself operating room. Tall white cabinets with counters lined three walls. The fourth wall held a peg board displaying hospital instruments, including knives of various sizes, scalpels, and saws, all within easy reach of an operating table where Carolyn lay strapped down, legs spread-eagled, arms above her head. Her butter yellow hair spilled about her face. She looked like the Barbie bride in the playhouse bed. Replacing the white bridal gown was a blue paper robe.

"Carolyn, it's me," she whispered.

"Lydia? Oh God, get me out of here."

Carolyn's face was a deadly white, her eyes mascara-smudged, huge and terrified. The torn blue paper robe scarcely covered her long, pale body.

Lydia rushed to another door at the opposite end of the room and shot the bolt lock in case Urzaga tried to enter while she was freeing Carolyn. The lock looked flimsy and maybe wouldn't hold very long, but at least it would provide some delay. She inspected the door through which she'd just entered. No bolt lock, nothing to keep Urzaga out. She turned to Carolyn, who was moaning and pleading with her to hurry, hurry.

Lydia's hands shook as she tried to undo the strap that held Carolyn's wrists together. She attempted to hide her own fear by speaking soothingly, assuring Carolyn she'd have her free in a few minutes.

"He's coming back," Carolyn sobbed. "Unstrap me. My hands and feet are numb."

"Where's the woman with the striped scarf?" Lydia asked.

"That's when it happened. When I asked about her, he said I was imagining things. Freaking out again. What's taking you so long?"

The strap around Carolyn's wrists was tight, fastened to the very last notch, the leather new and stiff. And she was all thumbs. "I'm sorry if this hurts."

"I'm too numb to feel anything. Oh God, oh God, oh God."

"Please stop your oh godding, it just makes me more nervous."

"He'll be here any minute," Carolyn wailed. "And he's the one who's crazy, not me. His eyes looked strange—like splintered glass. It was terrifying. I knew I had to act. And act fast. Oh God, can't you hurry?"

"Carolyn, I'm trying. Telling me to hurry only slows me up. Keep talking. It'll go faster for both of us. Why did you go over there to begin with?"

"To poison him."

"With the rat poison you lifted at the supermarket?"

"Insect poison. You saw? I was going to pay him back for being unfaithful. I knew it wouldn't kill him, just make him sick. But he caught me slipping it into his martini, and made me drink it. I threw up on him when he was dragging me in here. Deliberately. It made him furious. He strapped me down and said he'd deal with me later. Oh, God, I've been here for hours. Can't you work any faster?"

Lydia could scarcely see what she was doing. And she needed three hands. Two to unstrap Carolyn and one to hold the flashlight while she did it. She beamed the light around the room and found a switch. When she flicked it on, Carolyn shrieked. "Turn that off. It's blinding me."

What seemed like a thousand-watt bulb cast a brutal

spotlight on Carolyn, leaving the rest of the room in shadow.

"I'm sorry, but I have to see to work at this."

A knife would be quicker, but her hands were too shaky. She'd end up slicing Carolyn instead. Lydia finally loosened the strap, freeing both hands.

"I can't move my fingers," Carolyn whimpered.

"Keep trying. Flex them. Get your circulation going."

Lydia went to work on an ankle. Carolyn's feet were blue and swollen. Lydia rubbed them to reduce the swelling, but it didn't work.

Colombo, who'd been sniffing the cement floor, gave a sudden deep growl and leaped at the door leading to the house. The one she'd bolted, fortunately.

"Oh God, he's out there. He'll break in and get us both," Carolyn said, starting to cry.

Something hurled against the door with the force of a battering ram. And kept hurling. Either Urzaga was using an implement or had the superhuman force of a madman. Lydia expected the bolt to give way any minute. Colombo barked and growled fiercely, daring Urzaga to come in.

No time to waste. No time to be scared. Lydia grabbed a knife from the peg board. The knife had a sharp, shiny blade. "Please God, make my hand steady," she prayed. God or someone up there listened. It took only a few seconds to slit the straps. She hated to think of what the knife would have done to Carolyn if she'd missed.

The bolt was giving way, splintering wood.

Quickly she helped Carolyn down from the table and onto her feet. Carolyn's knees buckled. "I can't stand up," she said, voice quivering. Tears came to her mascara-smudged eyes. "Go ahead. If you don't, he'll kill you, too."

"He's not going to get either of us," Lydia said, more staunchly than she felt. She grabbed a butcher knife from the wall and gave the smaller knife she'd used to cut the straps to Carolyn. "If you can't hold this, put it between your teeth."

"I can hold it. And I can damn well use it."

"Let's go." She put an arm around Carolyn's waist and half pushed, half dragged her along.

"My clothes are in that closet," Carolyn said.

"Forget them."

Lydia gave Carolyn a good shove and succeeded in getting her out the door and into the tunnel just as Urzaga came raging through the other door, white jacket flying, hair sprawled over his forehead, eyes shining with hate, madness, or both.

Colombo, snarling, went for Urzaga's throat. Urzaga shouted in Spanish as he tried to fend off the flurry of orange and white. Lydia didn't wait to see what happened next. Saying a silent prayer for Colombo, she hurried out of the room to Carolyn, who clung to the tunnel wall as she tried to make her way on numb feet.

It was like running in a nightmare, trying to pull Carolyn along and being held back by the drag of Carolyn's weight and her own rain-sodden boots. At least Carolyn had stopped her oh godding.

"How long does this go on?" Carolyn asked. Lydia supposed she meant the tunnel.

"Stairs up ahead. Come on, you can make it."

Lydia heard a faint strangled yelp, and her heart took a dive. Poor brave Colombo. This time her prayer hadn't worked. It would take only minutes for Urzaga to catch up with them.

Almost as soon as she thought it, she heard Urzaga's footsteps echoing in the tunnel behind them.

"He's coming," Carolyn whispered.

"There's two of us, one of him, and we've got knives," Lydia told her. She didn't mention that Urzaga would have grabbed a knife, too. "Just keep going. The stairs aren't far away."

But they were farther than Lydia remembered, the tunnel twice as long as before. Behind them, Urzaga's footsteps grew louder by the second, gaining. She doubted they could take him—Carolyn was still too weak. Besides, it was dumb to even try. All Urzaga had to do was nail down the trapdoor, and they'd be buried alive.

In the meager light of her pocket flashlight, Lydia spotted the stairs just ahead. With a strength stemming from fear, she managed to drag Carolyn up the stairs and through the trapdoor just as Urzaga reached the first step. She dropped the door and stood on top of it, hoping that her weight would hold it down. "Run," she yelled to Carolyn. As an afterthought she added, "Stoop or you'll hit your head."

It was too dark to tell if Carolyn stooped, but she heard her run out the door. She also heard a shot, a woman's scream, and men's voices.

"Get him, he's over there," a man shouted.

A jumble of men's voices. Someone yelling, "Call the ambulance."

Through the scarf-draped windows she saw lights. Lots of them. Darting like giant fireflies.

Lydia switched on her pocketlight to see what was going on.

"Who's in there? Come out, hands up. You're covered," a voice ordered.

She felt the trapdoor lift underfoot. Heard Urzaga's grunts beneath her. Feeling herself tilt forward, she looked down and saw a hand had crept out. A hand with a knife. She raised a booted foot and came down on the hand with her heel, hearing a gratifying howl of pain.

"Who's in there?" a voice yelled, gruff, familiar. A voice she'd once hated, but at the moment was glad to hear. "What's going on?"

"That's what I'd like to know, too," she yelled back.

A light flashed in the doorway, followed by a head of thick gray hair. "Jesus," Barolini said. "What's that under your feet?"

Lydia looked down at the knife-clutching hand sticking out of the trapdoor. The hand was twisting, trying to work free. She slammed down her boot again. The knife dropped. "Got him," she cried triumphantly.

"Nah, he's not the one. We got the murderer outside. Winged Carolyn Auerbach. Took her for you."

"Just like you did," she told him.

"I don't know what you're talking about," Barolini said. He stooped and came in the door. "Jesus, what have you been playing in here? Whose hand is that you're standing on?"

"The hand of the serial killer," she replied, as calmly as she could.

CHAPTER 40

Neil handed Lydia a warm mug. "So how you doing, friend?" he asked. He wasn't speaking to her but to Colombo, who lay beside Lydia on the couch in Adam's living room, his neck swathed in bandages.

"He'll be okay. I hope," she said. She took a sip from the mug—some tea, a little honey, and a lot of rum. Her diet these days seemed to consist of alcohol and Wheat Thins. She huddled in a blanket, still shivering. Both she and Colombo were convalescents. Colombo more than she. The vet said the knife had just missed his artery.

"You're one ballsy dog," she told Colombo.

He thumped his tail weakly.

"He has one ballsy mistress," Neil told her.

It was eleven in the morning. Carolyn was in the hospital after being shot in the shoulder by Todd Bigelow. A case of mistaken identities. Bigelow was in jail now. Ditto Urzaga. Where she hoped they'd both rot. Barolini was basking in a flood of TV lights, hailed as supercop for finding both the serial killer and the confessed murderer of Adam Auerbach.

"What made Todd confess so readily, I wonder?" Lydia said.

"You'll have to ask Kramer. Maybe Barolini beat it out of him."

"Good."

"And you call yourself a liberal?"

Neil parked himself in Adam's chair. He looked haggard, drawn. And all because of her.

"I thank you for my rescue," she said.

"You can also thank Steve and Kramer. Good thing you didn't tell me you were going back to town."

"How did you happen to be here?"

"I kept calling and getting your machine. I knew you were with that madwoman and started worrying. Steve said I was driving him crazy, that I should go to your place and find out. First thing I saw was Adam's car in the driveway. Then Carolyn's and yours. I didn't notice your tires had been slashed, but I thought it was damn strange for you to be entertaining all these visitors in a dark house. I rang the doorbell, and when you didn't answer, knew something was wrong. "More?" he asked when she set her mug on the coffee table.

"Thanks, I haven't finished this yet." She'd finished it, but Neil looked dead on his feet, and she didn't want him to have to wait on her. "So then you called Kramer?"

Neil nodded. "He was more upset than I was. He said you'd told him you'd found Colombo and were going back to town, but if your car was there, something was definitely wrong. What made you think it was Colombo at the door?"

Lydia sighed. "I guess I was in such a big hurry to get out of danger that I ran right into it."

"Yeah, well, Kramer wanted to come over and investigate, but he couldn't leave his little girl alone. He called Barolini, who told him he was acting like a nervous old maid. Barolini got pissed at him earlier in the evening, Kramer said, when he'd called and told Barolini about all the stuff you'd discovered. Thought it made him look like a bad cop."

"He is."

"Sweetie, not everyone's as good a sleuth as you. Anyway, I volunteered Steve as a baby-sitter, and as soon as Kramer got here, he discovered your slashed tires and knew damn well something was wrong. So he phoned Barolini again, gave him the details, and said he was calling in some men. That got Barolini here fast. We scattered out in the woods and started looking, and then we heard the gunfire. The rest is history," Neil said, and yawned.

"Go home and get some sleep. I'm safe now."

"Don't be so sure. Vanessa is still at large. And your

bodyguard," Neil said, nodding toward Colombo, "is presently out of commission. You two are coming back with me. We have more guest rooms than Adam. More than God."

"You mean Colombo is no longer persona non grata?"

"If it's love me, love my dog, I guess I have no choice."

"Neil, you're a friend."

"Did you ever doubt it?"

CHAPTER 41

A thin, elegant man walking a thin, elegant greyhound cast a suspicious look at them—and the greyhound at Colombo—as he entered an ivy-covered redbrick house almost identical to the house they were inspecting.

"Good thing you're a cop. We could be arrested for loitering," Lydia said.

But Kramer's interest was elsewhere. "Do you think he'd know which house Steinbeck lived in? No, I guess he's not that old. This was back in the late forties or early fifties. Goddamn it, there ought to be a plaque. No one cares." He shook his head sadly.

Kramer was dressed up. He wore a white shirt, tie, tan trousers, and a chocolate sport jacket that showed the strain where it buttoned over his stomach but went with his brown eyes. His shoes weren't polished, but at least when he went out he wore shoes and not bedroom slippers as Adam had done on occasion.

Kramer had called her in the morning. She was getting ready to go with Carolyn's cousin Frank to visit Carolyn at Oak Grove in Connecticut. Carolyn was getting better, but still wasn't great. She'd flipped out in Hamptons Hospital. Little wonder, since that was where Urzaga had worked, but by then he was in maximum security. Seven bodies had been found under the swimming pool excavation where the cement was to be poured. It was all in the news, including the terrible details. Urgaza had stalked his victims and murdered them one by one, after seeing their pictures in the *Long Island Newsday* in an article on outstanding women. There had been ten women in all; three of them, he hadn't gotten around to killing.

Kramer had told Lydia when he called that he was coming in to take a look at the house where Steinbeck had once lived on East Seventy-eighth Street. "It's just a block from you. Care to join me later for dinner? I know this is last minute, but I wasn't sure I was coming in. I had trouble getting a sitter for Andy."

Lydia said she'd join him for a look at Steinbeck's house if she got back in time, and yes, dinner would be fine.

Kramer interrupted her thoughts. "Pick out a restaurant. You know this neighborhood better than I do. I guess there aren't any places still around where Steinbeck would have gone."

"Le Lionceau has been here for a long time. He might have gone there. The food is nothing special, but behind it is a garden and a huge rock with a waterfall—after a heavy rain. It's near here. But first I have to take Colombo home and feed him."

Instead of waiting downstairs in her building as Adam used to do, Kramer insisted on following her and Colombo up the three flights, saying the exercise would do him good.

"Barolini is always after me to go with him when he works out," Kramer said between huffs and puffs as they made their way up. "Guess I could use it."

"How is our ace detective?" Lydia asked, unlocking the door.

"In homicide heaven. Busy lining up a publisher and writer for his book."

"A book? He's a writer?"

"Looking for an as-told-to. Joe McGinniss has declined. He's not as bad as he sounds. Barolini, I mean. Not as cocky as he used to be. With reason. Both of us should hand our badges over to you considering how you showed us up," Kramer added, after he'd caught his breath inside the apartment.

"Colombo deserves the credit," Lydia said, loading his dish with Alpo. "He was right at Todd Bigelow's throat the night he attacked me, and then he took on Urzaga."

"True. I wasn't putting you down," Kramer told Colombo, who was too busy eating to take offense.

Lydia excused herself, went to the bathroom, put on lipstick and brushed her hair. She was still wearing what she'd worn to see Carolyn. The usual black ensemble. She added gold earrings and decided she'd pass muster.

"Did you hear about the super?" a sweet, little-girl voice called, as Lydia and Kramer left the building. "The police picked him up. Him and his no-good friend Willy."

Mrs. Nagy was leaning out her front window, a well-worn cardigan draped over her shoulders. "That Sal and Willy, they tried to get rid of the tenants in that building across the street. They let pit bulls roam the halls, broke into apartments, and beat up an old man. Our landlord, he owns that place, too. Now he's in trouble. He paid those two to do it."

"It's a wonder Sal didn't try his terror tactics here," Lydia said. "The worst he's done is let the place run down." And lied about when she'd gone out to see Adam.

"He didn't try that stuff here because he knew I was watching," Mrs. Nagy said. "What he didn't know was, I was watching over there, too. When I heard what was going on, and saw Sal and his thug friend Willy sneaking in and out, I got suspicious and reported them to the police. They came and caught those two in the act," she said jubilantly.

"Good work," Lydia said, and tugged Kramer away before Mrs. Nagy launched into another neighborhood story.

Since it was early, they got a table at Le Lionceau without a reservation. A new maître d' led them past a life-sized stuffed lion guarding the fireplace to a table by the window that overlooked an enormous rock, all lit up even though it wasn't dark out.

The young, good-looking waiter—an actor—greeted

Lydia effusively and took their drink orders. Vodka martini for her, bourbon and soda for Kramer.

"Bourbon?" she asked when the waiter left.

"What Steinbeck used to drink. I read that somewhere." He nodded toward the waiter. "Have you been here before, or do you always get such warm greetings?"

"I used to come here with Adam. He was a big tipper, to make up for his bad behavior. Mostly it worked."

"What does Le Lionceau mean?" Kramer asked.

"Young lion, but that one looks quite elderly." She nodded toward the stuffed lion by the fireplace.

"Maybe he was here when Steinbeck ate here," Kramer said hopefully.

"Has the date for Todd Bigelow's trial been set yet?" she asked.

"November fifteenth. You might be called as a witness."

"I still haven't figured out why he killed Adam. I was so sure it was Urzaga in the beginning."

"Urzaga's specialty was murdering women. Successful women."

"Why?" Lydia asked.

The waiter appeared at their table. "Would you like to hear tonight's specials?" he asked.

"Later," Lydia said, and turned back to Kramer. "Why?" she asked again.

"According to the psychiatrist who made the diagnostic evaluation, Urzaga thought a woman's place was in the home."

"But Urzaga told me his mother spent most of her time in bed suffering from depression."

"Who knows what went on in his twisted mind? I've read a lot about serial murderers, but their motives baffle me. Maybe they're just plain evil."

"What's the answer to Todd Bigelow? Why did he murder Adam?"

"At first he claimed self-defense. Said Adam and the dog attacked him."

"Incredible!"

"We didn't buy it, of course. Now he's saying he did it because Vanessa Auerbach cared for her ex-husband more than she did for him. He thought with Auerbach out of the picture, she'd be all his."

"You mean it was love, not money?"

"According to Bigelow, everything he did was for Vanessa—including going after you with that flare gun. He thought scarring you for life would please her. And if he killed you, she'd love him forever."

"And what does Vanessa say to all that?"

"She doesn't. She's in Portofino."

"Portofino? How do you know?"

"I made it my business to find out, in case Bigelow was covering for her and she was out to get you. She took off with her leading man, that soap opera star, Kevin Drake."

"I still don't know if Adam's tape had a gap on it, or who stole mine," Lydia said. "Vanessa wouldn't have known I had it."

"She guessed. She got Bigelow to steal yours and erase Adam's. She didn't want anyone to hear how she begged Adam for money. It hurt her pride. Adam was supposed to love her more than any other woman."

"I think he did. It was all Sturm und Drang with them. It was what Adam needed to take his mind off his depression."

"Maybe so. Love is funny."

"I'll drink to that," she said, raising her martini. He raised Steinbeck's bourbon.